Lily

and the

Ghost of

Michael Thorne

by

NP Haley

Lily and the Ghost of Michael Thorne is a work of fiction. Names, characters, places, brands and incidents are either the product of the author's imagination or are used fictitiously.

Made in the USA

Copyright 2018

Revised 1st edition

ISBN#13: 978-0-692-06379-8

Formatted by: Ron Haley

Edited by: Ron Vincent

Cover photo: Copyright 2018 by Katie Vincent

Cover design: Pink Ink Design

Library of Congress Cataloging-in-Publication Data

Except for the fact that my father was called Bugpappy as a child and Caruthersville, Missouri is an actual small town on the edge of the mighty Mississippi River in the boot-hill of Missouri, **Lily and the Ghost of Michael Thorne** is entirely fiction. This book evolved from my father's stories of superstitions and ghost sightings along the Mississippi River which were passed down from one generation to the next.

In loving memory, of my parents:

Catherine Patterson Pruiett and

Rev Arthur Coydon Pruiett

Acknowledgements

This book is dedicated to Ron Haley; you are the wind beneath my wings and supporter of my efforts. Without you I would have given up long ago. For my beautiful daughter, Kathy; you are the precious gift God gave to me when I needed something good in my life, and to Ronnie; you will never know how much you inspire me. I love you all.

Steve Martin, thank you for opening the door of opportunity and making my dream possible.

"Ron, if I had this life to live again, I would find you sooner so I could love you longer"

About the book cover

      The front cover photo was taken by my daughter, Katie Vincent, while visiting New Orleans in December of 2017. Having no idea there was an apparition standing at the edge of a window-frame of one historical building along Burgundy Street in the French Quarters; she snapped numerous shots of the beautiful buildings near the St Pierre hotel. It was not until after she returned home did she notice the apparition lurking and seemingly peering around the frame of the windowsill at her camera. Out of numerous shots, only one photo showed the apparition.

      This photo has been copyrighted: 2018

The verbiage and grammar used in this book is normal for the time frame. After reading Lily and the Ghost of Michael Thorne, you will notice some of the slang is still used in today's conversations.

1

The Levee

Sweat ran down her back and saturated her shirt as she squatted in the pickle barrel, the sickening sweet smell of vinegar and pickling spices making her stomach churn and roll as if trying to expel its contents. She was quite certain she would never again eat another pickle.

There she sat...holding her nose and listening as rats scurried around the barrels in their frantic search for food, scratching and squealing at one another as if one of them had found a pot-full of gold pickle pieces. Pushing the top of the barrel up a bit, she watched rats rushing and dashing about in their frenzied pursuit.

She could also hear the two river drunks stumbling and knocking over empty barrels in their own desperate search, yelling for her to come out and show herself.

"Boy, ya best come on outta whur ya be a 'hidin'." one of them yelled in a drunken slur as he stumbled and fell over an empty barrel.

"Come on now, boy. Get out here," the other drunk echoed the first one's demand. Then he belched loudly as he tried to continue yelling but the burp overpowered his voice, making the entire sentence come out as one long, mumbled, disgusting belch.

Again, he belched long and loud, ending the gross episode with an unbelievable loud, rumbling fart, as if maybe he had filled his drawers.

Lily covered her mouth with her hand, hoping she wouldn't lose the contents of her already upset stomach.

"Ahhh," the drunken sailor sighed, as if in great relief, "I'm a'feelin' much better. All that thar' runnin' with a belly-full of whiskey and slop from that say-loon ain't settin' too good in my innards."

"We jest want ta talk ta ya, boy," the first drunk called out again. "We jest want to talk ta ya and see iff'en ya be cold or hungry. We done got some vittles right cheer' in our pockets."

"What'd jah say that fur', Jug?" the second drunk spoke up sternly. "We ain't got no vittles and iff'en ya do, we ain't gonna share 'em. Iff'en ya got some vittles I want 'em."

"I know'd it, Pug. I'm just a'tryin' ta coax 'em on outta his hidey-hole. I'm a'thinkin' he's hungry. He must be cuz he's skinny as this here stick I'm carryin'."

"So," Lily thought to herself, "they think I'm a boy. Well, good! If they find out I'm a girl they will never give up looking for me."

She had been up on the river road, looking for her brother and sister, Benny and Tessa, when the two drunks spotted her and quickly began stumble-running after her. She had taken off running and was well ahead of them when she got a stitch in her side.

"Chicken poo," she had gasped as she stopped to catch her breath. She then put her hands on her knees and hung her head down; trying to catch her breath and get rid of the pain.

That was when the strangest thing happened. It was as if a dark cloak was placed around her shoulders engulfing her entire body. It lifted her off the ground a few inches and swept her along towards the dock...a whole lot faster than she could ever have run. Once she reached the dock beside the levee, which was jammed full of empty pickle barrels waiting to be refilled and shipped down river to New Orleans, the cloak vanished and she was standing alone in the middle of the empty barrels.

The pounding of her heart as it jumped into her ears, was deafening. It seemed as if it was trying to jump right out of her chest and take off running on its own.

Quickly and quietly she then moved into the crowd of barrels, selected one close to the levee wall, lifted the lid and dove inside pulling the lid shut as she went in.

2

Now, here she sat in a pickle barrel listening to rats scurrying around hunting for food and two drunks searching for her. "What in the holy Hannah was with that darkness," she whispered to herself. When the dark cloak had first wrapped itself around her, she thought it was because she was going to faint, but here she was – she hadn't fainted. In fact, the darkness had felt warm and comforting.

She was quite certain all her blood had, by now, drained into her feet. She felt light-headed and her brain seemed to be as fuzzy as a baby chick's down. The thoughts of the dark cloak and the thick smells of pickle brine were almost too much for her.

Maybe she had imagined the whole thing, she thought to herself as she tried reasoning it out in her mind. She didn't know what it had been or where it had come from but she was certainly glad it appeared out of nowhere because she was quite certain the drunks would have caught up with her in the agony of the painful stitch in her side.

Knowing the two drunks did not want to "just talk to her", especially once they found out she was actually a girl, she sat quietly in the barrel. If she was caught, she would be sold and put on a riverboat heading down to New Orleans to be secretly sold to the highest bidder and taken away to unknown parts in the island nations where enslavement of any person was still abundant.

All the folks living along the mighty Mississippi River knew the stories of illegal child/young adult slave trade and how rampant it was in the port cities along the Gulf and it didn't matter what color your skin, a kidnapped person could possibly put a dandy bag of gold dust into the kidnapper's pocket. It was a widespread practice whispered and gossiped about among elite society, but those in charge of making the laws did nothing about the dirty deeds. Most times, nothing came of the search for children who vanished and were reported to some of the local authorities.

"Whur the heck is that thar' brat," one drunk called out to the other, "Dang it all to hades and back. I know'd he were runnin' down onta this here riverboat dock. I see'd 'em with my own eyeballs."

Lily listened as they stopped knocking barrels over and was quite sure they were standing there looking around trying to figure out how she had vanished so quickly.

"I bet'jah he slipped inta that thar' river and swimmed away," one of them said loudly.

"Yep, that thar's jest what he done did! Stupid young'un," the other replied.

"Let 'em drown. That thar' water's too cold ta go in an fish 'em out an I ain't gonna do it even iff'en it was warm."

"Damn it, I ain't got no other idee whur' he might be a'hidin' and I ain't seein' 'em a'floatin' in the river. He's done gone and drowned his own self. What'cha think:"

"Well," the one called Jug said, or so Lily thought it was, "ya won't be seein' 'em yet cuz he ain't done drownin'. His body has ta fill all the way up to hit's neck fur' 'em to start in floatin'."

"I ain't knowin' bout that thar!" Pug replied strongly, "Let me tell ya 'bout a feller I once'st know'd that up and got snatched inta this here river — right chere' at this very spot whur' we be lookin'. Me and some other fellers was out on one ah them thar' boats that take ya 'cross the river ta Ten-see when all of ah sudden-like that thar' feller was gone! Hit' was jest like a water-haint reached right on up and grabbed holt' ah him and snatched 'em right off'en our boat and that feller had no warnin' a'tall and he was the meanest feller I ever did see. He was so mean he would'ah sold his own granny fur' ah fried chicken leg. Hit' was like God himself came right on up outta that river, snatched 'em up and drown't 'em in this here water. I'm thinkin' that feller is still sittin' in that far'y furnace jest ponderin' on what happened."

Peeking through the crack between the lid and the lip of the barrel, Lily watched as one of the drunks told his story with gusto flapping his gangly arms around as he told his tale.

"Now, I weren't a'lookin at the feller when hit' happened but some of the other fellers was and they swear'd on thur' mamas' graves that haint hand came right on up outta that water and latched onta 'em with the grip of ah giant. They said that haint hand was as big as the ferry-boat we was ridin' in and hit' was plum scary I tell ya, plum scary. He weren't in that water but fur' one shake and all of ah sudden-like his body came shootin' right back up outta that water like a cannonball. He was dead, Jug, jest as dead as can be. His belly was already as big as a punkin and his face was lookin' like hit' was about to explode. We took on outta' that thar' water a'fore that body came back down into the water. I ain't never seen

4

anybody row as fast as we did. That ferry boat driver threw us all some paddles and off we went lickity-split. We reached that Ten-see shore, jumped outta that boat and never looked back. All's we hear'd was ah mighty big *ker-plunk* when his body came plungin' down into the water an I swear on my mama's grave thur' was ah loud rumblin' sound of laughin' comin' outta that water.

"Well, I ain't never been back on this here river and I ain't never gonna go back inta this river. This here river is spooked and full ah water-haints iff'en ya ask me. Nope, ya ain't never gonna citch' me goin' out on this here river—I ain't never gonna do it. And, hit ain't gonna take long fur' that young'un ta fill up with water. He ain't nothin' but ah stick."

"And, ya din't see 'em with your own *two* eyeballs, Pug. Ya only got but one eyeball, ya pea brain." The other drunk said brashly.

"Well, I know'd it! But I done did see 'em with my one eyeball, and anyways, we sure be needin' ta find' em."

"Yeah, I know," Jug replied briskly, "We be gettin' a pretty dang big bag ah gold dust fur' that'un. He might be scrawny now but he'll fill out good and proper once'st he gets his full grow goin' an all."

"I bet we could get a hun'erd dollars in gold dust fur' that'un."

"Yep, we could but hits lookin' like he done got away from us. Let's go on back to that say-loon and have another look-see tomor'ee. I be so winded I cain't hardly take a breath," Jug panted, "So iff'en yor wantin' ta keep on lookin', go right on ahead, Pug. I'm goin'' on back ta wet my whistle cuz that young'un done gone and jumped inta the river and prol'ly drow't his'self an is fish food by now."

"Yeah, I think I'm a'wantin' ta get outta here too, them haint tales got me all spooked like maybe one ah them water-haints could jump right up on this here dock an snatch us away. Come on, let's get outta here, Jug. We'll citch 'em tomorree."

Lily sat perfectly still as she tried breathing quietly. She squeezed her eyes shut and lifted her head toward heaven as she breathed a prayer.

Then she heard the drunks scrambling around as they attempted to get away from the dock as fast as their drunken legs could carry them before the "water-haints" snatched them up and dragged them into the river.

After a bit of huffing, puffing, farting, burping and cussing, they managed to stumble up to Waterfront Street; all the while crying about the bag of gold that just up and jumped into the river and swimmed away.

5

Thump, thump, thump

Lily could hear the huge paddle steam-wheelers bumping and rubbing against the sides of the dock as the river currents pushed and pulled them again and again into the wooden framework. Every time one of the boats hit the skeletal wood frame Lily's heart leapt into her throat. That sound was enough to scare the skin off her body!

The steam-wheelers loomed high above the landing with their towering smokestacks swaying back and forth with the rhythm of the river. Some of the boats were four decks high with three smokestacks so tall they could be seen from the other side of the long levee. They were a majestic, grand sight to see. Every day, people near the river would hear the look-out pilots calling out, "nooo bottom" or "marrrk twain", as he measured the depth of the river while passing small towns. Each time Lily heard the pilots call out the depth of the river it sent shivers down Lily's spine and put a longing in her heart to board one of these mighty steamers and travel the world.

The huge boats reminded her of the pictures she had seen as a small child of the queens in Europe. Like most of the queens in Europe, the passenger paddle-wheelers were always bedecked in frippery. Ruffled lattice-work wound around each deck railing making them look like squatty, chubby, Queens floating down the river in all their finery. In her mind's eye, Lily could imagine little short chubby Queenly legs floating along underneath the steamers as they chugged up and down the Mississippi.

The most magnificent paddle-wheeler of all was the *New Orleans Sirene*. Whenever the *Sirene* blew her unique whistle on the mighty Mississippi, all the folks living along the river's edge would walk out and watch her pass. She never had the need to stop at a small, little town like Caruthersville, Missouri, but the passengers from Natchez or New Orleans paid large amounts of money to ride the *New Orleans Sirene* so they could preen and display their wealth along the way.

The majority of the passengers were quite wealthy, so when life in New Orleans grew boring, when they became restless or weary of parties and teas they paid the outrageous fares to ride the *Sirene* all the way up north to the mouth of the Missouri River and all the way back down. A trip on the *Sirene* took much longer than usual, what with the passengers demanding the captain move slowly so everyone on shore would be able to have a grand look at them and their finery. They were not going anywhere in particular, or so it was rumored among the house servants who passed it on from house to house, they were just bored and needed a change of pace.

So, every time the *Sirene* passed, people lined up on the riverbanks to watch her pass. It was the dream of most families who lived along the river to one day be able to ride the *Sirene*. She was a beauty!

Musicians lined the upper deck playing the music of New Orleans as she passed and all the ladies on board patiently pacing up and down the deck as they waited for an audience. The single young ladies would bunch together and lean over the railings, laughing and waving at the small-town folks. They twirled their parasols and daintily waved their lacey white handkerchiefs, all the while throwing kisses to everyone admiring them. Quite often they would throw small pieces of tatted lace into the river so they could watch the young farm boys swim out and retrieve them. The children on board were dressed as miniature replicas of their parents. The little girls pranced up and down the decks as they twirled their parasols and waved their little girl handkerchiefs. The small boys wore suits and top hats and carried miniature canes. Their shoes were just as finely made and polished as their papas were and their little short walking canes were exactly like their papas.

The *Sirene* was midnight black with bright red, white and gold trim. All the smoke stacks were painted a shiny black with the words *New Orleans Sirene* embossed in gold down either side so it could be seen by viewers on both sides of the river. The top of each smoke stack was capped with over-sized gold crowns which gleamed and sparkled when the sun hit the shiny gold paint. Below the third level railing *New Orleans Sirene* was painted in bright red against a solid white back ground.

There had been times when Lily had watched finely dressed female passengers walk back into their cabins after strutting for the onlookers with faces black from the thick smoke as it bellowed from the smokestacks and winds pushed it onto the deck below where it settled on everything and everybody because it was such a slow-moving boat. But to the New Orleans ladies it was all worthwhile because they had been able to show the river folks just how beautiful they and their children were.

"The *Sirene* sure is the queen of the river," Lily thought as she sat in the pickle barrel peeking out through the crack between the barrel lip and the lid. Shaking herself, Lily came back to her present problem.

During the day, the dock was not a safe place for any child, but at night it was downright dangerous and scary. Drunken sailors staggered on and off their boats while beggars and thieves wandered along the levee looking for anyone who may be an easy victim.

Once again Lily pushed the lid up further and took a quick look out on the dock. The moon was peeking around the clouds causing its light to glisten off the riggings which stretched between each smokestack. The ropes were heavy with night moisture as the moonlight glimmered off the wet ropes turning them into giant, silvery spider webs. The swaying shadows of the spider webs, mixed with the silhouettes of the boats moving with the rhythm of the river appeared to be hiding evil spirts and creatures of the night. Moonbeams played ticks on Lily's eyes as she peeked out through the top of the barrel. The shadowy shapes of the ropes and pulleys morphed from silvery spider webs into terrifying, silver creatures skulking along the tops of the ropes and leaping down to the dock, dancing the devil's own dance on the wooden planks of the wet, shimmering dock as the moonlight flickered off the gleaming planks.

Pulling her old hat down a bit further and tightening her coat, Lily pushed the barrel lip up another inch.

Looking around once more, she slowly pushed the top of the empty barrel further up and was quite sure she would gag the next time she saw a pickle.

Thank goodness, the two drunks had been too drunk, or too stupid, to realize all the barrels were empty and waiting to be refilled and shipped out on the next pickle boat going down river. For some reason, probably the whiskey, they had not checked every barrel.

Raising her head above the barrel rim, she again checked to see if anyone was watching from the levee. Nothing moved and the only thing she could hear was the movement of the paddle-boats rubbing against the landing dock and the mumbling of voices coming from the top levels of each boat. The steam engines were quiet. It wouldn't become loud and noisy until just before dawn when the steam once again started building pressure in the engines.

The men standing on the top levels of the boats were guarding their boat in case someone tried to climb aboard without permission. All of the boats, even the cargo boats, had gambling rooms, so some of those standing on the upper levels were probably gamblers taking a break from losing all their money. Since all the winning gamblers never took a break, it was obvious these men were either losers or guards.

Apparently, the guards did not care about bums and drunks walking along the docks so they sure wouldn't care if they saw a skinny boy (or so they thought) snooping around.

"All the sailors must be in the saloons," Lily thought to herself as she pushed the top of the pickle barrel completely off. The wooden lid clanked loudly and rattled as it fell onto the thick planks of the dock. Immediately Lily ducked down into the barrel for a few more minutes then slowly stood up, slipped over the rim and stepped out onto the landing.

Benny's pants fit snuggly beneath Lily's shabby brown coat. Maybe she should have worn Gran-pappy's old pants, she thought to herself. She would have had to use a string to hold them up but at least they would have been more comfortable than Benny's.

Out in the river she could see more paddle-wheelers anchored for the night. The Mississippi was almost a mile wide here in Caruthersville, so the boats could drop anchor and wait for their turn to pull up to the docks when the first ray of sunlight slipped its fingers across the river and the boats which were already docked began leaving.

As soon as the captains could see, they would fire up the loud steam engines and slowly move away from or towards the docks.

Because of the large number of cotton farmers near Caruthersville and the Cedar wood mill, every cargo steamer stopped and loaded or unloaded before heading down river to Vicksburg, Natchez, and New Orleans.

Each boat anchored out on the river was lit up brightly with their gas lamps gleaming from every window; making sure night rafters or smaller boats would be able to see them. Every so often the pilot would sound his loud horn which would echo off the river and bounce throughout the countryside. Shimmering with lights and set against the dark sky, the big boats shone brightly with their lanterns swaying to the rhythm of the river current as their lights danced across the glassy water. But, these very boats which looked so enticing from the shoreline could be filled with evil doings. Some of them were actually used to secretly whisk away kidnapped children and young adults; sending them down river to be sold behind hidden closed doors in the underground slave-trade still prevalent along the river ports.

Yet, every paddle-wheeler tugged at the hearts of the young boys along the river. It was their dream to one day be the captain of such a huge paddle-wheeler.

"Benny!" Lily whispered loudly as she crouched over and scurried out onto the landing, trying not to alert anyone. She leaned over the side of the planks to get a closer look under the dock. The wooden boards were soaked and dripping with cold river water.

Laying on her stomach, she could feel the icy water seep through her coat and shirt as she hung her head further over the edge. Lifting one hand to hold onto her hat, she leaned further over; hoping she wouldn't slip into the river.

"Benny!" she called again a bit louder, "are you and Tessa down there? It's me, Lily."

Eerie glowing shadows glistened within the underbelly framework of the dock creating unknown creatures in a person's mind and the moonlight flickered and shimmered within the skeletal structure. The planks crossed each other so many times it looked like spindly spidery patchwork where a person could easily hide from unwanted eyes and that was what Lily was hoping Benny and Tessa had done. The whole structure creaked and groaned with the force of the water rushing in and surging out as the boats bumped against the framework, jolting the entire structure.

"Benny, answer me if you're down there. We have to get out of here before someone sees us or Aunt Birdie sends Elmer down here to find us."

A small, squeaky, little voice called out from under the dock.

"Lily, it's me, Tessa! Come and get me."

Lily could hear a lot of mumbling then Benny spoke loudly:

"Tessa! If you will just keep your voice down and do what I tell you to do, I can get both of us out of here without drowning. Lily, we're coming out on the right side of the dock. There are some wood planks we can use as a ladder so reach out and grab Tessa's hand before she yells out again or falls into the river."

Scurrying over to the opposite side of the dock, Lily leaned her head way over the edge and finally spotted them. Benny had a tight hold on Tess's waistband as he practically dragged her through the wet, slippery wooden planks.

Holding her breath in fear, Lily watched as Tessa's feet kept sliding off the narrow planks and Benny had to drag her back up by her waistband.

As Benny and Tessa inched along the wet boards, Lily could barely breathe. The waves were splashing against the wooden boards at times nearly covering both Benny and Tessa. If Tessa completely lost her footing, Benny may not be able to keep her upright. The water was extremely deep and rough under the dock and she doubted Benny could save Tessa.

Tessa wasn't a good enough swimmer to save herself and Benny probably couldn't save a frantic Tessa.

Barely breathing until they were within reach, she quickly stretched down her hand and grabbed Tessa's arm and pulled her up onto the dock.

Tessa was shivering, her lips were blue and all her clothes were dripping with cold water. Both she and Benny were soaked from the river water.

Taking off her own coat, she wrapped it around Tessa's thin, trembling, little shoulders.

Lily began to worry, if Tessa got sick, how would she and Benny be able to help her?

"Come on Benny," Lily whispered loudly, "Tessa is so cold her lips are blue."

"I'm coming as fast as I can, Lily!" Benny snapped as he reached up to pull himself onto the dock floor. Lily took his hand and gave it a sharp tug to help him and finally he was sitting on the dock. His hands were as blue and trembling as were Tessa's and his body was also dripping wet.

"What were you two doing down there? You had me worried sick!"

"Well," Benny said as he looked over at Tessa, "let's get Tessa warmed up and then I'll tell you all about it."

The three of them hurried along the dock and up onto the path leading to Waterfront Street. They ran as fast as they possibly could with Lily and Benny each holding one of Tessa's arms.

Whenever someone came their way, they ducked down behind barrels or boxes so no one would notice them. Lily couldn't help but wonder what had happened.

Approaching the Waterfront saloon area, all three of them bunched closer together so they could wedge Tessa between them. Farm hands, stevedores, longshoremen, drunks and ladies of the night were everywhere. The clanking of the tinny, out-of-tune saloon pianos echoed up and down the street as each of the saloon piano players tried to out-play the others. Drunken men wandered the streets keeping a keen eye open for any opportunity to snatch up a child and sell them to the slavers who, in return, would sell them to profiteers who would turn around and sell them to the underground slave market. The sailors were mostly mean, ugly men with very few teeth and faces so dirty it was hard to determine what they actually looked like. Their body-smell gave their presence away before a person spotted them. They smell of whiskey, sweat, urine and the filth which surrounded the entire saloon area of Waterfront Street and left a lingering odor floating around the cliental. Lily had seen men from the cargo boats urinating on themselves because they were too drunk or stupid to realize what they were doing. They were a disgusting lot of men.

"Hey, boys!" a drunk shouted as he sat on a woodpile outside on a saloon. "Wanna sell that thar little gal ya got with ya?"

Lily felt Tessa tighten her grip on her arm and give out a quivering gasp of fright.

Immediately they began running with Lily and Benny practically dragging Tessa along the road.

They all knew stories of parents who would sell one of their children to these men in order to feed the rest of their children.

"They probably didn't want their children in the first place," Lily thought to herself as they continued hurrying along the street, "They probably have children just to sell to the slavers and make more money!" Lily knew one thing for sure; she and Benny had to get themselves, and Tessa, away as soon as possible.

"Come one, come on," Lily whispered softly, "if we're caught, we'll all be in a fine kettle of fish."

Passing each saloon, they hunkered down so no one inside could see them through the window or the open holes where windows used to be before it was shattered by something (or someone) being thrown out onto the street. Some of the saloons had boarded up the openings. The owners had grown tired of purchasing glass and having it shattered every Saturday night by fighting men. At least planks of wood kept out both four and two-legged beasts.

When they passed the *Ruby Slipper Saloon* they turned right and went into the back alley and quietly slippe into a small shanty built behind the saloon.

"Okay," Lily said as she lit a lantern along with a small potbellied stove, "Tell me what happened."

"Well," Benny whispered as Lily began pulling off Tessa's dripping shoes and stockings, "just as me and Tessa came out of the back of the bake shop, Aunt Birdie walked past and saw us!"

"She started yelling and trying to catch us," Tessa whispered with wide-eyed fear as Benny continued with his story.

"I was so afraid she would get Tessa my heart was pounding right out of my chest. We took off running as fast as we could until we got to the boat docks. I knew if we hid underneath Aunt Hogs-waddle would never be able to find us. I sure was glad you came along when you did, Lily. I thought for sure she would go home and get old Elmer and have him find us and drag us back. That's why we were down at the far end of the dock. I knew if we went to the far side, no one would be able to see us because there's so many boards blocking the way.. Not many people know about that opening where a body can squeeze down underneath and hide.

Her name isn't Aunt Hogs-waddle, Benny. It's Aunt Birdie." Lily replied softly.

"Well," Benny replied, "she looks just like a hog waddling to me. I don't understand why Pappy H called her Birdie. She's too wide for a bird and she couldn't fly if she had a whole flock of eagles holding onto her arms. She looks like that ol' hog of Mr. Pruiett's waddling down the path through his corn field." Benny began mimicking a waddling hog as he told his story.

"She waddles so much she could knock a grown-up man down to the ground, or even out into the street if she hit him with her behind! And her face...I swear by the bottom of my britches, looks just like a hog's face. In fact, our ol' hog Sully looks prettier then she does, and Sully is much nicer." Benny laughed.

"Benny," Lily answered sharply, as she and Tessa turned away so Benny could change out of his wet clothes, "Aunt Birdie is not fat or wide or ugly. You think so because she is not a nice person. She is skinnier than mama was but she's not nice. That's the whole problem. She's not a good person but you really shouldn't be talking like this in front of Tessa."

"I already know she looks like a hog waddling from the back," Tessa giggled as her big green eyes widened and her eyebrows arched higher than usual.

"And, her face really does look like a hog. I think when she was born Pappy and Granny H got her mixed up with someone else's baby. Somebody must have crawled into Granny H's window during the night and switched babies. Probably because her real mama took one look at her baby and fell right over onto the floor in a faint and then wouldn't get up until she had a baby human," Tessa laughed loudly.

13

Benny laughed so hard he started coughing.

"That's it," He exclaimed. "Her name has to be Birdie Anne Hog-jaws and I bet you a gol-durn nickel she really isn't our aunt. She can't be Pa's sister, she's just to mean spirited. I don't think she is our Aunt Birdie 'cuz Pa would have warned us about her meanness. What we have here is a dilemma. We need to find a family with the last name of Hog-jaws and they'll have our real Aunt Birdie," Benny chuckled.

"We can just take their kin back to them and grab up our real Aunt Birdie and take her home where she belongs! We get the good aunt and they get the bad aunt along with her bad spirit. Hmm...but, they may like our real Aunt Birdie and not want this mean one back. Maybe we'll have to sneak into their house of a night and make the switch. They probably live up there in the Ozarks so maybe they'll be happy to finally find their long-lost kin. They won't really know how mean she is until it's too late and we'll be home already and too bad for them and they won't be able to do a gol-durn thing! What do you think about that, Lily?"

"I think you had better stop cussing right now. We have to be serious about this," Lily scolded.

"I am being serious, me love," Benny said with a twinkle in his eyes as he used one of Pa's favorite endearments, "Aunt Birdie Hog-jaws is seriously ugly and seriously mean and I was seriously scared when we saw her. What was Aunt Birdie doing at the bakeshop after dark? She never goes to town when it's dark, or even when it's close to dark, as far as that goes. Ah-ha...I know, maybe she stopped to get some hog feed and forgot the time of day," Benny smirked, "or, maybe, just maybe, she needed a new hog-trough for her supper plate." He grinned wider, giving Tessa a wink which made her start giggling again.

"I really don't know," Lily said out loud,

"But I bet I could guess," she thought to herself, "she was up to no good, that's for sure."

"You think she has some of those young'uns from over in Burl and is trying to sell them to the slavers?" Benny whispered in a serious tone of voice.

Burl was a settlement about two miles away from Caruthersville filled with freed slaves and their families. They work the land for their food just like all the rest of the farmers along the river. Some of them fished for a living, bringing their daily catch into town to sell. A few of them always stopped at the farms along the way to sell fresh fish to the farmers. Granny Tomason usually hired some of the young boys to help work her farm, the same as their Pa had done every year.

Tessa's eyes grew huge as she whispered, "I saw her with two of Mrs. Sophie's girls the very day before we left our house and they were crying for their mama and Aunt Birdie told them if they stopped crying she would take them on a nice boat ride with a big picnic basket and have a picnic. The little one, Sylvie, stopped crying but then her older sister Lizzy jerked Sylvie's hand away from Aunt Birdie and took off running as fast as she could out across the field towards her house dragging Sylvie with her. All the while yelling at Aunt Birdie that their mama had told them they were not to go anywhere with anyone and her and her little sister wasn't going anywhere with a mean old woman like Aunt Birdie.

"Well, Aunt Birdie yelled back something about getting the law after Lizzy for being sassy, but Lizzy just kept right on running. I was in the berry patch and I could see the whole thing," Tessa stretched out her arms and made a big circle, "Later that same day Aunt Birdie started asking me about those squatters down in the river bottom. You know, Lily, the ones with those three little girls who all look alike. They are little like me and they never have to go to school. They're so lucky! Lily, you know what else?" Tessa didn't wait for Lily to answer, she kept right on yammering, "Their names are Molly, Polly and Dolly! Isn't that funny? I like them. They have wonderful names and they all have real white hair and their eyes are the same color like my eyes! Can you believe that! Isn't that something."

Tessa giggled and continued chattering like a Magpie, "Our names should be, Tessa, Bessa, Lessa and Caitlin should be Messa since she's got herself in such a mess. They even told me they all have the same birthday and their birthday is the same day as my birthday is! Isn't THAT something?" Tessa's eyes were sparkling. Every time Tessa got excited about something her eyes widened and sparkled.

They're called triplets, Tessa," Lily said quietly, "They were all born on the same day."

"Really? Wow! Well that's a mighty fine thing to happen. And do you know what, Lily? Their Pa's name is Daniel just like ours." Tessa smiled and looked as if she were in deep thought.

"Well, anyways," she continued after a second or two, "Aunt Birdie Hog-jaws asked me all kinds of questions about them but I didn't tell her a single thing. I just kept my lips shut tight and acted like I didn't even know who she was asking about.

"I don't like her one single bit, Lily," she whispered quietly, "I think she would sell her own baby, if she had one. But she's too mean to have a baby. No man would want to put a baby in her belly. She's too scary."

"Tessa, you have to stop talking like that. It isn't very proper for a young girl," Lily scolded, "but we do have to stay away from her until we can find Caitlin. I think Aunt Birdie could be dangerous."

Tessa's eyes filled with tears as she looked at Lily hopefully, "What happened to my Caitlin, Lily? Did she really run away and leave us here with Aunt Birdie forever?"

"No, sweetheart. Aunt Birdie lied to us. She would like to snatch us up and tell everybody Caitlin left us and now she has to take care of us. Then she would say she is doing the best Christian thing and she dearly loves us, but all the while she would be planning on selling us and telling folks we ran away. So, stay away from her. If you see her again, run.

"Here, Benny, you and Tessa share these sweet buns Mr. Johnston gave me. He said he would have to throw them out since they didn't look the way he wanted them to look. I thought they looked fine, but he insisted no one would buy then so I accepted them. I'll go out and see if Granny Tomason's mulch cow will give us some milk for the morning."

As Lily put her Grandpappy's old hat and coat back on, she watched Benny take Tessa over to the pile of old rags by the stove. He helped her take off her wet coat then turned around so she could have some privacy while putting on a long warm, dry dress.

The pot-bellied stove had warmed the little shanty enough to keep them warm for the night.

Just in case someone stumble along the alley and decided to check out the light coming from the holes in the shanty, Lily blew out the lantern but left the fire burning in the rusty old pot-belly stove so it wouldn't get too cold for Tessa.

The weather was still chilly at nights, but during the day it was growing warmer and warmer. Spring had finally arrived and the grass and trees were already turning green. The early spring flowers were now in full bloom and the open fields and forest clearings were evolving into a colorful rainbow as wild flowers displayed their petals of vivid colors.

Lily was worried about Tessa. Tessa was only five and small for her age. She could say some things that surprised the rest of them and she had a quick-thinking imagination and a quicker mouth. Whatever popped into her mind popped right out of her mouth.

Lily's mind drifted to her brother and sisters. Tessa looked like their mama with her soft, red-blonde hair and mossy green eyes. When Lily thought of her mama, sometimes she pictured her with light red hair and other times with light golden-blonde hair. It was as if God could not make up his mind whether to give her and Tessa red hair or blonde. Occasionally Pa would refer to them as his jewels and say their hair was part ruby and part spun gold. When it came to eye color, Mama and Tessa's eyes could look as green as the leaves on the oak trees, and other times they looked like the green leaves of the lily-pads growing in the pond behind Granny Tomason's house. They both had fair skin, a sprinkling of freckles across their noses and expressive dark brown eyebrows which moved up and down with their thoughts and moods.

Benny looked like Pappy H with his dark red hair and blue eyes. Many times, Mama had told them Pappy H had his freckles until the very day he died so Lily was sure Benny's freckles were on his face to stay. His arms and legs seemed to belong to a much taller person but Granny Tomason assured her his body would, one day, catch up with those long arms and legs. Lily sure hoped so because he looked rather funny at the moment.

Benny was a lot taller than Lily and one could already see the muscles developing in his thin arms and legs. Mama said Benny acted like Pa, easy to get along with, full of mischief and always taking care of everything he possibly could. Even when their parents were alive, Benny was busy helping out whenever he wasn't in school. He would come home from school and immediately start working on the farm with their Pa. He often said he loved working the soil more than anything else. He was a good person and Lily was proud to call him her brother.

Caitlin and Lily looked like their Pa with their dark black hair, amber gold eyes and long black lashes surrounding their eyes.

Whenever Mama was worried about the crops coming in during a bad harvest; or anything else going wrong, Pa would laugh, give her a hug and tell her they had enough gold in the eyes of their two oldest daughters to last the two of them a lifetime. All he had to do was talk Caitlin and Lily into giving him their eyeballs and he and Mama could run away from their mischievous offspring and live forever on a tropical island. Then he would jump towards the two girls and chase them out the door of the house and around the yard yelling at the top of his booming voice; "Give me ye gold, ye pirating wench's!"

Caitlin and Lily would be running and screaming as if the demons of hell were upon them. The would run off into the woods and Pa would act as if they had escaped and go back into the house to tell Mama the gold had slipped through his fingers, but he would try again another day.

Mama would laugh at his foolishness and once again be in a good mood.

"What a happy man Pa had been. He had been the best Pa a person could ever want," Lily thought as she prepared to leave for Granny Tomason's farm.

Thank goodness Benny had Pa's personality; he was very dependable and responsible. Instead of just running off when Caitlin disappeared, he had stayed by Lily and Tessa and helped get them all out of the house. Without Benny Lily would have had to take Tessa with her every time she left the shanty.

"Where is Caitlin?" Lily wondered, "Has Aunt Birdie talked old Elmer into carrying her off to the boats?"

Elmer was Aunt Birdie's handyman and was a scary person. He looked just as mean as Aunt Birdie acted. He is tall as Pa had been but he looked unkept. He had crooked, dirty, greenish teeth and smelled like one of the sailors from the docks. His hair was always dirty, slicked back and tied at the nape of the neck with a piece of rawhide. It was black as coal and hung straight down his back. Sometimes he wore it in a long braid which touched the top of his britches. His skin had a red hue to it which made him look like the Kickapoo Indians who lived in the area, or at least part Kickapoo. His face was leathered from working in the outdoors for many years, he had the high cheekbones of the Kickapoo, but his eyes were not the coal black of a true Indian. They held a touch of green around the outside of the iris and he had a piercing stare. If Elmer stared at a dead body, Lily was quite sure it would roll away or jump right up and take off running. Also, he had no eyebrows at all. Instead of eyebrows, he had scars as if he had been in a fight and his opponent had held him down and sliced off his eyebrows. Many times, Lily was tempted to ask him what happened to his eyebrows but she chickened out every time she looked at the angry scowl on his face.

18

He had huge hands and massive muscles and could probably carry away a full-grown cow without breathing heavy. Sometimes Lily wondered why Aunt Birdie and Elmer had not gotten married, since Aunt Birdie claimed Elmer had been her handyman for as long as she could remember.

Maybe Elmer just stayed around because he had a warm place in the barn to sleep and Aunt Birdie gave him plenty of food to eat. All he had to do was take care of the small amount of work around the farm and Benny helped him with that. Aunt Birdie must be giving him money for his whiskey but, Lily and her siblings had never quite figured out where Aunt Birdie, herself, got all her money unless it was coming from the plantation in Natchez.

When Mama and Pa died, Caitlin promised to take care of Benny, Lily and Tessa. She also told them since she was twenty-three no one could take them away from her. Surely that included Aunt Birdie. Aunt Birdie and Elmer arrived the very day after Mama and Pa's funeral with Aunt Birdie saying she and Elmer were already on their way for a visit when they got the sad news of the deaths.

A little at a time, Aunt Birdie took over everything in the house. She began cooking and cleaning as if it were her own house and gradually moved Mama and Pa's things out of the house and into the barn. She told them it made her too sad to look at anything that reminded her of her beloved Daniel.

Every time Aunt Birdie moved something out of the house Caitlin would move it back into her own bedroom. Caitlin had moved into Mama and Pa's bedroom the night after the funeral and Lily was sure Aunt Birdie would have gone straight into their room and stayed if it had not already been occupied by Caitlin.

As it was, Aunt Birdie told Lily and Tessa they would have to share the same room so she could have the room Tessa was in for herself.

She began telling everyone what do and when to do it. Caitlin tried stopping her by telling her there was no need for her to stay since the house now belonged to the four children but Aunt Birdie smiled and said stiffly, "Oh mercy me, dear. I do realize that, I surely do but I am sure your dear mother and my sweet Daniel would want me to stay and take care of you children to the best of my ability. This will all work out for the best, yes indeed it will."

When Caitlin disappeared, Aunt Birdie told all the folks in town the house was now hers; seeing that Caitlin had run off with a lover and left all the children for her to take care of.

Lily's stomach grew tight as an ache rose up in her chest just thinking about all of it. Caitlin would never leave them, even if she had run off with a lover, which she did not do, she sure wouldn't leave her younger sisters and brother here with Aunt Birdie and old Elmer. Something bad happed to Caitlin; Lily could feel it in her bones.

2

The Fog

Hurrying along the dark alleyway, Lily felt uneasy about leaving Benny and Tessa alone for any length of time, but she had no other choice. It was safer for Tessa if Benny stayed behind with her than if Lily herself stayed. He could probably do a better job protecting Tessa against anyone snooping around the shanty and Tessa shouldn't be out in the cold after getting so wet. So that left Lily to go alone to Granny Tomason's house.

Flickering rays of light danced in the windows of homes and buildings; temporarily giving a shadowy glow of light brightening the path as she scurried along the dark alleyway. Lily knew she would soon be away from the dwellings and the Missouri forest would become black as pitch.

Thick fog began tumbling along the alleyway as it was pushed in by the breeze coming up from the chilly river water. Like tumbleweeds rolling across the prairie, the fog rolled along the path with its misty tentacles grabbing ahold of and curling around every obstacle in its path; swirling upward and pulling everything into its chilly, damp shroud. Trees, buildings, and shrubs were heavily veiled within the murky, sinister vapor. It reminded Lily of a mythical creature trying to devour its food before it was taken away. Shifting shadowy trees swaying in the night breeze looked like imaginary creatures waving their long, spindly arms above their heads as the fog swirled its way up their trunks, devouring small leaves and pale spring blossoms. Then, with an audible hiss the breeze blew the fog away, bringing everything into focus again but then, immediately another push of the breeze swept the damp, misty fog back into the alleyway.

Finding herself holding her breath, Lily looked down and watched as the wet fog swirled around her feet, creeping up her legs in its effort to envelop *her* in its wispy blanket. Goose bumps popped out on her arms and she began tingling with panic as the mist crept slowly up her body.

Brushing at it, she tried getting it away from her body but it stuck to her hands creating little puffs of fog when finally she shook it off. Then once again, a quick rush of the breeze pushed the fog all the way up to her waist.

Feeling fear slide up her back and into her brain, she envisioned herself being wrapped tightly in its embrace and carried down the alley and into the river by these wispy fingers of haze. Frantically she began swinging her arms up and down her body as she tried pushing the clinging mist away.

"Okay Lily-girl," she said to herself loudly, "Stop it. It's just fog."

The sounds from the saloons became fainter as she forced herself to quickly walk away from the waterfront with her feet pushing the fog into puffs around her ankles like dry powdery dust.

The yipping of a dog echoed eerily down the alleyway causing Lily to stop and look back.

As the dog continued yipping, as if it were terribly frightened, she could hear it was coming closer and closer. Standing still she tilted her head a bit to listen more closely and maybe, tell how close the dog was when suddenly it burst through the fog like a bull bursting through a white curtain and it was running straight at her. Frozen with fear, Lily watched as the big hound bounded quickly along the alleyway, reached her and dashed past without giving her the slightest glance. It was as if the dog had not seen her at all, even though it brushed her pant leg in passing. Wherever it was headed it was in a big hurry as it left swirling clouds of tumbling fog behind. It raced down the road as if being chased by an evil spirit as it kept glancing behind itself as if expecting to see something or someone following. The

22

fog looked like it was chasing the hound as it rolled and tumbled in billowing puffs behind him and then it gobbled the hound up and instantly there was silence...as if the fog had swept the hound off the road into the clutches of the unknown. Once again, the hazy, fog-filled night became silent as a tomb with an eerie feeling of foreboding hanging heavy in the air.

The lonesome hooting of a large barn owl and the croaking of bull frogs finally broke the silence as Lily continued down the shadowy alley at a faster pace. The sounds of the night always seemed creepy to Lily, even in her own home with the rest of her family. But, tonight with the fog rolling in and out of the shadowy alleyway, the sounds became downright sinister; sending shivers through her bones.

The clanging sounds of the saloon pianos grew fainter and fainter the further she moved from town. Soon they were too faint to hear, and the sounds of the night creatures would be the sole noise within the forest.

Once again, the breeze began pushing fog swiftly along the road like giant tumbleweeds. It quickly swirled, twisted and danced to the melody of the winds. It was strangely captivating in a spine-chilling kind of way, as if it were alive and watching.

Then, in just a few seconds, it became thick and dense, too dense to tumble. The river flung out a strong arm and gave the fog a sharp push into Lily's path. Her view was totally blocked and limited to a few short feet in front of her. Slowing down, she began walking in a slow shuffle displacing the misty fog with every step. She felt claustrophobic; as if she were being woven into a small cocoon with the fog pressing tighter and tighter around her body. The fog was so thick and close there was no way she could see the road.

She had to stop because she couldn't move one foot without the fear of running into something, or someone.

Panic rose up in her throat and terror swelled up within her soul.

Then once again, just as quickly as it had appeared, the fog was sucked out of the alleyway and vanished and the strong winds left, leaving a soft breeze to settle the fog's wispy remnants, rendering the alleyway visible. The breeze now felt warmer, like a gentle summer wind.

With the wet remnants of fog settling to the ground, Lily's mind wandered back to the tales her Pa had told of the dark evils that happen in the Black Forest of Germany when the moon and stars hid their faces from the earth as if they too were frightened to watch. She remembered him telling of how wolves would come out at night to hunt for human flesh and howl, sometimes surrounding cabins built deep in the heart of the forest, as they called for someone to come out.

In those dark, long ago, tales of the Black Forest, the occupants would swear the wolves could speak to them in a language they understood. The wolves would tell them of all the gold and silver to be given to anyone who would risk opening their doors. The evil beasts would promise not to harm the humans if someone would just bring food out to them. The old tales told of the foolish who believed the lies and opened the doors only to vanish forever.

It was told that the inhabitants of the cabins would have to put boards across their windows and doors to keep the wolves out along with cotton in their ears to block out the alluring, captivating words of the wolves. Supposedly the wolves were so wise, (and the men so foolish) if any man, woman or child heard their soothing lies, they would heed their call.

When the first distinctive howl of the strange wolves echoed across the forest, candles would be placed on windowsills and behind closed doors the candles would burn brightly throughout the night to keep the evil whispers from slipping like vapor through the cracks. The inhabitants had to keep fires going in the fireplaces, even in the hot summer nights, or the words from the wolves would creep into their homes through the chimneys.

Lily also remembered tales Pa told about wicked apparitions and leprechauns from Ireland — tales of how night evils would ride in with the wind when the fog was thick and the nights were so black it was impossible to see your hand in front of your face. He told of times when just as in the Black Forest of Germany the moon and stars would hide their faces, as if afraid, behind heavy black clouds, as the evil winds echoed off the rolling green hills. A man, alone on the dark cobblestone streets of Dublin, would feel the clinch of fear as something brushed its hand across the back of his neck, making goose bumps rise along his arms and legs. When shrinking, yellow orbs of streetlamps, which had become muddied by the blood-chilling fog, were the only sources of light. The fog seeming to have crawled inside the fixture and push the flame of light into tiny orbs.

This fog would ride in on great gusts of wind from the ocean; thick enough to stick to the sides of buildings and creep up their walls to the roof tops. It was called the *Devil's Fog*.

All the people of Ireland knew of the *Devil's Fog*, and believed it truly could take your soul — or parts of your body — and leave behind an empty hole where your spirit had once lived.

When the *Devil's Fog* rolled in, villagers would rush into their homes, shut and lock the shutters, turn the locks on the doors and not look out until the next morning. If a poor soul was caught in this evil fog, they would hurry to the nearest house begging the residents to let them stay the night. There were many, many tales of what happened to poor souls who could not find a safe haven. Some would be found the next morning, their arms and legs gone, or maybe with all their blood drained from their bodies. Worse yet, their life may have been spared, but at the cost of their soul, which was taken by the presence of the *Devil's Fog*. From then on, night after night they would wander the streets of the village hunting for their lost souls. They were like the zombies in the African tales, never eating or sleeping, just trying to fill the empty hole where their soul had once lived.

In case the fog came upon the village unawares, most of the shops along the village streets kept cots in the back where their workers could sleep for the night. Each shop had extra bedding for strangers who might rush to their doors during the fog's sudden appearance.

25

When Pa told his tall tales of ghouls and goblins he would lower his voice to a ghostlike whisper and speak slowly as he leaned over his children sitting on the floor in front of him staring up at him with eyes wide and mouths open. It was as if speaking any louder would conjure up vile creatures who would suddenly appear behind them. Lily always scooted as close to Pa as possible and wrapped her arm around his leg, keeping Benny behind her just in case the creatures tried to sneak in. Benny would try to laugh and Pa would look at him and say in a low rhythmic Irish lilt, "Don't believe it do ya now, laddie?" Pa would ask as he chortled wickedly, "Let us all wait and see into the future, me boy. You'll come to see your dear ole Pa and be telling me the fearsome things ya had seen and heard as a wee laddie and be asking for me knowledge on how to be telling it to ye own wee lads and lass's."

Mama would always scold Pa, saying, "Hush you're scaring me own wee ones with such foolish tales, Daniel Henry Quinn. Don't ya believe his foolish tales, me wee ducks. Come on over here and I'll be telling ya tales of good leprechauns who give all good children, like yourselves, sweets and hugs."

"No Mama!" They would all say together, "We want to hear more of Pa's foolish tales," Pa would laugh, wink at Mama, and start another. On those nights, so long ago, Lily, Caitlin and Tessa would all sleep in the same bed. Even though Tessa was just a little infant and unable to understand any of the tales, having her in bed with them made Lily and Caitlin feel safer.

* * * *

Feeling someone or something looking at her, Lily peered into the shrouding forest and buildings surrounding the alley. Blinking rapidly to make sure her eyes were not fooling her, she spotted a lone shadow leaning against the side of a building. She stopped, swallowed and blinked her eyes to get a better look. Was it a leprechaun? Was it a haint? Her heart was in her throat and the hair on the back of her neck stood straight up and once again goose bumps popped up on her arms and legs as the blood in her veins turned icy. The shadow didn't move, but Lily could feel him watching her. She could not see the shadowed eyes, but her heart gave a lurch when he waved his arm beckoning her to draw closer.

26

She tried to run, but her legs refused to move. They were not reacting to her brain's commands. Fear had frozen her muscles.

"Come on, come on!" she screamed in her mind, all the while staring at the shadow who once again beckoned her.

"Move, move, move," she brain-screamed again, but nothing happened! Her legs refused to budge.

The shadow moved as if coming toward her, but stopped when a shutter on a second-floor window above him banged open. A woman stuck her head out the window and looked around.

"Well, Jack," the woman called out with a booming voice, "it could be God's own boots stomping right outside our window, but this fog is so thick we couldn't see him even if he was wearing candles on his boot straps," Turning her head, she yelled loudly to someone behind her, "Tis as thick as river mud, this fog is."

Turning to look out the window once again the woman yelled, "Get off your lazy duff and get out there ya'self iff'en ya want to be a'seein' what the noise is, I'm not going out in the stuff!"

Lily had not heard the noise the woman was talking about. All she could see was the shadow. Again, she squinted her eyes to get a better look and this time she could see his clothing and ...it was a man and he wore a military uniform.

"Whoa!" she muttered, "Who in the hind-leg-of-a-hound dog is that?"

The man was in a full soldier uniform as he slowly began walking toward her again with his hat pulled down over his face, preventing Lily from making out his identity. He had a full beard and mustache with a slight smile; Lily didn't know if she should feel relief or fear. The shadow wore a long military coat, open along the front with military emblems on the shoulders.

As he drew closer, Lily could see he was holding something in his hand, as if he wanted her to take it. She couldn't make out what it was, but it lay in his open, outstretched palm.

"Lily-Beth," the shadow called to her in a soft, low voice, "Lily-Beth, come here. Please, I need to talk to ya."

Lily thought her poor heart would surely stop right on the spot. The only person who had *ever* called her by that name was Michael Thorne.

But Michael Thorne was dead, he died in the war.

The shadow was not quite half way to her when the fog suddenly tumbled back in with a quick, distinct '*whoosh*' and totally covered him and pulled him into its dense shroud. The upstairs window slammed shut and Lily's muscles woke up. She started running as fast as she possibly could, expecting, at any moment, to feel the icy hands of death grab her ankles and pull her back into the fog.

She ran for what seemed like forever with her chest burning from breathing so hard and water was running down the corners of her eyes. She ran and ran, all the while quietly singing under her breath, interrupted by loud gasps for air, one of Pa's merry Irish tunes about the washer- woman; hoping it would calm her nerves:

> When I was at home...*gasp*...I was merry and frisky. My pa kept a pig, but my mother sold whiskey...*gasp*...My uncle was rich, but ne'er was lazy, till I was enlisted by Corporal Cazy...*gasp*...

She ran and sang until she was out of breath and had to stop and catch her breath.

Finally, she was able to make out the light in Granny Tomason's window. Glancing over her shoulder, she saw no one following but that didn't mean they weren't back there somewhere. Still breathing heavily, she bent over and rested her hands on her knees trying to catch her breath. Lifting her head, she peered back down the road again. No one followed.

Straightening up, she knew she had to keep moving, in case the shadow had taken a different route to follow her. the tension in her body eased as she turned toward Granny's house and started hurrying along the path.

"Thank you, good Lord in heaven," Lily sighed, "I sure hope I got away from whomever that was."

Granny Tomason's small farm was in the middle of a field of wild flowers and oak trees. Some of the wild flowers had already bloomed and the oak trees were full of lush green leaves. The wide path going up to Granny's gate was free of weeds.

The house was a double shotgun house. Reason being, if you were to shoot a shotgun through the front door, the shot would go straight out the back door. Granny's house was larger than most shotgun houses. When you opened the front door, you immediately entered a straight hallway which enabled you to see the door leading to the back porch. There were four bedrooms off the left side of the hall, a parlor, dining room and very large kitchen off the right side of the hall. The kitchen took up half of the right side of the house. It had a large walk-in pantry and a big eating table in the center of the room. A huge wood-burning cook stove stood along the back wall of the kitchen with wood piled as high as Lily's head on one side and the water pump in a dry sink was on the other side. Granny said that was built so she didn't have to tote water all the way across the room just to heat it up.

The nicest thing about Granny's house was in the summertime when it was covered with white and blue Morning Glory vines it smelled like a field of flowers all on its own. The vines grew all the way up to the rooftop and covered her entire roof. During the heat of the Missouri summers there were flowers all over her house.

Mama once told them Granny and her husband had wanted a lot of children when they were first married, but it never happened, so now Granny had a big beautiful home but no children to fill it. But Granny said the good Lord knew what was best and she was fine with his decision.

Most days Granny paid Benny or one of the boys from town to come out and chop wood and do her heavy chores. She either gave the boys cash or food for their families and the boys worked hard for her and kept her farm in good condition.

As Lily walked along the pathway to the house she could hear the rustle of small critters among the wild flowers growing tall and thick across the meadow in front of the house. During the summer months a variety of flowers like Blue Bonnets, Clémentine's, Cone flowers and in particular, wild red rose bushes, painted the meadow with color.

Granny Tomason was not really their granny, but she had known Mama and Pa for a long time. She was the Quinn children's best friend and loved them dearly just as they loved her. They knew she would help them out with anything they needed.

She had once told Lily she was a distant relative, but Lily could not remember which side of the family Granny said she was related to

3

Granny's House

Lily approached Granny Tomason's house through the front gate as Pie-Eater, Granny Tomason's dog, stood up on the porch and began barking. His tail was wagging so hard his whole backside and back legs were moving back and forth with each bark. Pie-Eater's hair was copper-red and he was as big as a small mama bear.

His bark was deep and resonated across the field making him sound ferocious, but he was a big loveable teddy bear. All he wanted was a free hand-out of food and as much belly-scratching as he could beg off a person.

"Hi, Pie-Eater!" Lily laughed. Pie-Eater had gotten his peculiar name because every time granny sat a pie on the windowsill to cool, he would make a beeline for the window and try his best to gobble the pie up before Granny caught him.

He loped down the steps and in four giant strides jumped up on Lily as she came in through the gate. Lily smiled at the happy dog and scratched his head as he flopped onto the ground waiting for her to scratch his belly.

The door to the house squeaked opened and Granny's peeked out, "Well, Lily Quinn, hurry up child and get on in here. It's too chilly to be out in the

31

dark of night. What are you doing coming all the way out here? What's happening at your house? Something I should know about? You children need some help?"

Sighing with relief, Lily replied, "Yes, Granny, we do. Caitlin's disappeared and we left our house because Aunt Birdie slapped me. We just need a little milk until Benny and I can find Caitlin. Mr. Johnston, the baker, has been giving us some of his sweet buns throughout the day, so we have something to eat, but I'm worried about Tessa." Lily blinked and swallowed, afraid she would start crying.

Deciding not to tell Granny about the shadow she encountered on the way out, Lily gave Granny a big hug.

"Whoa, hold on a minute, gal," Granny held up her hand and stopped Lily from talking, "Come on in here where it's warm and have a set-down at the table. So, Caitlin's missing? What in tarnation is going on here? What is wrong with little Tessa and where are Tessa and Benny right now?" She pulled out a chair and motioned for Lily to sit down.

Granny put some wood into her cook stove and stoked the fire then bustled around getting Lily something to eat as she waved her hand at Lily as if to say "start talking". Lily told Granny all about what had happened and where they were staying. She told her about the drunken sailors at the levee, getting sweet rolls from Mr. Johnston's bakery and not being able to find decent food for the three of them. She assured Granny that they would pay her back if she could manage to help them out with food and milk.

"Lily, don't you be worrying about paying me back for anything I give you young'uns. But," she paused, "I don't think this will work out too well. Might be that old aunt of yours has done her dirty work again, I'm afraid. Maybe she had our Caitlin carried off. I think you three children better come out and stay with me. I have plenty of rooms for sleeping and food for eating. You can all help work this farm and we'll be just fine and dandy. Come on, Lily, eat some of these here warm biscuits and put some of this warm honey on them. Warm honey is good for the body and the soul. I have more than I will ever be able to use. You take plenty

32

of these biscuits and honey on back to little Tessa and Benny. Go on out to the barn and get some milk from Bells, and you children hurry on back here as soon as you can. If you want to come back tonight, that's quite alright. If not, just be sure and be here first thing before daylight. You don't want anyone seeing all of you leaving and coming out my way. We'll keep your whereabouts a secret for a while."

Granny Tomason always had the right solution for every problem. She also had plenty of food and never wanted for anything. She lived very comfortably, but didn't sell much from her farm. She owned a few heads of cattle, a mulch cow, and chickens for eggs and eating. The garden she planted every year was big enough for her and maybe the whole Union army so the overabundance of vegetables from her summer garden was given away to families in need. All she asked in return was for someone from the needy family to come out and help with such things as planting, hoeing, harvesting and canning. She gave money to anyone who was in need, and food for anyone who was hungry and her left-over eggs she sold to the baker in town and sometimes she sold a few head of cattle to other people, but that wasn't really enough to live on.

Lily didn't know where she got her money, but she did know Granny Tomason had once been married to a very mysterious man from Europe who came home only for a few weeks each year.

Lily remembered seeing him a few times in her life. When her husband was home, Granny and Mr. Frederick Tom-a-son (that was the way he introduced himself), would come over and visit with Mama and Pa. He was a big man with twinkling blue eyes, a pirate's mustache, pirate boots and a loud, blustery voice which seemed to fill the room with laughter. At times, he walked with a limp as if he had at one time been in a battle with an opponent, or so the story goes. And for some reason he always smelled of rum and cinnamon. Mama once told the children Mr. Frederick Tomason was a gentleman and a scholar. He had been educated in Europe and was the smartest man Mama had ever met, and since Mama's father and grandfather were well educated in Europe also, she would be the one to know.

Mr. Frederick seemed to always have his arm around Granny's shoulder and Lily remembered staring at him and watching him give Granny a kiss on the check whenever he said something funny and he, himself would let out a loud laugh. Granny would gaze up at him and smile. She had explained to them that Mr. Freddy, as she called him, had many business dealings in England and India and could not come home often. Most people in town thought "Mr. Freddy" was a pirate and was too afraid of America to live here.

A short while before Mama and Pa died in the carriage accident, Granny came to their house and told the family that her Mr. Freddy had gone down with one of his ships off the coast of Madagascar. She was heart-broken and cried the entire time she was doing the telling. Mama insisted Granny stay with them for a few days so she could have people about and not be so alone but Granny said she wanted to be at the home Mr. Freddy built for her.

Pa said Granny had gotten a large sum of money from Mr. Frederick's holdings; Lily was sure that was the reason Granny was able to help so many people, but the town gossips said Granny inherited all of Mr. Freddy's ill-gotten treasures from his pirating days. "A pirate?" Lily would mumble whenever she heard someone talking about Mr. Frederick's acts of piracy, "There are no pirates in this modern age."

Lily's mind popped back to the present and she looked at Granny, "Oh, Granny, thank you so much. but if Aunt Birdie finds out we are staying here, she will take us back. What would we do if she took it into her head to give Tessa, Benny or me to one of those slaver boats?" Lily asked.

"Oh, pooh on the old Bird," Granny said, "Don't you be worrying about her. You just get those other two young-uns out here just as soon as you wake up in the morning."

Lily looked at Granny as if for the first time. Granny was a tiny little woman, full of energy and quite pretty for a granny. She still had dark red hair and eyes the color of the blue sky over the blue Mediterranean Sea. That was what Mr. Freddy always told her when he was home – he called her his "blue-eyed beauty with the hair of a hot fire". A ready smile was always on her lips and she kept herself neat and clean. She had the energy of a much younger woman and was always dashing around like a humming bird as she did her chores.

When Mama and Pa died, Granny had wept like they were her own children. She tried to talk Caitlin into moving all of them out to her house to live, but Caitlin said it would be best if the four of them stayed where Pa had built them a home. Then Granny said she supposed that was the best, but if need be, she would move in with them. Caitlin assured Granny it was not necessary but Granny stayed with them until Aunt Birdie arrived, then decided it would be best if she moved back to her own house.

"Don't you be worrying about anything right now except getting the three of you out here as soon as possible, Lily girl!" Granny's voice brought Lily back to her present problem. "Let's just worry about that for now. The three of you need to get out here so you can stay warm and start eating something that will stick to your ribs. Let me ponder this problem we have and maybe I can come up with a solution.

"Since Birdie is supposedly your Pa's sister, I guess she has the right to try and take you away. But, if it comes to that, we'll just give her a fine race in the courts. I don't like the thought of you three living in that shanty and begging for your food. It isn't right. Your mama and Pa would certainly not approve and Caitlin is old enough to take care of all of you. Let me help you try and find her. I'll start asking around and keeping my eyes and ears open. Everyone in town thinks I'm too old and don't understand much, but I understand every word I hear and every look I see in that town. Why, just the other day I heard some street bums say, "Those three would be worth a pot of gold". Don't know what or who they were talking about, but as sure as I'm standing here, they were up to no good. Those men at the docks would sell their souls to the devil for gold."

Lily then thought to herself, "They may have been talking about the three little girls down in the river bottom, or maybe even Tessa, Benny and me. I need to let the triplets' ma and pa know."

With that thought in mind, she looked at Granny and asked, "Granny, do you know the squatters living down in the river-bottom?"

"Well, not very well, Lily. But Mr. Peterson does work for me once in a while. He seems to be a right nice fella. He never has brought his wife or kids along so I really can't say I know them. Why do you ask?"

"Well, Tessa told Benny and me about how Aunt Birdie had been asking her a lot of questions about them before we left our house. I wonder if she might be thinking of snatching those three little girls from their ma and pa and selling them down the river."

"Well now, that could very well be but don't you worry about them Lily girl, I'll take care of it. I'll go down there tomorrow and let their ma and pa know to keep an eye out for anyone coming along. Their pa has a shotgun and won't hesitate to use it if he thinks someone is trying to get his girls. Now you get on out there and get some milk for you and those other young'uns and don't be worrying none about something you can't control."

"Thanks Granny, I'll talk to Benny and see if we can't figure out a way to come out here. At least you won't be by yourself and Benny and I can help you out."

"Well get going Lily girl. Bring that milk bucket back inside and I'll put some in a jug for ya'all."

Lily jumped up and gave Granny a hug and kiss, "I'll be right back in."

The back door squeaked as Lily stepped out into the darkness and walked to the barn carrying a lantern. Pie-Eater came around the corner of the house and followed her out and Granny's cow turned and gave a soft lowing sound as Lily walked into the stall and started petting Bells head.

"Hello, Bells," Lily said, "It will only take a minute and then I'll leave you alone."

Pie-Eater sat right down beside Bells as he waited to see if he could beg some milk off Lily. His tongue was hanging out and his eyes were fixed on the milk bucket.

Lily laughed as she looked at Pie-Eater. Every so often she would spurt some milk towards him and he would catch it and lick his lips. As she milked Bells, she began thinking about how she and Benny could find Caitlin, "What could have happened to her? Lily's thoughts went back to the night Caitlin disappeared. Lily had been woken up by sounds coming from the outside the house as if tree limb was rubbing against her window and thumping against the house. Then she heard a man whispering to someone else as she lay there listening, she thought it was Elmer and his old drinking buddies again, since they were snickering and breathing heavy.

"That's it," Lily thought, "I bet they were carrying Caitlin away! They must have gotten into her room and pulled her out through the window!"

The next morning was when Aunt Birdie had informed them that Caitlin ran off during the night with a lover and left them because they were too much trouble and Caitlin wanted a life of her own.

Lily had looked straight into Aunt Birdie's eyes and said, "That's a lie! Caitlin would never ever leave us!" and that was when Aunt Birdie slapped her across the face.

"Don't you ever call me a liar again, girl!" Aunt Birdie screamed, "You try that again and all of you will be sorry!"

Lily, Benny and Tessa were stunned as they sat there speechless. They didn't finish eating until Aunt Birdie had left the room.

Benny then went out to the barn and Lily and Tessa started cleaning up the kitchen. As soon as the dishes and kitchen were cleaned, they went out and found Benny and that was when they decided they had to leave — there was no telling what Aunt Birdie would do next.

It was easy getting a few things together and slipping away. Aunt Birdie was always too busy digging around in the attic to pay much attention to the three of them. Lily took their mama's small amount of jewelry and her Pa's smoke pipe. After Tessa and Benny got their things together and Lily checked to see if Aunt Birdie was out of sight while Benny made sure Elmer wasn't around, the three of them walked through the woods into Caruthersville and once they got into town they found the old abandoned shanty behind the *Ruby Slipper Saloon*, and that's where they had been ever since they left their farm. It had been three days since Caitlin disappeared, and Lily was getting more worried as each day passed.

What would they do if they never found Caitlin? Maybe they should try to get on one of those wagon-trains going west. Maybe that was where someone had taken her. Maybe they could sneak aboard one of those boats going down the river to New Orleans and find some work down river. But, Benny was only fourteen and she was only thirteen. Maybe she could get a job in one of the bakeries. Mama had taught her how to bake all types of cakes, pies and tarts.

She sat back on the milk stool and put her face on her knees. "What are we going to do?" she sighed.

She finished milking Bells and took the milk inside so Granny could pour some into a jug for Lily to take back to the shanty.

The fog had vanished as Lily retraced her steps back to the shanty and she was able to make it back in no time at all. She could hear the hoot owls and the rustling of small animals again. Her eyes darted behind each tree and down each path as she hurried along the deserted road to town. When she got to the place where she had seen the shadowy soldier, she crossed to the opposite side of the alley and walked a little faster. Nothing appeared and the night was once again like every other night along the Mississippi.

She was still a bit jumpy. Every cat or dog she saw made her flinch for a second or two, and voices coming from the homes and buildings made her heart beat a bit faster. If given the choice, she would rather run into a wild animal, large or small, than a shadowy person!

Once she got close to the shanty, the fog was again thick, but it didn't remind her of the *Devil's Fog*, as it had earlier. No breeze made the fog come alive, and no strange shadows — male, female, military or non-military — lurked among the houses and buildings. When she was close enough to hear the saloon pianos, she was relieved. Her heart slowed to its normal pace and she felt a little more secure.

"I wonder who that soldier was and what did he want with me?" she wondered to herself. She had not seen a soldier in full uniform in a long time. A lot of ex-soldiers still wore their jackets or military pants, but not the whole uniform. Plus, she was sure she would not be able to help any of them with anything. She was only thirteen, and the only reason a stray soldier would want to speak to a thirteen-year-old girl was if he was up to no good.

The only thing giving her pause was the fact he had called her "Lily Beth". Now, that was really strange! How had he known Michael had called her Lily Beth? Maybe he was an old friend of Michael's during the war and was now a little off in the head from living through such a dreadful time.

The whole experience had been a downright scary encounter; that was for sure. She was thankful to the good Lord on high for stomping outside that woman's window and to the woman herself for slamming the shutters open. It may have prevented the shadow from reaching her before she could talk her legs into getting her out of there. She shivered at the thought.

"Well, I don't really want to find out, that's for sure." she muttered.

Her mind kept going back to the shadow. For some reason the man seemed familiar to her. It could not have been Michael Thorne unless he had been lying sick for all these months since the war ended. But, if that were the case why didn't he just come on into town and talk to everyone? It sure was a strange thing.

Slipping quietly into the shanty, Lily kept thinking about it. Why would a man in a soldier's uniform approach her? What could he have possibly wanted and who was his family? Maybe he was just a renegade soldier, wandering from town to town. Maybe in his mind, he really didn't know where he wanted to go or, even worse, who he was.

Even though she was afraid, she had felt he had not meant her any harm. Why was that? He was out in the thick fog beckoning for her to come toward him. Of course, he meant her harm! The question was — what was wrong with her own head in thinking maybe it was a nice ghost wanting to chat? "Well, I'm just glad I got away," she once again mumbled to herself.

Tessa was asleep on the pile of rags and Benny was snoring loud enough to wake the dead. "So?" Benny said, as he woke up with a start, "What did Granny Tomason have to say?"

"She wants us to go out to her house in the morning and stay with her until we find Caitlin and are able to return home," Lily whispered quietly, "What do you think, Benny? Think it's a good idea?"

"Well," he stretched and yawned, "It's not a bad idea. At least we would have a decent place to sleep. And Granny would let us work for food to eat. Why don't we give it a try? If anything happens and Aunt Birdie finds us, we can always go out to one of those caves on Granny's back acres."

"Okay, sounds like a plan," Lily herself yawned and sat down on the same pile of rags Tessa was lying on. Let's try and get some sleep. In the morning, we'll take off for Granny's house."

After they settled down for the night, Lily decided to tell Benny about the shadow soldier. When she came to the end and stopped speaking, Benny sat up and looked at her for a while.

"Lily, you can't go out alone at night any more. It's too dangerous and there are too many renegade soldiers about. He could have gone after you and had you within minutes. What if he was the one who has Caitlin and is just waiting to catch each of us alone? No, Lily, you cannot do that again."

"It was the strangest thing I have ever experienced. For some reason, I had the feeling he meant no harm and maybe he was, like a friend of some kind," She paused, looked Benny in the eyes, as if trying to convince him and herself, "I know it sounds crazy, but maybe he was from someplace else. Maybe was the spirit of a soldier or something. I know that sounds unreal, but that's the feeling I got as I was standing there looking at him. Actually, there was nothing scary about him. The scary part was just the whole situation put together. The sudden stopping of the hoot owl calls, the thick devils-fog blowing in with a gust just before he appeared and then the slamming of the window shutters from the person on the second floor of the building. I think he wanted to say something to me, but something else didn't want him to. The thick fog tumbled in towards him with a strange rumble and he just disappeared into it, almost like it had swept him away. When I think about it, I think he was holding something in his hands. Not a gun or anything dangerous, just something he wanted me to see. It was just the strangest thing ever."

Benny and Lily both lay back on the makeshift beds and within minutes they were sound asleep. Neither of them heard a sound when something was placed outside the door of the shanty.

4

Sheriff Beaumont

Before the sun slipped its bright fingers above the tree tops the next morning, Lily, Benny and Tessa gathered up their few belongings and walked out of the shanty door on their way to Granny Tomason's farm.

"Hey!" Tessa exclaimed as she bent down with a puzzled look on her face, "Look what I found. It was right here in front of the door! Look Lily, is looks like one of Caitlin's hair combs. Did you bring one with you from our house?"

"No," Lily replied as she and Benny turned to look at what Tessa was holding in the palm of her hand.

"I didn't either. Did you, Benny?" Tessa asked as she intently examined the hair comb with a perplexed looked on her face.

"No, I didn't," Benny said, as he stood looking down at the hair comb, "Maybe this doesn't belong to Caitlin at all. It was probably dropped by one of the saloon girls who came out here last night."

"No," Lily replied, gingerly taking the hair comb from Tessa and holding it up in the early morning haze to get a better look, "This is Caitlin's hair comb, all

42

right. See the design on the edges? Pa carved it for Caitlin on her fifth birthday. We weren't even born yet but one time when I wanted to wear them, Caitlin told me about Pa making them for her. She gave one to Michael when he went off to the war and she kept one for herself. She told Michael she wanted him to have a part of her with him and for him to carry it at all times until he came home to be with her again. After he didn't return and Mama and Pa died, she said she would never wear hers again because she didn't want it to break." Lily spoke softly as she slipped the hair comb into her pocket, "Who would have taken this from Caitlin's room? Maybe Aunt Birdie is selling our things off for money. If she is, she is going too far. This has to stop! I wonder what else she's sold off, and who dropped Caitlin's hair comb in front of the shanty."

"If it was one of those low-down saloon girls, I'm going to have the sheriff arrest them," Lily thought to herself.

As they started out to Granny's house, Tessa chattered on about everything along the way. She stopped to check out a line of ants marching along in single file and the bugs and flowers, or to just pick up a rock and examine it. Lily and Benny were too lost in their own thoughts to talk with her.

When finally, they got to the gate in front of Granny's house, Benny called out, "Hello the house", and opened the gate as Pie-Eater came bounding around the corner of the barn and into the front. They could smell the delightful, inviting aroma of bacon and biscuits cooking on Granny's stove and quickened their steps without saying a single word to one another.

Granny called them in and when they entered, the house felt warm and smelled oh so delightful. Rubbing their hands together to get them warmed from the chilly morning air, they made a bee-line into the big kitchen and smiled with happiness as they took a look at her dining table.

Once again Granny called from one of the bedrooms, "You young'uns have a seat and don't wait for me, You go on ahead and start eating. I'll be with you in a jiffy. I want to put more blankets on this bed for Benny."

The three of them smiled at each other as they felt the fire warming their cold feet and hands.

"This kitchen smells sooo nice," Tessa said as she looked around. "I want to stay at Granny's forever. Or at least until we find my Caitlin."

"I think Granny will let us," Lily replied, "or at least until Aunt Birdie finds out where we are and tries her best to take us back." Tessa's eyes grew huge again and Lily was sorry she had said anything about Aunt Birdie. "Don't worry Tessa," Lily said as she put her arms around her little sister, "Aunt Birdie won't find us." Lily hid her concern from Tessa.

"You children eat up, eat up and don't be shy about it," Granny said as she hurried into the kitchen.

The food on the table looked like a king's feast. Eggs, bacon, hot biscuits, grits, milk-gravy, fresh butter, fried apple pie and fried potatoes with fresh cold milk from Bells. "It's cold out there and you need something to warm your bellies," Granny said as she took her seat at the table.

Sitting down, all four of them began eating without saying a word. After surviving on sweet rolls from the bake shop, they couldn't find the words to describe the taste of Granny's food!

Suddenly, Pie-Eater started barking loudly. All their forks stopped in midair and they stared at Granny. Time was frozen for a few seconds as no one moved. Granny looked up, with just as much surprise as the three children, and said, "Now I wonder who that could be this time of a morning?"

"You children stay right here and don't come out of this kitchen. I'm going to see who it is and if it's anyone it shouldn't be, I'll get rid of them. In fact, I'll get rid of them no matter who or what it is."

The rapping on the door rang sharply as Granny walked out of the kitchen. Whoever it was waited for a few seconds then knocked harder.

"Lily, I'm really scared, I think it's Aunt Birdie and Elmer," Tessa whispered frantically.

"Open up Granny, it's Sheriff Beaumont," A loud booming voice called out, "and Ah walked the whole way out he'ah and it's damn cold."

Sheriff Beaumont's family was from way down around the Louisiana swamps, and even though he was raised in Missouri at times he would slip into his parents' slow, Cajun "Naw'leens's" drawl. He had a low, melodic voice which seemed to flow like warm molasses whenever he talked. His voice made a person feel all warm and cozy inside like the comfort of a thick, warm blanket on a cold winter night. He was the main target for every mother with a daughter who was of marrying age.

The Sheriff was probably six-foot-tall with black, curly hair which seemed to tumble onto his forehead and a thick, full mustache. His eyes were as black as pitch, with lashes that were too long and thick for a man and his teeth seemed to shine like the night stars when he smiled and his shoulders almost touched the sides of Granny's front door frame. With his black mustache and tan skin, he looked like he should be sitting on a river boat in the New Orleans harbor, making money at the gambling tables or riding the gambling boats up and down the Mississippi fleecing all the wealthy men as they came aboard to gamble. It was said that his pa come over from France and his mother was a beautiful full-blood Indian. His pa's name was Pierre Michel Beaumont and his ma's name was Cathereen Morning Dove. She was taken away from her Indian village and put into one of the Indian schools outside New Orleans where they changed her name from Morning Dove to Cathereen, and taught her the ways of the local citizens. But, after she married Pierre, she started using her Indian name again. Pierre Beaumont had loved his Indian wife and called her "Dovey". Whatever the case, Sheriff Beaumont was quite the handsome man in most ladies' eyes.

"I'm coming, I'm coming Sheriff! Hold your 'taters and I'll be there in a second and I don't want to hear another cuss word out of you again, young man," Granny said sternly as she opened the door a crack, Sheriff Beaumont grinned broadly and pushed the door open a little further.

"Ah'm coming on in Granny, it's too damn cold to stand outside — and that's the last cuss word Ah'll say today, ma'am," he drawled, as he continued to smile at Granny.

"Well, André Beaumont, I surely hope so, and I guess I don't have a choice if you come in or not, seeing as how you pushed yourself right on past me and are already inside. What do you want coming all the way out here to call on me this early of a morning anyway? I don't have much coffee made or I'd offer you some. All I have is some warm biscuits and honey."

"Well, ah'm looking for those three Quinn kids, Granny. Their Aunt Birdie is worried about 'em and ah thought maybe ya seen 'em around he'ah. Have ya?" Sheriff Beaumont bent down and stared straight into Granny's eyes.

"Why would you be looking for the Quinn children out here, André? You know they have a home of their own. Why would they be here with *me*?"

Trying to intimidate her, the sheriff continued starting straight into Granny's eyes and frowning, "They've been gone from their'ah Auntie's house comin' up on three days now and she wants them back. Granny, if yor'ah hidin' 'em, it's against the law and ah will have to take 'em back to Birdie Quinn's house and arrest you for kidnapping. You know that don't ya?"

"Well, of course I know that, André Beaumont." Granny had her hands on her hips and was tapping her foot, "Do you think I was born yesterday? And for your information, young man, that house is not Birdie's house. It belongs to Benny, Lily, Tessa and Caitlin. Birdie just decided to take it over, and no one has bothered to correct her. It's about time you set her straight, André. You should be more worried about finding that little Caitlin than worrying about me and if I have those three young'uns. Caitlin's been gone for three days now and no one is looking for her. Maybe you should check with all those sailors and dock drunks to see if they saw her about the time she disappeared. If I see those children, I'll make sure and do the right thing for them. And, as you well know, I'm a law-abiding person; and you very well know that, André Beaumont. Now wait right here young man, and I'll get you a warm biscuit to take with you on your way back to town."

"Ah'll just come along with ya, Granny," Sheriff Beaumont drawled, "cuz it's sure smellin' mighty good in yor'ah kitchen."

"Well, come on if ya have to," Granny said a little louder than usual.

"Granny, word is that Caitlin ran off with her lov'ah."

"Oh, humph!" Granny snorted then turned and looked directly into the Sheriff's eyes, snorted again then turned back around and began stomping toward the kitchen with Sheriff Beaumont right behind her. When she got to the kitchen door Granny glanced around and continued walking in with a grin on her face. The table was clean as a whistle and all the food, except for the biscuits, was gone.

"Here you go, André," Granny said, reaching over and wrapping four warm biscuits in a cloth., "Now hurry on back to town and start looking for that little Caitlin. She didn't run off with a lover, André Beaumont. As a matter of fact, she doesn't even have a lover. That's ridiculous since the only one she loved was Michael Thorne and, as you know, he died in the war."

Sheriff Beaumont sighed and rolled his eyes upward.

"Granny, thanks for the warm biscuits, but ya sure do cook a lot for just one little granny. A body might think ya were havin' company. It sure smells mighty fine in he'ah, like bacon and maybe some eggs. Ya sure ya haven't seen those Quinn kids, Granny?" he asked, as he looked closely at her once more and said softly, "Ah sure don't want to arrest a granny, but maybe it wouldn't be such a bad thing ta do 'cuz then ya could cook for me. That might just be a right-fine idea," He drawled softly, as if talking to himself, with a cockeyed grin.

"Get on out of here you, young whipper-snapper and mind your manners! I have a farm to take care of and you have plenty of women to cook for you. And don't you be snooping around my farm of a night. My old dog will let me know if someone's around and that shotgun over my door can't see too well in the dark of night and just might go off and blow someone's leg clean off. Not knowing who is out there sneaking around and all."

Sheriff Beaumont laughed and patted Granny on the head. Granny slapped his hand away and stomped towards the front door.

"Yor'ah an old softy Granny," he said. "But Ah do swear'ah, Ah will arrest ya if Ah have to. Ah'll be on my way and Ah'll stop by and tell Miss Birdie that Ah guess those young'uns aren't around he'ah after all. Maybe they took off in one of those wagon-trains going west. That would be the exact place ah would go if Ah were a young'un and wanted to get out of Caruthersville. So long Granny, and make sure'ah ya have some pie and coffee the next time Ah come out to see ya, ya he'ah."

"I'll do that André, and you be careful out in the dark of night doing your Sheriffin', Bye now, and tell your Miss Tidbury hello for me."

Miss Tidbury was Sheriff Beaumont's old widow-woman landlady who was old as Methuselah and the town gossip.

"Ah'll be sure and do that," Sheriff Beaumont replied as he sauntered out the front door and shut it behind him.

"Damn, it's cold out he'ah," André thought. "That Granny sur'ah is a character. She thought she could pull the wool over my eyes. They might have gotten away with it too, if one of those kids hadn't sniffled as they sat in the pantry. They must have taken every crumb of food except the biscuits in ther'ah with 'em. I sure could have used a warm plate of eggs and bacon.

"Maybe Ah should look for that little Caitlin Quinn," André thought to himself as he ambled along the path to the Quinn farm. She sure was a pretty thing. Twenty-three and considered an old maid. She kept to herself, taking care of her brother and sisters. If he remembered right, she did have a beau before the war but the fella had gone and gotten himself killed. She was the same age his sister Renée would be — if she were still alive.

An ache pressed against his chest as he thought of Renée. She had been the light in his bleak life for so many of his young years. After their mother died, André pretty much raised Renée on his own, since his pa gave up on life itself on the day of his Dovey's funeral. One would never have guessed Pierre Beaumont had two children. All he did was sit in the rocking chair in front of the window and watch the world pass by as he held his one and only picture of his Dovey.

Andre and Renée tried to get him to talk, but no conversation could be coaxed out of him. The only time he spoke at all was after he finished his meals and said a soft "thank you, sweetheart," to Renée or a "thank you, son." to André.

The only time he got up from his rocking chair was to eat, go to the privy or to bed. That was it. He had not taken a daily wash in months and never again did he shave his face or go to work. Not a single day, for the rest of his life, did Pierre Beaumont step foot away from their property.

Andre tried to keep food on the table by doing odd jobs in Caruthersville, and Renée cleaned the house, washed their clothes and did whatever cooking she could. Renée was only nine, and André was thirteen at the time of their mother's death and those days had been difficult for both André and Renée. Not only did they lose their mother to the jaws of death, they also lost their father to grief. Pierre Beaumont's spirit and soul was buried in the exact burial plot as was the body of his Dovey. Three years later on the same exact day, Pierre Beaumont died; André found him in his chair with his picture of Dovey clutched to his chest with a soft relaxed look on his face. His father had taken a bath, shaved off his long beard and put on his best Sunday suit. It was if he knew he was going to die and had gotten himself ready to see his Dovey. André's heart broke but felt relief for his father, knowing death was what he truly wanted. For in dying, Pierre was sure he would be with his Dovey.

After that, André and Renée moved into a very small, two-bedroom shanty outside of Caruthersville and by that time, André had grown into a big muscled boy and was able to take on jobs paying him more money. Renée was twelve and went to work at the local bakery, helping out with the early morning baking. She told André she loved her job and wanted to someday open her own bake shop.

Mr. Johnston, the baker, told Renée she had a great talent for baking and he would help her in any way he could.

But, one cold spring morning, as she walked to the bakery in the early pre-dawn hours, she was grabbed by a drunken sailor. When she tried fighting him off, he hit her on the head with his fist hoping to only knock her unconscious, but she had not survived the blow. The owner of the *Ruby Slipper Saloon* found her lying in the back alley where whoever hit her decided to dump her body. André went a little crazy that day. He really didn't remember what happened after the Sheriff came to get him from the cedar wood mill. All he remembered was staring down at Renée, thinking how small she looked lying on the doctor's table in her pretty blue dress, with her dark hair curled around her face. The doctor had fixed her hair so as to hide the mark from the man's fist, but André had been able to see the broken skin. The doc had also closed her eyes and washed the dirt and mud away from her face and clothes. She looked the same as she did when she was sleeping.

Andre remembered thinking, "Ah can't do this, Ah just can't bury her in that cold ground. She's all Ah have and Ah'm all she has. She will be so afraid all by herself in that graveyard. Ah just can't do it." He must have spoken out loud because the old Sheriff put his arm around André's shoulders saying gently, "She won't be alone son. Your ma and pa will be with her. She was a beautiful young gal and a wonderful sister to you, André. Let her go now. At least that river scum didn't have time to get her on that boat. Let her go, son. We'll find who did this if it takes us the rest of our natural life."

André buried Renée next to his ma and pa. It had been the worst day of his sixteen years. He then went back to work that very afternoon, vowing to find the person who killed her.

When he turned eighteen, André applied for the position of deputy Sheriff in the sleepy little river town of Tennemo, Tennessee, and got the position. Tennemo was a little town with very few problems or crimes. André enjoyed the work in Tennemo, but he returned to Caruthersville when he was twenty-five and heard the position of Sheriff was open. André stepped into the job with ease, seeing that the retiring Sheriff was the same one who had been there when André was younger. The same old Sheriff who had helped André in his hunt to find Renée's killer and until the day he died, the old Sheriff continued his search for information about Renée's death, but to no avail.

"Will it ev'ah stop hurting?" André wondered as he ambled towards the Quinn farm, "No, God don't let it stop. I want to remember Renée and what that person or persons did. They ended a young girl's life before it even started. they viciously ripped her out of this world and into the cold ground. I will nev'ah stop trying to find them."

As the image of Renée came back into André's mind, the pressure in his chest seemed to well up into his throat and he had to keep swallowing and blinking his eyes to keep from sobbing like a small child.

"Ah wonder if maybe the same thing has happened to the Quinn girl, Caitlin?" André puzzled over in his mind.

Slowly he walked down the narrow path. It was cold and he was in a foul mood, "What the hell is going on with these Quinn kids? Where is their'ah sister and why are they at Granny Tomason's house instead of their'ah own house?"

Just the thought of those slimy sailors getting the young Caitlin Quinn made André sick to his stomach.

"Ah guess Ah'm gonna have ta start lookin' somewhere'ah," he mumbled, "It might as well be at their'ah own home. What an old biddy that Birdie Quinn is. She is just a mean old woman who has nev'ah been married and probably nev'ah will be. What man could live with that old woman? Maybe that fella Elm'ah would, but no one else would even give it a second thought," André concluded.

When he got down the road a short distance from Granny's house, he turned right onto a narrow field path and started walking up to the Quinn's house. The Quinn's farm had been a nice farm once upon a time. André could remember Mr. Quinn working hard every day trying to keep the farm going. André had worked for him during a few heavy harvest seasons. He always had a smile on his face and a laugh to share about something. And Mrs. Quinn was a

51

looker. She loved her husband and kids, but she sure was good-looking, even to a kid of sixteen. She was definitely Irish with that red-gold hair, fair skin and eyes like a soft green leaf, she was one handsome woman. It sure was sad when they both died in that carriage accident. Sometimes it seemed as if bad things happen to good people and the bad people have very few problems.

As André got closer to the Quinn's farm, he could hear Birdie yelling at someone.

"You should have been there and made sure it all went as it should have! Now look what happened we lost that entire load of cotton to the river! What's wrong with you, old man? My money is the money that feeds you and keeps you out of the weather. Maybe you should strike out on your own and see how you like it!"

"Wonder what she's talking about," André thought.

"Maybe you should do the dirty work from now on, Bird!" Elmer yelled back. "There are a few things in life I won't do and tak..."

Andre stomped on the first step going up onto the porch causing Birdie and Elmer's voices to shut off. André heard low whispering, but couldn't make out what they were saying.

Birdie quickly appeared at the front door. Her apron was spotless white and her hair perfectly slicked back into a tight, neat bun at the back of her neck. Not a hair or piece of clothing was out of place. She was a tall woman; not what one would call fat, but very well endowed on the top and her hips were broad. She looked the perfect, matronly woman but everyone knew she was an old biddy who, at time, shrieked at people.

Elmer was standing a few feet behind her looking out at André, then he looked down and a big grin spread across his face. Elmer looked the part of a rascal with dirty, slicked back hair, his clothes were rumpled as if he had slept with the horses for days on end.

52

"How-do, Miss Birdie," André nodded his head in a polite gesture, "Elmer."

"Well hello, Sheriff." Elmer looked up again and said with the big grin still spread across his face, "Come in, come in and have a cup of hot coffee. Birdie, run on to the kitchen and get the good Sheriff a cup of coffee. It's kindly chilly out this morning, ain't it Sheriff?"

Birdie gave Elmer a look that would have killed him dead, if possible.

"Well, yes, it is," Birdie said turning back to the Sheriff and smiling sweetly, "and please do come on in out of the chill, Sheriff. Have a seat in the parlor and I'll get us all some coffee and sweet biscuits."

Andre could tell Birdie did not want to let him in, but Elmer had put her on the spot and she had to agree.

As André looked at Miss Birdie's handyman, Elmer kept right on grinning, and when Miss Birdie turned around André saw the reason why — Birdie's skirt and petticoats were caught in the waistband of her drawers. Skirt, petticoats and all were tucked up. Her whole backside was exposed and there was a large hole torn in her bloomers and her derrière was shining through like a big jagged round sun. It was as if maybe a mouse had gotten into her under-drawer's drawer and eaten a belly full of cotton. Her stockings came up to her knees and six inches above that her bloomers started. Her bloomers were black and the "sunshine" hole was right in the middle of her left cheek.

Elmer started laughing right out loud and Miss Birdie whirled around and gave him a stern look, as if to ask, "What are you laughing at?"

Andre had a hard time keeping his smile to himself as Miss Birdie turned and walked back toward the kitchen, her hips started swaying and the hole started moving around her backside. First it moved to the right, then it moved to the left, back to the right, and back to the left. As the hole moved back to the right, part of it got caught in the crack of her behind and stayed there. The hole stuck there and the crack stayed in view. André squeezed his eyes shut and when he opened them again she had stopped, bent over and was picking something up off the floor. The hole stretched further down her derrière and André was sure he felt his eyes bug right out of their sockets.

"Holy Moses," Elmer croaked quietly, "I ain't never seen anything this funny a'fore."

"Get out of he'ah quick boy," André told himself, "Pick up your feet and get them movin' quick before it's too late."

Elmer sat down hard on the chair in the foyer, hung his head and quietly laughed so hard tears were running down his face as he looked at Birdie than back to André.

"Sheriff, if that don't look like the light of the high-noon sun, I'll eat my hat. Makes a feller just want to snatch her up and kiss her all over, don't it Sheriff?" Elmer gasped as he rubbed his hands together acting the part of an excited kid.

It was the funniest sight André had also seen in a long time. He guessed it was mainly because Miss Birdie considered herself so prim and proper.

"Holy Hannah!" André thought. "How am Ah gonna talk to this he'ah woman without laughing right out loud?"

Andre finally went over and pulled Elmer up off the chair and dragged him into the parlor. Not a word was said between them. They just sat there. André knew if he looked at Elmer, he would start laughing and not be able to stop. Every few seconds Elmer would snort out a laugh and André would give him a glare.

Elmer had his dirty handkerchief out and was wiping at his eyes and blowing his nose. "If this fella doesn't stop laughing," André thought, "Ah'm not gonna be able to stay he'ah."

"Jest as sweet looking as sugar-biscuits on a Sunday morning, ain't she, Sheriff?" Elmer croaked out. Both of them became silent and did not look at each other when they heard Miss Birdie coming down the hall.

"Here we go, Sheriff Beaumont," she said sweetly, "you dear man, have some nice hot coffee and sweet biscuits to warm yourself up a bit. I just took them out of the warmer and they're still nice and fluffy."

"You had to hand it to Miss Birdie," André thought to himself as he watched her, "she's one of the best cooks and cleanest women in Caruthersville and she could charm the feathers off a blue-jay if she wanted to. But then again, she usually shrieks like a wild banshee."

"Thank you kindly, ma'am, Ah believe Ah will" André said, not looking at Miss Birdie's face, "These he'ah biscuits sure'ah look tasty. Ya are a mighty fine cook, ma'am."

"Why thank you Sheriff. I do try. The Lord in heaven knows I try to be the best living soul I can be. I live my life the way the Good Book says." Birdie looked over at Elmer, "Don't I, Mr. Elmer? Why, Mr. Elmer has been my handyman for many years and I don't think he can think of a single time when I haven't done my Christian duty for every soul I come in contact with. Isn't that so, Mr. Elmer?"

Elmer looked like he was going to choke on the whole biscuit he had stuffed into his mouth. He was having a problem talking, grinning and keeping the food in his mouth at the same time.

"Why, Sheriff Beaumont," Elmer finally managed to say with a mouth dropping biscuit crumbs, "Sometimes Miss Birdie gets up early, early in the morning to cook for the needy. That's right, Sheriff Beaumont, at the crack of dawn she gets up and cooks; trying to bake for all the needy folks 'round. Yes sir, Sheriff, at the crack of dawn," Elmer muttered with a snicker.

With that stated Elmer took on a choking spell and had to suck down some of his hot coffee.

55

"Here, Elm'ah, please, help yor'ah self to my share," André passed the plate to Elmer, thinking if he could keep Elmer's mouth full of biscuits, maybe he would stop laughing.

"Thank you kindly, Sheriff, and yes, Miss Quinn you surely, surely are a good cook. You are one good Christian woman, a wonderful Christian woman, as a matter of fact. That's exactly what you are ma'am. You surely are one big," he paused, "... hearted woman. You are certainly a ray of sunshine for Caruthersville!"

Elmer started choking on his biscuit again and had to take another big gulp of hot coffee to make it go down. As he brought the cup away from his mouth he said in a very solemn preacher type voice, "Yes ma'am, you are one big hearted woman. Without you there would be a big hole in all our hearts."

With that being said, Elmer looked at André and grinned from ear to ear.

Andre didn't think he was going to be able to get through this conversation with these two characters. "Okay André," he told him- self. "Don't think about anything but the missing girl."

"Well, Sheriff," Miss Birdie asked, "Have you seen those-" she stopped to correct herself, "- my children? I miss those three, ah, four children so much. First Caitlin runs off with her lover and leaves the other three with me, and then those three little ones come up missing. Have you found them or heard anything about them? I'm just worried plum sick. Their Pa, who was my dear sweet brother, you know, God rest his soul, would be so worried about them. When he passed on, God rest his soul, I promised I would make sure those children grew up to be God-fearing. Now I've already failed with that Caitlin. My brother, God rest his soul, would be so upset at that girl."

"Well ma'am," André replied, "Ah don't rightly know for sure'ah where they are, but Ah'm sure'ah they are fine. Ah thought Ah saw them at the oth'ah end of the street, down from the Sheriff's office, last night, but Ah couldn't get there fast enough to make sure'ah. Where ev'ah they're staying, Ah'm sure'ah they will be okay."

"And just how do you know they will be alright?" Miss Birdie voice grew harsh and demanding, "Do you know where they are and you aren't telling me? If that's it, Sheriff, I will personally send for the governor. You not telling me where those children are would be breaking the law, as you well know! Did you check over at that old Mrs. Tomason's house like I told you?" Miss Birdie demanded. "That old woman is nothing but trouble. I told you she's an evil old woman, and I'm worried about my children and what she might do to them. Her husband was a pirate, you know, and no telling what on God's green earth she has influenced them to do. She probably has a house full of stolen treasure from her husband's pirating days. I heard he was an evil blood-thirsty pirate! Just ask some of the good Christian folks in town. She says she's some kind of a relative to their mother, but I don't believe it. I am truly Daniel Quinn's sister and I never heard tell of her in all my born days! I want those three children back and I want them back today!"

"Now calm down, Miss Birdie, I am not a li'ah," André stated sternly, "and Ah went to Granny Tomason's house this morning, and no, Ah didn't see them ther'ah a'tall. Granny has a hard-enough time, as it is, running her farm without havin' to take care of three children. Ah'm sure'ah Granny will let me know if she hea'ahs anythin' about the children. What about their'ah older sista, Caitlin? Have ya heard anythin' about her?" André asked, looking at Elmer.

Elmer's face went straight and immediately flushed; he quickly looked away from André.

"No, Sheriff," Miss Birdie spoke up for Elmer as her voice lost its harsh tone, "Mr. Elmer and I haven't seen hide-nor-hair of that Caitlin. I tell you, she ran off with some lover and we won't hear from her again. It's better that way really since I wouldn't want her bad reputation to ruin those two young sisters of hers. Yes, it is better that she stays away and never returns."

"How about you, Elm'ah?" André looked him directly in the eyes. "Ah'd like to hear'ah it straight from yor'ah own mouth. Have ya heard anythin' about Caitlin and this person she supposedly ran off with?"

57

Elmer looked back at André. "No sir, I haven't. But if I do, I'll be sure and let you know right away."

"That's strange," André thought. Elmer sounds like he is pretty sincere about this.

"Well, folks, thanks for the coffee and biscuits. Ah appreciate yor'ah time and Ah'll be back here'ah if Ah hear'ah anythin." André stood up and walked to the front door.

Miss Birdie and Elmer followed him to the door. She had returned to her sugar-sweet attitude once again as she spoke, "Thank you kindly for helping us Sheriff, and don't you be worrying any about that Caitlin. She's done made her bed, let her sleep in it."

She waited until André was out and down the steps before she turned to Elmer and began hissing like a snake at him. André could hear Elmer's laughter ringing through the open door and Birdie's stomping feet as she walked back down the hall. Evidently Elmer was telling her about her drawers and the "sunshine hole."

5

The Hunt Begins

Lily, Benny and Tessa tumbled out of the pantry with a thud and sighs of relief.

"Whew, that was a close one," Benny said.

"I can't believe we got away with that, Granny," Lily laughed.

"Yeah," Tessa whispered. "I was so scared I almost wet myself when I heard him stomp into the kitchen with you, Granny."

"Well, I don't know if we really fooled him or not, Sheriff Beaumont is a right-smart young fella and one of the kindest Sheriff s we've had. I'm sure-a-shootin' he heard that sniffle. But, André is a good boy. If he thinks you young-uns are better off with me, instead of that Aunt Birdie of yours, he won't be telling anyone about you being here."

"Do you trust him, Granny?" Benny asked

"With my own babies, if I had any, Benny-boy,"

"What will he tell Aunt Birdie if she asked him?" Lily asked with a frown.

"Well," Granny said, "I'm thinking he's a smart enough fella so he'll be able to get some information out of your Aunt Birdie and not tell her about you young'uns being here."

Tessa smiled broadly, "Just like you did, huh Granny?"

"You don't have to worry about me telling a lie to anyone, Tessa-girl. I know how to protect those I love and dance around the old devil before he can catch a hold on my arm," Granny said as she looked at Tessa with a big smile, "I didn't tell any lies today and don't plan on doing it in the future," Granny put her arm around Tessa and gave her a squeeze.

Lily knew Caitlin did not have a lover, or anyone else she would abandon them for. Caitlin still loved Michael Thorne and no other man, as far as Lily knew. Not that it would do her any good — Michael had not returned home after the war ended and after a good long while Caitlin finally realized he must have died in the field during some battle and was probably buried in a makeshift graveyard along with so many other young soldiers.

Along with Michael's parents, Caitlin had planned a funeral for him. There was no body in the grave, but having an actual funeral and a headstone on top of the empty grave gave the missing soldier's family and loved ones a little closure.

Many families had done the same thing after the war ended and their loved ones never returned to them. Lily guessed the funeral and the burying of an empty casket must soften the sorrow of their loss.

Although some families got a wonderful surprise when after a very long time their son or husband wandered home. Some of the soldiers had been too sick to let their families know where they were and others couldn't remember who they were or where they were from until months after the war ended. But Michael Thorne never returned.

Caitlin had waited and watched. She would walk into town most every day close to the time the afternoon train arrived, using one excuse or another, but Lily knew she was watching for Michael to come home on the noon train. No one found his body or any of his belongings. And if they had, they had not bothered sending them on to his family.

So many boys were buried in unmarked graves back East and most of the dead soldiers had no type of identification left on their bodies after the opposing side stripped them of all their personal belongings. Every type of identification was carried back to a commanding officer to be collected and checked for any evidence one of the fallen soldiers might be an officer. That was the way both sides checked to see if there were groups of enemy soldiers still fighting without an officer leading them. If so, those groups would become easy targets.

At other times, injured soldiers crawled off into the surrounding woods or brush, thinking they would recover while hiding in the thick, overgrown trees and then be able to return and fight again. But instead of recovering, they died alone. Some were buried in the dense woods, never to be found by their families. Their fellow soldiers hurriedly buried them in hidden places where enemy soldiers would not dig up their remains and steal their personal belongings; all the while thinking they themselves would remember where the fellow soldier was buried and return to retrieve them after the battle ended. Other times, fellow soldiers took all the personal belongings of the fallen friends; thinking they would be able to send them to the soldier's family, but in the melee and confusion of battle, they themselves perished. Most battles were too intense for any living soldiers to carry the dead back to their camps – even the injured, may times, were not taken back to their camps but left to agonize among the still-fighting soldiers.

At one time Caitlin told Lily she guessed the soldiers had done the best they could, seeing that they were fighting in very hot weather and there was absolutely no place to put the dead except in the ground. For quite some time Caitlin cried every time she spoke about Michael. She would frequently comment on how Michael probably wouldn't want to come home injured like some of his friends had done, so maybe it was best he didn't come home at all. But as she was saying so, tears were rolling down her face and Lily knew Caitlin would have taken him back — no matter how injured he had been.

It sure was a sad time for all of America, Lily would think to herself as she listened to Caitlin talk about the north and south and how they both lost so many of their sons and husbands.

"Maybe when Caitlin comes home, she will find a nice beau like Michael and then she will be happy again," Lily said in a soft whisper to Benny, "When she gets home, maybe we will go out and help her find a new beau. What do you think, Benny? Maybe Sheriff Beaumont?"

"Well, we'll have to see if he is worthy of being with Caitlin. I guess if Granny Tomason thinks he's nice he might be okay. We'll just have to see," Benny whispered back.

"Benny," Lily said when they finished eating and had the kitchen back in order, "let's go into town and see if we can find any clues as to what might have happened to Caitlin. While we're there, we can see if the baker needs any of Granny's eggs today. Could we do that for you, Granny?"

"That would be just wonderful, Lily. It would save me a trip into town and I'm sure Mr. Johnston is about ready for more eggs. But you two be very careful about who you run into and make sure you stay away from those river boats."

"Is it okay if Tessa stays here with you Granny? Or do you want us to take her along? Whatever you want us to do will be okay."

"Of course, Tessa can stay here with me. I haven't had the company of a sweet little gal in a coon's age. The very first thing Tessa and I will do is take a ride down to the Peterson's house in the river bottom and tell Mr. and Mrs. Peterson to be on the lookout for anyone snooping around their little gals, and then we can make some chicken and dumplings for supper, and maybe some gingerbread cookies to go along with it. What do you say, Tessa? Is that a good idea?"

"Oh yes, Granny," Tessa said excitingly jumping up and down, "that's just what me and Mama used to do. Let's get started right now. What do you want me to do first?"

"Well, let's see your sister and brother off first, and then we'll start out for our visit and after that we'll come back and start in cooking. But before we leave for our visit, we can fix up a big basket to take along with us. That way we can have a nice lunch with Mr. and Mrs. Peterson and those three little gals. How does that sound?"

"Yippee! We are going on a picnic and I get to play with Molly, Polly and Dolly!"

"Benny, you and Lily stay together and be very watchful in town, and also keep an eye out for that Elmer and your Aunt Birdie. You stay away from those saloons. I hear Elmer is down around the riverfront most every day. Your Aunt Birdie goes into the mercantile pretty much every other day, and she also goes down to the boat landing. I really don't know why she goes to the docks. I hear tell she says she gets fresh fish, but I don't really think so. You two young'uns keep an eye open and don't speak to anyone you don't know, and stay together. Now give me a hug and get out of here. We'll be watching for you before dark comes on."

"Thanks, Granny, and I'll make sure Lily stays safe and we'll be sure and stay together," Benny replied, "both of us can out-run that old Elmer or Aunt Birdie if they see us and give chase."

"Yep, that's right," Lily spoke up, "Unless Elmer catches us from behind he won't be able to catch either one of us. Aunt Birdie can't run fast enough to catch a turtle, much less one of us."

After they collected Granny's eggs, Lily and Benny started down the path to town. Lily pulled her hat low and buttoned her coat all the up to her neck. Granny had given her some mittens to keep her fingers warm until the morning chill burned off and she pulled them up as far as they could go. The mittens were too big, but they were better than nothing at all.

Benny pulled his hat low over his ears and buttoned up his coat. Benny's pant legs were a little too short but his socks were pulled up to cover the space between his pant legs and his shoes.

63

But at least they weren't hungry and Granny had given them everything she could find to help keep them warm this early in the morning. The wind blew softly — not enough to bother them much, but it was still quite chilly.

"Benny, we have to find Caitlin," Lily stated firmly as soon as they were clear of the house, "She has to be on one of those boats waiting to go down the river, or on a wagon train going out west. But I'm thinking she's on one of the boats tied up in a hidden room where no one can hear or see her. If someone put her on one of the wagons going west, she would have screamed louder than a mountain cat and people would have helped her get away. Let's go down to the boat landing and see if we hear or see anything."

"I thought maybe you wanted to do that very thing," Benny replied, "That mean-hearted Aunt Waddle has gotten her last bag of gold. She shouldn't have been so greedy as to take away her own niece. We'll get her back, Lily, you can count on that."

As the two walked toward town, they remained quiet; each of them again lost in their own thoughts about how they were going to find Caitlin. Benny was pretty sure he could sneak onto some of the boats and hide among all the barrels until he could manage to slip around and see if Caitlin was being held in one of the cabins. Maybe if he acted like he was interested in being an errand boy, or something on the boat, they would let him on board. But he would have to make sure they didn't lie to him — just to get him on board — and then tie him up and not let him go until they were down around New Orleans and he had no chance of getting back home.

Quite often, the slavers would use black walnut juice to darken a person's skin so as to make it easier to sell them; luckily, his red hair made that option unlikely.

He also thought about seeing if there were any wagon trains going west before he tried to get on board one of the river boats. He hadn't heard of any coming though lately, but since it was now spring, the wagon trains would soon be coming through more frequently. He had not seen any coming through in the last few days, so the likelihood of Caitlin being taken west was small.

The Wagon trains were always an interesting lot of people. Whenever a wagon train came ambling through the river towns, everyone who could would go out to visit with the travelers and ask hundreds of questions. Some of the town people were always thinking about taking off for the wild west with each wagon train that came along. Other people swore they were going to join up with the next one passing through.

Few, if any, actually did. Most of the people just dreamed about going — it was an exciting thing to think about. Everyone wanted to know why the people on the wagon trains were going and how they would make a living once they arrived. Addresses were often exchanged and promises were made to keep in touch with each other.

Very seldom did the townspeople hear from any of the travelers and only a few travelers kept their promises of letting people know they had made it to their destination. One family in particular, the Fitzpatrick's from Boston, Massachusetts turned around before the wagon train made it to the great desert and returned to Caruthersville to open a general store. The things they told about their trip were thrilling and terrifying. Tales of being attacked by hostile Indians and renegade soldiers happened so many times the first chance the Fitzpatrick's got they took it and returned east. There were tales of attacks by mammoth grizzly bears, mountain lions and deaths from Cholera and Typhoid ran wild once it started. Most native Indians were friendly, but the renegade groups of ex-soldiers and thieves were fearsome. Mrs. Fitzpatrick had kept a diary and in it she told of how many graves they passed each day. Not a single day went by, she said, in which they did not pass at least seven to ten graves. The wagon trains were all going to California or Oregon. Some of the pioneers wanted to start a business or a farm. Quite a few of the single men were going to strike it rich in the gold fields. They had their wagons full of necessities: food, water, guns, cooking utensils for cooking outdoors, and a bare minimum of furniture. The travelers were always filled with excitement.

Some of the trains were fifty wagons long. All the children would be whooping and hollering when the day came for them to continue their journey west. It sure had been tempting to Benny after his ma and Pa died, but he felt responsible for his sisters. Going to California on a wagon train sure would be one grand adventure, though.

"Wait," he thought to himself, "going west on a wagon train may not be where Caitlin is, I'm thinking the locomotive train was the ideal place to begin our search!"

"Lily!" he said with excitement, "The train station! Let's check out the Pullman cars waiting at the train depot! Maybe Caitlin has been put in one of them. Whoever took her might have put her in one of the Pullman cars waiting for the train to come through and hook up with it. That way they could take her down to New Orleans on a train faster than they could a boat, once they hooked up to the engine."

Lily stopped and looked at Benny with her mouth and eyes wide open, "Jumping Jehoshaphat, you're right! I didn't think of that. You're probably right Benny! Let's get on over to the train depot and ask Pete, the ticket master, if he's seen Caitlin or anyone who seems suspicious. Maybe Pete really doesn't sleep while he's sitting there at the ticket-window as much as people think. Maybe he caught something with his half-closed eyes that no one else saw."

6

The Depot

Lily and Benny took off running toward the train depot. It didn't take them long to get there and just as they were running up the platform steps, the morning train was blowing its ear-shattering whistle; signaling its departure in thirty minutes on the nose. The trains stopping in Caruthersville were a mixture of different types of cars. First, of course, was the engine and hooked up to the engine was four passenger cars and then the baggage/cargo car. Last but not least was the stock car where all the animals where braying and mooing and carrying on something awful. And then, of course, a caboose brought up the tail end.

Local passengers were hugging and crying and carrying-on as their kinfolk boarded the train on their way down river to visit relatives. Porters were loading baggage into the baggage car at the same time two cowboys were trying to coax their stubborn horses into the stock car. The porters were yelling at the cowboys to get out of the way and the cowboys were yelling at the porters to shut-up and the horses were bucking and trying to kick anyone who came within reach.

Lily and Benny laughed loudly at the madness when one of the horses gave one of the porters a swift kick in the behind sending him and all the baggage he was balancing on his shoulders flying through the air.

The vendors and the locomotive were competing over who could be the loudest as the huge black locomotive rumbled and belched black smoke and coal-ash as the vendors yelled at the top of their voices peddling their goods from window to window. Food, and whiskey were quickly being exchanged for money through the open windows of the passenger cars. People were leaning out the train windows shouting at the vendors and the vendors were practically throwing soup into bowls as fast as they could, knowing at any moment the train would be pulling away. The passengers were trying to buy from the overwhelmed vendors, who in turn were yelling at each other in their attempt to satisfy all the customers. The stop in Caruthersville wasn't long enough for passengers to get off the train and go into local eateries, so the cafes and saloons came to the trains. The noise coming from the sound of feet stomping and the multitude of voices yelling was almost as loud as the train itself. Black smoke continued to cough and spew from the coal engine as the breeze pushed it onto the platform; but no one seemed to notice the black ash falling. All their attention was on the vendors and what they were selling.

"Fr-iii-eeed chicken!" a vendor screamed at the top of his lungs, "get your fr-iii-eeed chicken right here!"

"Whiskey, gravy and biscuits!" another yelled, "get your whiskey with fresh biscuits as fluffy as the noon-day clouds."

"Taters, maters and beef stew!" still another shouted out, "fresh from Rosie's diner to you!"

"Get your whiskey from the Ox Yoke Say-loon," a tall skinny vendor yelled as he waved his arms in the air trying to attract customers. He was a tall, lanky fella standing well over six feet tall, "along with biscuits as light as goose feathers smothered in creamy, buttermilk gravy."

A young, very bored, boy about five years old was standing beside the fried chicken vendor holding up a large, haphazard sign with a dead chicken drawn on one side with a bottle of whiskey leaning against the dead chicken.

Vendors were slapping food into bowls or filling whiskey tins as fast as jackrabbits. The returned soup bowls were refilled for the next customer without being wiped clean. If the bowl still contained uneaten food, too bad, the vendor dipped it back into the pot and filled the bowl full. The same spoons were used for all the customers and no one seemed to mind at all. They were snatching and grabbing food just as fast as the vendors were snatching and grabbing their money. Money was changing hands so fast a person couldn't keep track; even if he wanted to. All the passengers must have brought along the correct amount of money because no change was being given to anyone. It was complete pandemonium.

The busiest vendors were those selling whiskey from the local saloons. There were three boys running up and down the platform selling whiskey as quickly as they could dip it out of the barrels. Before the train arrived, the saloons had their whisky barrels waiting on the platform. As fast as a passenger gulped down the whiskey, the boys snatched the tin cup away from them, dipped it back into the barrel for a refill and scurried away, handing it to the next paying passenger. Some of the men gulped down their whiskey and threw the tin cup out the window and the whiskey vendors would have to run and grab it before one of the street bums standing on the platform snatched it up and tried to get a free gulp of whiskey from one of the barrels.

Lily and Benny stood mesmerized with their eyes wide and big smiles on their faces as they watched the mayhem.

"They have all gone loco," Lily laughed loudly. "As many times as I have seen this chaos, it still makes me laugh."

"Crackers and craw fish!" Benny hooted with delight in his voice. "Every time I see this I am thrilled! I love it!"

"Son, if ya don't close yor'ah mouth, yor'ah gonna catch a fly and choke on it," came a husky voice from behind them.

Lily and Benny whirled around and stared into a face peering down at them.

"Oh," Lily jumped and gasped, "Hello, Sheriff Beaumont."

She wanted to grab Benny and run for the hills as fast as they could to get away from the Sheriff. She was sure he was going to grab both of them and haul them back to Aunt Birdie or maybe even throw them in jail and hold them until Elmer came to get them.

Looking up at the Sheriff, Lily hastily said, "You scared us. We're trying to find out if our sister, Caitlin, might be around the train depot. Have you seen her? She looks a lot like me, except older and well...more of a lady."

"Nope, Ah haven't Lily. But, Ah'll keep my eyes open for her. When was the last time y'all saw her?"

"It's been a few days now," Benny said anxiously.

Without stopping to breath, Lily began talking as fast as she could she stood there nervous as a cat and fidgeting with a curl of hair hanging in her face, "When we got up and went down for breakfast one morning, about three days ago, Aunt Birdie told us Caitlin had run off with a lover during the night and left us. But that's not true, Sheriff. Caitlin would never do that and we haven't been able to find her and she hasn't come back to us. I know she is trying to get home but someone must be holding her someplace. You have to help us find her, Sheriff. We have to find her before something bad happens to her."

Lily's voice broke as she tried telling the Sheriff about Caitlin, "She would never, never leave us and we're getting pretty worried. How about it Sheriff? Help us and I promise Granny Tomason will bake biscuits for you every day if you want! What do you say?"

"Okay, okay. Ah'll help. But ya kids have to stay away from anyone who looks the least bit suspicious. Don't be going into any of the saloons and don't be out at night wandering around down at the dock. And by the way, yor'ah Aunt Birdie is looking for ya and she told me she was worried about y'all," André bent down so he could stare directly into their eyes. "And...anoth'ah thing, wher'ah is yor'ah little sista, Tessa? Birdie seems to think ya two ran off with her and she wants y'all to go back home. What do ya have to say about that?"

Lily swallowed hard as she looked at Benny then back at the Sheriff.

"Well," she hesitated a bit, "we do try to stay away from Aunt Birdie, seeing that she is so mean and all — even when we are home. We get up early, do our chores and take off. Sometimes we go down to the river bottom to visit folks," Lily lied. She nervously began twisting the ends of her curls hanging around in her face and looked away from the Sheriff. "We stopped at Granny Tomason's and Tessa stayed and help her out while me and Benny came into town to look for Caitlin," Lily figured she hadn't told but a little fib to the Sheriff, so it might not look really bad in God's book.

"Don't worry about Aunt Birdie, she's not worried about us none." Lily looked straight at the Sheriff and kept her eyes staring directly into his eyes. Her face didn't show any emotion.

Andre couldn't tell if Lily was lying to him or not. He squinted his eyes and frowned as he looked at her, "What a good lie'ah," he thought, "she could fool anyone if she put her mind to it. If Ah hadn't heard those rascals in Granny's pantry Ah would think for sure'ah she was telling me the truth."

Smiling, André looked at Lily then glanced over at Benny. Benny's face was beet-red, but not as red as his ears were. "Lily needs to get a new partner-in-crime," André thought with a smile, "Benny's face is a sure give away."

When André's eyes met Benny's eyes, Benny looked down and began shuffling his feet on the platform.

"Okay kids," André finally said after a second or two of silence trying to make Benny squirm, "Ah'll be looking for yor'ah Caitlin startin' right now. But ya two go on back to yor'ah Aunt Birdie's house. Ah mean yor'ah house, sorry."

"Thanks Sheriff!" Lily shouted. She gave André a surprisingly big hug and kissed him on his cheek. "I knew you'd help us. But we have to go to Granny Tomason's house and give her the money we're getting for her eggs. Granny said you were a nice fella, and now we know it for sure."

71

Andre hugged Lily back and ruffed Benny's hair, "Go on now, get on out of he'ah and don't let me catch ya two snooping around any place you shouldn't be."

"Okay Sheriff," Benny quickly replied, "we're going."

"See ya later," Lily called as they hurried away.

Andre watched them run off the platform and take off down the street, until their figures disappeared amongst the crowd of travelers and townspeople.

"Ah'm sure they aren't going to both'ah listening to anything Ah just told them," André thought. He watched them as far as he could than turned around to look at the train. As he stood looking at the train cars, he wondered if Caitlin Quinn could have been put on one of them and taken out of Caruthersville, or maybe she was in one of the private cars parked on the sidetracks.

"Damnation," he thought. "Where should I start looking? She could be on a boat going down the Mississippi or on a wagon train going out west, or she could be right here in Caruthersville inside someone's home."

As André leaned back against the wall of the train depot he looked around at the people on the platform. What an excellent example of human insanity. With the black smoke billowing out of the engine and black oily ash falling onto everything in sight, the noise of the engine and the screaming vendors was enough to drive a man crazy.

Except for a few strangers, all the people on the platform looked familiar to the Sheriff. A couple of dust-covered, sweaty cowboys were trying to get their horses loaded and a porter gathered up scattered clothing from some poor soul's bag which had fallen open. A few local men were standing on the depot watching the amusing sight the same as the sheriff was. A woman dressed in an expensive, emerald green dress and hat stood beside a train window talking to a gentleman who was seated inside the train. As André watched, the woman's face grew red with anger and he could tell she was raising her voice as she spoke to the man. André couldn't hear above the racket as to what they were saying, but the woman was obviously upset and the man kept staring out the window, glancing down at the woman than up again as if he was looking for someone. It was evident someone else should have been there to catch the train. The gentleman didn't look pleased at all.

Slipping his badge into his front pocket, André sauntered to the far end of the passenger cars and began moseying down to get closer to the man and woman. As he walked past the train windows, he spoke to all the passengers he knew. Lucky for André, when he got one window away from the woman in the green dress, he spotted old Mr. Tillman.

"Hey Tillman," André called out as he stopped and leaned against the trains windowsill, "how are ya? Goin' down to see yor'ah daught'ah in Na'leens?"

"Well, how-do, André. Yeah, I'm goin' on down ta visit Paulette and her wild young'uns fur' ah bit. That gal o' mine has eight of them thar' rascals and they're all boys! But I cain't stay there too long 'cuz those young'uns of hers is untamed as swamp critters. Those rascals are always a'climbin' on me and a'pullin' my hair. Then, they'll snuggle up ta me and whisper in my ear what a c'est magnifique pa-pa I am so I cain't get onta 'em a'tall. I jest have ta leave and come on home so I can regain my sanity. Sometimes I'm wonderin' how I ever get home with any hair left on my head a'tall."

Mr. Tillman chuckled deeply as he spoke of his grandbabies.

"Why, last time I was down thar' visitin'," he continued, "one of them young'uns came a'struttin' outta the house ta the front porch like ah ol' banty rooster struttin' his stuff. He's 'bout knee-high to ah grasshopper, but he was jest a'swaggerin' and a'grinnin' from ear to ear as he high-stepped it in a pair of my best trousers and my Sunday-go-to- meetin' shirt. He even had my Sunday hat pulled down so low his ears were a'stickin' straight out like barn doors! I swear he had the devil's own mischief in his eyes. He stopped right dab in front of me and says really loud, 'Bon jour, Pa-pa, ain't ah looking mighty fine?', then he takes off a'runnin' and a'whoopin' down the steps and out onto the road a'fore I could blink an eye. I had to nab a couple of her other young'uns to run after that little rascal

73

and fetch my duds back. All the rest of them thar critters, and their dogs, took off a'runnin' after that little feller. The dogs were a'barkin' and the boys were a'whoopin'. Even the youngest one took off toddlin' after the rest of 'em. They caught that bugger and darn near tore my duds up gettin' 'em off'ah the little rascal. Then here he comes a'struttin' on back to the porch jest as naked as a jay-bird and a'laughin' like that there was the funniest thing he ever done. He walks right up to me, naked as he was, and says with a big smile spread across his face and says, 'Pappy, Ah sure do love them ther'ah duds o' yor'n.' So, I go on ahead and gave him my shirt. It weren't worth wearing anyways with it being torn up."

Mr. Tillman was smiling with a twinkle in his eyes the whole time he was telling the story.

"But, I tell you, André, it was purt near worth the price of them duds just to see the fun those critters had wrestling each other. All eight of them thar' young'uns is pretty as a bugs-ear. But, they be wild as swamp critters and are ah handful for my Paulette. She just laughs and tells me they mean no harm cuz they're just being boys. I'd a'never thought my blonde-haired, blue-eyed pretty little piano-playing Paulette would marry up with that wild Cajun cousin ah your'n and havin' a passel of wild young'uns with all of 'em a'lookin' just like their pa with that curly black hair and them black eyes exceptin' that thar little 'un. He's lookin' jest like my Paulette with his curly blond hair and blue eyes." Mr. Tillman's eyes sparkled with happiness.

"But now, my Paulette, she's a fine mama to them wild heathens, that's fur' sure."

Laughing, with a grin spread across his face, Mr. Tillman looked out at André and winked, "I reckon that wildness comes from that crazy Cajun blood of their pa's family an all."

"Ah reckon so," André drawled slowly as he too laughed and looked at Mr. Tillman with a smile, "yeah...Ah reckon it is."

"Well, my Paulette is expecting another young'un come harvest time. She really hopes hit's a little gal-child. I told her maybe she should be a'hopin' hit's another boy-child, seeing that the rest of them thar' critters be so wild and all. Iff'en hit's a little gal it'll be just as wild as the rest. But whatever hit is, hit's just fine with me. I got myself one child but the good Lord done gave me neigh on nine grandchildren. Life is good, yep, life is good to me," Mr. Tillman flashed André another big smile.

Everyone knew Mr. Tillman loved his Paulette and her wild young'uns. His wife had passed on when Paulette was quite little, so Paulette was all he had of value...as Mr. Tillman himself always said. Paulette married Michel Beaumont, André's cousin, two weeks after they met and then she up and moved to New Orleans with him, trying her best to get Mr. Tillman to move down with her but he said he couldn't stand living with those 'skitters and gators'. Truth be told, he probably figured it was safer for his health if he only saw his wild grandkids four times a year.

"How's your Sheriffin' coming 'long? Catch any crooks lately?" he asked André with a chuckle.

Just as Mr. Tillman said the word "Sheriffin", André felt, more than saw, the woman standing at the next window stiffen. Instantly she began speaking loudly to the man sitting inside the train and it was pretty obvious she wanted André to hear what she was saying.

"She should have been here by now. What's keeping them?" the woman said pleasantly, "Oh dear, I am starting to worry about the dear girl. I surely am starting to worry. Maybe I should go and check on the dear child."

Out of the corner of his eye André could see her look over at him, but André kept his face turned toward Mr. Tillman as he continued talking about Caruthersville being such a sleepy little town with very little crime.

"Well, dear," the woman continued speaking loudly to the man, "have a safe trip and I'll see you when you return home. I'll go out and check on our dear niece immediately and see what the problem is." The man leaned out of the window and the woman kissed him on the cheek. As they pulled away from each other, they whispered quietly then the woman turned and quickly walked off the train platform. André kept talking to Mr. Tillman as if he had heard nothing.

The monstrous locomotive hissed and rumbled louder as it built up steam and the grinding of the huge, steel wheels began churning slowly. Black smoke billowed from the smokestack in great clouds of black ash and the train began pulling away from the depot.

Andre yelled goodbye to Mr. Tillman and told him to be sure and say hello to Paulette and Michel.

"I'll do that, Sheriff, as soon as I get there. And, if I have any sense left by the time I get back I'll let you know what he has to say." Mr. Tillman leaned out the window and yelled over the deep rumble of the train as it slowly built up speed and once again blew its ear-piercing whistle.

Andre laughed, waved and walked away from the moving train. As he glanced at the window where the gentleman sat behind Mr. Tillman, he could see the man had raised the window glass up and was staring at him. André smiled and nodded but the man did not return the gesture.

Andre hurried off the platform and out onto the street as he began looking for which way the woman in green had gone.

Looking down the main street, he could not see one buggy or a wagon with a woman dressed in green, and he couldn't see the woman walking anywhere. "She must live fairly close," he thought to himself as he walked slowly towards the sheriff's office. She was nowhere in sight and as hard as he tried, he could not remember ever seeing her before.

7

The Saloon Escapade

Walking slowly along the back alleys, André looked in every hidden nook and cranny for the lady in green. He kept his eyes open for even a glimpse of a green dress, but not a speck of evidence could be seen. It was as if she had vanished into thin air. As he rounded the corner behind the *Ruby Slipper Saloon*, there stood two waitresses, Opel and Pearl, outside the back door taking a break from the rowdy drunks demanding whiskey.

"Hey Sheriff," one of them called out to him, "how are ya? Come on in for a drink. We haven't seen ya in a while."

"Hello ladies. Not today, mind you, but maybe anoth'ah time. Did ya ladies happen to see a lady in a green dress and hat pass by the alley, maybe going up to Church Street about two or three minutes ago?"

"No, shu'gah, we haven't, but we haven't been watching for ladies either. Now...if it was a good-looking man you were looking for, we could probably tell ya right off if he had passed by," Both girls laughed at the same time.

Andre smiled, shook his head, turned around and walked towards Church Street.

"Nice talking to ya, Sheriff," Pearl and Opal called out in unison. "Come on in and keep us company for a while."

"Ah don't think so, ladies," André turned and smiled at them as he looked back over his shoulder.

"What a pair," André thought to himself as he shook his head, "I sure hope they find themselves a good husband to take care of them so they won't have to work at the *Ruby* much longer."

Cutting up one block, André walked along Church Street for a short distance but saw no one in a green dress and hat. As he turned back toward Waterfront Street, he heard loud yelling coming from one of the saloons.

"Don't let me see you two in here again," Yelled a booming voice from one street over in the saloon district. "Ya hear me? Next time I'm gonna get the Sheriff and have both of ya thrown in jail. I don't care if you are two skinny kids. Get out of my saloon and don't come back!"

"Damn," André muttered to himself as he began running towards the racket, "Ah bet it's those two Quinn kids again! What are they doin' in a dang saloon?"

"Hey! Hey! Come back he'ah ya two." André yelled as he spotted Lily and Benny running in the opposite direction. "Ah thought Ah told ya to stay away from these he'ah saloons."

Coming to a screeching halt with dust billowing up to their knees, Lily and Benny stopped in their tracks.

"Aw, horse manure," Benny muttered. "He caught us."

"We were just asking some questions, Sheriff," Lily said to André as they turned around to face him.

Benny pulled Lily behind him and hissed, "Shhh. Let me do the talking."

"Sheriff," Benny began talking as fast as he possibly could, "let me explain. I was going into the saloon, all by myself, to see if old Mr. Tillman was in there. He goes to that particular saloon most days around this time to get a bite to eat and I was going to ask him a few questions. You see, his daughter Paulette got married and moved on down to New Orleans, so Caitlin always takes him meat pies and the like a couple times a week and I thought maybe he had heard her say something that would help us figure out where she is.

"Lily was supposed to stay outside," he continued with a deep sigh, "but, she went in any way." Benny rolled his eyes up into his head. "Then, when she heard a man talking nasty about all the Irish, including our own family, living around here she yelled out that she had heard just about enough insults about the Irish. Then, and you won't believe it...she jumped right up on that fella's back and started biting his right ear."

Benny began laughing as he tried to continue with his story.

"Nothing would have happened if Lily would have obeyed me and done what I told her to do in the first place, but...you know Lily."

Lily glared at Benny.

"Obeyed? Did he just say obeyed?" she thought furiously to herself as her face turned red with anger.

"Obeyed! I'm going to kick his behind all the way across this river!" Lily fumed. She could almost feel steam coming out of her ears.

Benny continued talking as if he had not noticed Lily's wrath.

"I've been in that saloon many times before and the barkeep doesn't really care. The only time he gets mad is when a bunch of us young guys go in and bother his regular customers.

"Well, as soon as Lily jumped on the big guy's back, he started swinging his arms around trying to grab for her and then she bit a chunk right out of his ear.

79

That piece of ear was dangling by a little bit of skin, flapping in the breeze like a pair of britches hanging on a clothesline," Benny laughed so hard he could barely tell his story, "and he was cursin' and swearin' and spinning around trying to get a hold on Lily's arm or leg. But then he swung around by the bar and she snatched up a bottle of whiskey and hit him with a sharp crack on his injured ear then...*BOOM...*he hit the floor like a boulder dropping off a mountain top with Lily still on his back. When he hit the floor, she jumped right up and started in kicking at him. Then, every man in the bar started in laughing and the guy with the bitten ear started rolling around on the floor moaning and groaning and all the other men started in moaning and groaning; mocking the poor fella, and then, to make it worse, two of the fellas fall down on the floor beside him and started rolling around moaning. Well, the laughter got louder and louder, and that was when the barkeep grabbed me and Lily and tossed us out."

Benny stopped, leaned his head back and gave out a whoop of delight.

"Sheriff, I was so shocked at her I couldn't do anything. I couldn't even think as to how to get my legs moving and get us out of there. Thank goodness that barkeep shoved us out the door or I would still be standing there with my mouth hanging wide open staring at Lily and the bloodied ear. I just couldn't believe it Sheriff. Lily was hanging on like a chigger on a dog. It was the funniest gol 'durn thing I have ever seen in my whole life. That big galoot is going to be hotter than a boil on the bottom of your bu... behind."

Grabbing a tight hold on each of their shoulders, André was almost running toward his office, pushing them in front of himself. "Ya two are going to stay right he'ah inside my office for a while until Ah say ya can leave. That fella is going to be plenty mad when his head and ear stops ringing, and he's going to come looking for ya Lily."

"Sheriff," Benny said as he hop-walked alongside the Sheriff trying to keep up, "I just couldn't believe it. Lily jumped right up on that fella's back like a flea jumping on a dog and started in biting his ear!" Benny was laughing so hard he could barely talk.

80

Once again Benny went through the motions for the Sheriff.

"You should have been there, Sheriff. What a sight to see! It was great! She sure is a wild thing when she had her temper up. It was a great sight to see! Imagine that, Lily got the best of a grown-up man! She was like a mad-dog!"

Grinning from ear to ear and almost dancing a jig, Benny continued his telling.

"She sure is something, isn't she Sheriff? Yeah, it was a funny sight, alright. Those men in the saloon will be talking about this for a long time. How a small boy, which they thought Lily was, bested that galoot. It was exciting I tell ya, it was just plain exciting and you should've been there to see it. Those other men were having the biggest laugh ever. When Lily was latched onto the back of that galoot I heard some of the other fella's taking bets on how long she would stay on his back. The whole crowd was cheering Lily on and yelling things like, 'Hang on thar, short stuff!' or, 'Grab his hair boy, grab his hair and don't let go!' If I'd had any money in my pocket I would have put in a bit myself. I knew Lily could hold on as long as he was standing up, but I didn't have any money and I was too stunned to even think about it."

"She's something all right," André said as he stopped and stared down at Benny. "That big galoot, as ya call him, is going to be as mad as a hornet once he stops hurting. Lily, you are going to get yourself hurt really bad is what you are gonna do. Ya two have got to start behaving yourselves."

André mumbled something as if talking to himself, "Lily, ya need to start wearing a dress, ya hear'ah? Like right now today. If ya wear a dress, that galoot won't know you're the boy who jumped on his back in the saloon. Now get in my office. We need to talk."

Pulling both of them into his office, André shut the door and turned around to glare at them then he walked to each window and pulled the shutters closed.

81

"Okay, let's have an honest-to-goodness talk. No more telling lies. If ya want me to help ya find Caitlin, yor'ah gonna have to be truthful with me. Lily, from the time ya discovered Caitlin was missing until this morning, what happened?"

"We already told you, Sheriff Beaumont," Lily sputtered, wiping some of the galoot's blood off her coat sleeve. "We woke up in that morning and she was gone. Aunt Wad... Birdie told us she ran off with a lover during the night and wouldn't be back. I told her she was lying and then she slapped me."

"Well, what actually happened during that night? Did either of ya hear'ah any strange sounds a'tall?" André asked with a frown still on his face.

"Well, I woke up around midnight because I heard some mumbling and bumping around outside the house. I laid there thinking it was Elmer and one of his drunken buddies just coming home from the saloon—because they always stumble and mumble around the yard when they're drunk and trying to find their way into the barn. I didn't get up and look out because I didn't want them to see me peeking out at them because they can be kind of scary sometimes, you know. Anyway, the next morning Aunt Birdie told us Caitlin ran off. It's not true Sheriff. We know it's not true."

"Yep, that's right," Benny spoke up quickly and agreed with Lily, "and that's the truth, Sheriff, Caitlin would never run off and leave us with Aunt Birdie. That mean old Aunt Waddle is telling lies about her and I plan on doing something about it. Caitlin loves us too much to leave home and not tell us."

"Wait, wait, wait," André raised his hand to stop Benny from continuing. "Hold on a minute, who the heck is Aunt Waddle?"

"It's really Aunt Birdie," Lily sighed. "Benny, we have to stop calling her 'Aunt Waddle, it isn't something Tessa should be hearing from us."

An instant picture of Miss Birdie and her "sunshine" hole drawers popped into André's mind causing him to smirk, but said nothing.

"Okay. You two have to try and help me out he'ah. Do you really think Elm'ah had anything to do with Caitlin's disappearance? When Ah spoke to him and yor'ah aunt this morning, he didn't act like he had anything to do with it. It was kind of like he knew something about it, but hadn't done anything bad himself. What do ya two think?"

Lily and Benny looked at each other for a second or two then looked at André, then back at each other.

"You know Sheriff," Lily finally said, "we kind of liked Elmer at first, didn't we, Benny. When he and Aunt Birdie first came to our house, he seemed pretty much okay, sort of different and kind of dirty, but he was okay. He never said much to us, or Aunt Birdie, come to think of it; all he did was work and drink. Well, he and Benny did the work. Did he ever say much to you, Benny?"

"Not really," Benny said. "But he really did help with all the work. Most mornings he was up and about before I could get out to the barn. He never said anything bad about anyone to me. In fact, he didn't say anything about anybody, good or bad. He just worked, ate, and went off to the saloons with his saloon friends. He would mumble a 'thanks' when he needed to. I remember he always said 'thank you, ma'am' when Caitlin did something for him. It seemed as if he had more respect for Caitlin than he did for anyone else. With everyone else it was just 'thanks' and that was about it. That is, unless he got with his drinking friends, then he would become pretty loud and rowdy. But that's true with most of the drunks around town."

"Why do you ask, Sheriff?" Lily inquired.

"Well, Ah have some thoughts about this whole thing. Ther'ah was some shady characters at the train depot this morning and Ah'm just wondering about some things that went on ov'ah ther'ah. Lily, do ya have a dress to change into at Granny Tomason's house?"

"Ahhh... why should I have anything at Granny's, Sheriff?"

83

"Lily, Ah know ya'all are stayin' out ther'ah, and to tell the truth, Ah think yor'ah bet'ah off ther'ah than at yor'ah own house until this whole thing is settled. Now, always tell me everything you know and don't hide anything and Ah'll do the same — if Ah can. Okay?"

"Okay," Lily replied softly. "Yes, I have a dress at Granny's house. I'll put it on as soon as we go out to her house. You just keep your word, Sheriff Beaumont and help us find Caitlin."

"Ah'll do my best. Try not to worry and please," he paused, "stay out of trouble. Now, get on home to Granny's house and stay ther'ah. You've been in enough trouble for one day. Get on out of he'ah and don't let me see ya in town again today. Ya hear'ah?"

"Alright Sheriff, but we have to run back and get Granny's basket of eggs Lily left under the train platform and drop them off at the bake-shop and then we'll go on back to Granny's house."

Lily and Benny walked out of the Sheriff's office and turned back toward the train depot. Lily had completed forgotten about the basket of eggs under the platform.

"Come on Lily," Benny said, "let's go. If we hurry maybe we'll see something at the depot. Keep your eyes and ears open."

84

8

Pete Turnkey and Pearl

Running as fast as they could, they got to the train depot in no time at all; fully realizing Sheriff Beaumont would be mad as a hornet if he found out they were still snooping around, but the two of them pushed his warning out of their minds. Finding a clue to Caitlin's disappearance was more important than listening to Sheriff Beaumont.

Approaching the depot, Lily and Benny slowed to a walk, "Okay," Lily said, "Let me grab the egg basket first and then we can take a quick snoop around."

"All right," Benny replied, "but keep your eyes open for those men from the saloon and pull your hat down some more. You still have on the same clothes, and they'll know you right off. Here, give me your coat and you take mine. Maybe that will help."

As they switched coats, Lily looked up and saw the ticket master, Pete Turnkey, dozing as usual with his head resting on the edge of the ticket window.

"Come on," she whispered to Benny, once again forgetting about the basket of eggs.

"Hey Pete," Lily called out, as they walked over to the ticket window, "How ya doing today? We were wondering if any strange things have been going on here at the depot. Like maybe you've seen our sister Caitlin in the last couple days?"

"Hello Lily, Benny. How you two doing?" Pete replied, leaning out his ticket window to get a better look, "Nope, sorry, I haven't seen Caitlin in a few days now. Let me come out there and we can chew the fat a while. How is she? I sure do miss talking to her every day. She usually brings me a sweet roll or something tasty. Why would you be looking for her here at the depot?" Pete said as he stepped out of the ticket booth.

"She disappeared a few days back and we're trying to find out if anyone has seen her or if anything suspicious is going on."

"Disappeared? Well...ya don't say. I'll be! Let me ponder that for a while. Let's see here," Pete tapped his finger on his chin as if he were in deep thought,

"Weeelll," he drew out his words, "I'm not real sure, but there was a couple of men standing over by the tracks having a long talk, and I did overhear one of them saying something strange. Let's see, what are the right words, oh yes, his *exact* words were: 'She's a looker, should get a whole bag-full for that one. The problem is, we have to get her all the way down here to the train from way out Yoder's way.'

"At the time, I thought they were talking about that new filly everyone has been talking about. But after they left, I said to myself; 'self, now that new filly is out at Jeff Goodwin's place. Wonder if Yoder has a new filly too? And then," Pete hesitated for a second, "Again I said; 'self, Leroy Yoder moved on over to Memphis with his daughter.' But right at that very second the train came barreling in and the whole thing just flew right out of my mind like a bird. But now that you mention it, and I know Caitlin is missing, maybe they weren't talking about a horse filly. Maybe they were talking about a young gal filly."

Pete looked off in the distance as if he was doing some heavy pondering once again as he frowned into the sun.

Sucking in her breath with a quiet gasp, Lily said. "Oh, my goodness, you think so, Pete? Were those the exact words they used?"

Pete darted his eyes back to Lily and began drumming his finger again, but this time on the side of the ticket booth. Then he answered her in his get-your-tickets-here voice, "Yes sir-ree! As sure as I'm standing here, those are the *exact* words they used right there. Those…are…the…*exact*…words." Pete thumped his finger harder on the wooden booth as he said each word.

Pete Turnkey reminded Lily of a giant barn owl. He was tall, even for a man, and his face was quite pale. His shoulders were hunched over as if he had carried a heavy load during his lifetime. Huge thick glasses sat on the bridge of his long, narrow nose and were pushed up so tight against his face they causing his eyebrows to flare out above the frames of his glasses like feathers. His face matched his nose: long and narrow and his blond hair stuck straight out all over his head. His clothes and body were always clean, and his hands looked as if they had never done a full day's work. The greatest thing about Pete was that he could read any legal paper anyone asked him to read and he could tell you exactly what it meant. If it pertained to the law, Pete was the one to see and if a person couldn't read… he was the go-to person. He read for most of the non-readers in town and never told another soul anyone else's business. Pete could walk down the worst street in Caruthersville without being bothered – everyone knew one day they may need him. Even though he knew everyone's business, all that information was safely tucked away in Pete's brain. No amount of threats or gifts could make him dishonor a promise he made with the people who trusted him.

Gossip was that Pete had been a big-time lawyer in New York City but had unknowingly gotten involved with some shady characters and had to flee for his life after he found out they put a price on his head for being an honest person and talking to the federal government when they went into his office to ask questions. But no one really knew the whole story, and he wasn't telling. In fact, some folks say Pete Turnkey is not his real name.

Honest, clean, an excellent reader and maybe… (only maybe) a shady past. That's the description everyone gave of Pete Turnkey and he seemed to sleep most of the day as he sat at the ticket window on the train platform he called his own.

Pete looked at Lily and Benny with bugged-out eyes through his thick glasses. "Whoaaa doggies," Lily thought as she stared up at Pete, "he looks more like an owl today than he does most days. He must have washed his hair last night — it's sticking out all over his head."

Pete had a frown on his face as he said in a quiet voice; almost as if talking to himself, "Oooooh.... this is in-ter-est-ing! Have you two been to see Sheriff Beaumont? I'm sure he'll find this very interesting. Go on over there really quick-like and tell him what I heard. Have him come on back here and be nippy about it and while you're gone I'll do some more pondering. Maybe I can remember some more important facts." Pete shooed them away with his hands like swatting at a fly, "Hurry up now. Go, Go." Benny grabbed Lily's arm and pulled her off the platform.

"Come on, let's go! Maybe he has something here. Maybe he can help."

Benny and Lily burst through the Sheriff's office door and stumbled inside. Instantly they skidded to a stop and stared. There sat Pearl, from the *Ruby Slipper Saloon*, on the Sheriff 's desk with her long legs crossed, leaning towards him as if waiting for a kiss.

"Great gobs of goose grease," Benny thought as he smiled, "I do think she likes the Sheriff. Yep, I would say so."

Sheriff Beaumont jumped up from his seat at the desk so quickly he knocked Pearl onto the hard floor in the process. Pearl landed hard on her backside and instantly fell back and banged her head against its surface. Her legs whooshed up over her head and all you could see were bloomers and legs. She let out a loud "oof" as the air rushed out of her lungs.

After a few seconds of awkward silence, Pearl sat up with a groan and yelled out: "Dang it Sheriff, you didn't have to push me, I'm quite capable of getting down from your desk by myself, and in a more ladylike fashion, I have you know. Damn! Sheriff André that hurt my backside, ya big oaf! What's the matter with you? I couldn't breathe there for a minute. Have you gone loco or something?" Pearl sputtered as she gasped for air.

"Pearl," Sheriff Beaumont stammered, "Watch your language around these kids"

Benny's mouth was wide open in an enormous smile as he stared at Pearl. His smile was the biggest smile Lily had ever seen on his stupid face.

"Good Lord, what's a pretty girl like this doing sitting on the sheriff's 's desk all leaned over waiting for a kiss? She must work over at the *Slipper*." Benny thought as he kept on staring at Peaarl. "Wow, she sure is a pretty thing!"

"Gol-durn, Sheriff!" Benny croaked, all the while gaping bug-eyed at Pearl, "What-cha doing with this gal in your office sitting on your desk? Don't you know this is no place for that kind of thing? I'm just young and I know that. What's the matter with you? Anybody can walk right into your office since it's a public place and I really don't think a good Sheriff should be having ladies sitting on their desks like that, do you? What's the matter with you?" He asked again, "ya gone loco, like *she* said?"

Lily couldn't stop staring. Pearl. Pearl's skirts were still up above her knees and she was just sitting there with her black stockings and high-heeled shoes as if she were still too stunned to move.

"Maybe the Sheriff isn't the one for Caitlin, if he carries on with women like this," Lily muttered to herself. "He's a dog-eared scoundrel and a womanizer. That's what he is, a womanizer and a scoundrel! What a flop-eared, egg-sucking hound!"

Lily turned around and stomped out of the Sheriff's office, "Come on Benny, let's go. Dad-blame him, he's a womanizing rascal of a mule's hind end!

89

We are not asking him to help us find Caitlin! We can do it ourselves. Come on," Lily said again angrily, "We can do this with Pete Turnkey's help. We don't need the help of an old, scaly-wagging, flop-eared dog."

When Benny didn't answer, Lily turned around to look at Benny and discovered he wasn't behind her. He was still in the Sheriff's office. Lily stomped right back into the office and stopped with her hands on her hips. Benny was leaning down to help Pearl up off the floor and he had a tight hold on one of her arms.

"Well that's a fine howdy-do," Lily stammered, "now my stupid, pea-brained brother thinks he has to help this woman up." If she had a stick, she would hit both Benny and the Sheriff upside the head and maybe knocked some sense into their empty brains.

"Let her get up by herself; she just said she was capable," Lily stated loudly.

"Here ma'am, let me help you up," Benny spoke gently to Pearl; all the while ignoring Lily as she stood in the door tapping her foot and watching. "Sheriff, take hold of her other arm and we can lift her up onto this chair."

Sheriff Beaumont was still standing there staring down at Pearl with his mouth open until Benny spoke up. Quickly he stepped around and grabbed one of Pearl's arms and both of them lifted her onto the chair.

"Well good grief," Lily thought to herself, "I don't remember Benny ever helping me up, even after he pushed me down. Even if I stumble and fall down, he has never bothered to rush over and lift me up real gentle-like. Heavens-to-Betsy, they don't have the brains God gave a goose, and geese brains are about as big as a pea."

"You're a dumb ox. You are just as bad as Sheriff Beaumont," Lily wanted to say, but didn't since she wouldn't want to hurt Pearl's feelings. After Pearl was seated in the chair, Benny told the Sheriff that they needed to talk to

90

him in private. "Alright," Sheriff Beaumont said softly, "Pearl, do ya think ya can walk on back to the *Slipp'ah* by yourself?"

With her eyes flashing fire, Pearl glared up at the Sheriff. "I walked over here by myself, didn't I? I'm not a child and you're a stupid horse's patoot. I've been takin' care of myself since I was eight years old so I don't think I need some dumb-cluck of a man helping me find my way back down the street to *Ruby's*. That wasn't a very nice thing to do, Sheriff. I've never seen you be so rude to a lady."

"Pearl, Ah am so sorry," the Sheriff stammered. "Ah really didn't mean to knock ya off the desk. These he'ah kids surprised me and it was just a reaction. Please excuse my rudeness, Pearl"

"I think I am going to lose my breakfast all over this floor," Lily thought.

"Well, don't ev'ah do it again, Sheriff," Pearl shouted, as she mocked Sheriff André's accent, "Or you will nev'ah be seeing me again, ev'ah!"

Jumping up from her seat, Pearl stomped to the office door then stopped and turned to look at Lily and said loudly, "Young lady, men are dumb as stumps and they cain't even help it. Never, ever marry-up with one of these creatures. If you do, you will be forever sorry and depressed!"

With that, she walked out and slammed the door shut. At that moment, Lily decided she liked Pearl.

"Well," the Sheriff mumbled under his breath, "I just don't understand women. No matt'ah how Ah try, even when ya say sorry, they are nev'ah happy."

Lily scowled at the sheriff.

"Sorry," Sheriff Beaumont said as he turned to them, "Benny and Lily, that was kind of embarrassin' for me. Yor'ah right Benny, Ah shouldn't allow Pearl to sit on my desk whenever she comes to visit. Ah guess it isn't very proper-like."

91

"I don't reckin' it is, Sheriff." Benny smiled, "Even though she is a right pretty lady and all, it probably isn't very official-like."

"Okay, let's hear'ah what ya two have to tell me. It bett'ah be good, because Ah told the two of ya to get on ov'ah to Granny's house, remem'bah?"

"Well," Lily spoke up, "before we start in talking, both of you better use your shirt-tails and wipe that drool off your chins before it runs down onto your necks!"

Sheriff Beaumont and Benny turned and looked at Lily with puzzlement, "What in the world are you talking about, Lily?" Benny asked.

"Wipe your chins off. You're still drooling."

"Sheriff," Lily said stiffy, "When we went back to get Granny's eggs from under the train platform, Pete, the ticket master, was just sitting there with his eyes half closed doing nothing a'tall, so we started asking him some questions about seeing any suspicious- looking people hanging around the depot during the day. And, lo'-and-behold, he did hear something kind of suspicious about two days ago. He said he heard some men talking about a new filly out at Yoder's place and then he wondered why they said 'Yoder's place' because the new filly is out at Jeff Goodwin's, not Leroy Yoder's old farm. He now thinks they might have been talking about Caitlin, and not a horse. He wants you to hurry on over to the depot, because he is going to ponder on it some more to see if he can remember other things that might have been said on the platform in the last couple of days.

"But, if you're more interested in those girls at the *Ruby Slipper Saloon*, we don't need your help in finding Caitlin. We wouldn't want to upset your life of pleasure. Caitlin doesn't need a scaly-wag making cow eyes at her so if you'd rather go on over to the *Ruby Slipper*, that's fine. Benny and I can do this by ourselves."

"Lily, just calm down," André said staring sternly into Lily's eyes, "Ah'm not going over to the *Slipp'ah* and Ah'm not a scaly-wag. Pearl had a

92

legitimate reason for being in he'ah and Ah'm not in a mood to listen to any wet-behind-the-ears kid lecture me. Now, Ah'm going to the train depot and yor'ah both going home to Granny's. Now, get going!"

"We can't, Sheriff," Lily said forcefully. "We left Granny's eggs under the platform again. We're coming with you." André rolled his eyes skyward and mumbled a prayer.

"You know, since this whole thing started yesterday, Ah have started mumbling to myself and praying more than ah ev'ah have in my entire life. Come on then, let's get ov'ah to the depot so you can get those eggs."

Andre, Lily and Benny stepped out of the Sheriff's office and hurried down the wooden sidewalk toward the train depot with Lily having to almost run to keep up with Sheriff Beaumont and Benny.

When they got to the depot, Pete was pacing in front of the ticket window. "It's about time you got back here," Pete stated, "I remember some things that might come in handy with your case, Sheriff."

"Like what?" Lily and Benny said anxiously.

"Well," Pete replied, looking at Lily and Benny, "like seeing your Aunt Birdie out on the platform talking to some fellas who came in on the late train. They all stepped over to the side of the platform and talked for about fifteen minutes while the locomotive filled up with coal and then the whistle blew and the two fellas got back on the train and Miss Birdie left. Kind of strange, don't you think Sheriff? What would Birdie Quinn be doing talking to some fancy-pants city fellas? They were all slicked up in their city clothes and their boots looked like they just walked off the shelf of a Paris Bootery in New York City. If they were relatives or friends, she would have taken them on home for a visit. If they were salesmen, they would have spoken to more people in town than Birdie Quinn. And if they were church folk, they would have gone on down to the Reverend's house. It all seems kind of strange to me. How about you, Sheriff André? What do you think? Kind of strange, isn't it?"

"You're right Pete. that ther'ah does sound a mite strange."

"And," Pete continued, "Some strange fellers have been hanging out around the depot, like maybe they're waiting for something, or some- one. Ya think something's going on here? What-cha thinking, Sheriff? Maybe those bums have Miss Caitlin and are just waiting for an 'all clear' signal from someone so they can put her on one of the trains going down to New Orleans. What-cha think? Whatever you think I should do Sheriff, I'll do it. I've seen folks disappear many a time while I was working in New York City," Pete stopped and took a deep breath, "And it doesn't end up pretty, I can tell ya that."

Pete was so wound up he once again began pacing back and forth on the platform talking like a magpie. "Yes sir'ee, yes sir'ee, I'll do whatever it takes to help find Miss Caitlin. She's a real fine lady. I knew Michael too, he was her beau, ya know. He sure was in love with Miss Caitlin. She was mighty broken-hearted when he didn't come home from the war." Pete shook his head as he continued pacing.

"She sure was broken-hearted," Pete repeated, his voice grew soft as if talking again to himself. "Yep, she was mighty upset. Sometimes when she was in town she would come by for a chat and we would talk about her Michael. She had a hard time getting over him. Yes sir'ee, she surely did.

"You see," Pete continued talking, not caring if anyone was listening or not, "Michael was a good man. He and I became close friends the very day I arrived here in Missouri. I met Michael as I stepped off the train. I was having trouble with my carpet bags and Michael happened to be on the platform and when he saw how I was struggling trying to get them off the train and all, he came right over and lent me a hand."

Pete seemed to be talking more to himself than to anyone else. "Well, he took me right on over to the saloon and bought me a fine glass of whiskey. He asked me all about life back east and I asked him all about life here in Missouri and after hearing him tell of the good life here in Caruthersville where there is no hustle and bustle and folks are honest, I decided right then and there to stay right here in Missouri for the rest of my life."

Blinking his owlish eyes, he seemed to flash forward to the problem at hand, "She would have done well by marrying-up with him."

He stopped and glared at Sheriff Beaumont before continuing, "And he would have done well by marrying-up with her too. Miss Caitlin did not run off with a lover and don't you let anything happen to her. I guess maybe I should have been watching out for her," then began pacing again.

The Sheriff scratched his chin and thought for a few minutes then he too began pacing up and down the platform, just like Pete.

"Cri-min-y Christmas," Lily finally said, "Will you two stop pacing up and down this platform? What are we going to do now? Are we going to go out to Yoder's old farm and check it out?

"*We* aren't going to do anything," The sheriff stopped and stared at Lily, "*you* are going back to Granny Tomason's house and Pete and Ah are going to do something. You two kids are going on back to Granny's and staying ther'ah until ah tell ya it's okay to leave that house." André bent down, looked her right in the eyes and said very firmly,

"Now…do ya understand me?"

Lily wanted to punch him right in the nose, but she knew he would get mighty mad and maybe throw her and Benny in jail and throw away the key.

"Ah don't want two mor'ah missin' kids to be looking for. One is enough," he said sharply.

"Sheriff," Lily said indignantly, "Caitlin is not a kid; she is a grown woman!"

"Come on Lily, let's go." Benny pulled on Lily's sleeve and said, "Let's get Granny's eggs and get over to the bake shop."

9

Mr. Johnston and Aunt Birdie

Grabbing the egg-basket from beneath the platform, Lily and Benny hurried onto Main street and slowly ambled along the street watching the hustle and bustle of the town-folks and looking for any strange or unusual things going on. The day was warm and everyone seemed to be doing outside work as they ran here and there with their daily routine.

"I think spring is on its way out the back door and summer is running in the front door, isn't it?" Lily said as she looked up towards the clear blue skies.

"Yeah," Benny drawled, "You know, Pete sure seemed concerned about Caitlin. If I had known he was such good friends with Michael, I would have gone to him the first day Caitlin went missing. Did you know they were friends?"

"Nope," Lily replied, shaking her head.

Entering the bakery, Lily walked up and put the eggs on the counter. She called out a "hello" to Mr. Johnston, the baker, then pressed her face against the glass-enclosed display case and eyed all the sweets lined up in neat little rows. It reminded her of the tasty sweets her mama used to make.

"Hey Benny, don't these look delicious? What do you think?" Lily spoke up, "Shall we get some of those cherry tarts? Look at them, they are just oozing with cherries and calling out my name?"

"Lily," Benny said sternly, as he himself stared at the sweet treats, "Stop looking at them. These eggs are Granny's and she didn't say we could buy tarts or anything else."

"I know, I know. I'm just looking." Lily replied.

"How-do children," Mr. Johnston said as he walked in from the back of the bakery. It was obvious he had been in the back baking because he was covered in flour, "Ye got some eggs for me, yes? I was hoping Granny would come along today. At this very moment, I am out of eggs. How about a cherry tart for the two of ya? Doesn't that sound good? Fresh out of the oven they are and they're pretty tasty...if I have to say so myself. Don't want to toot my own horn, but they are the best you'll find in the state of Missouri. I cannot tell a lie," Mr. Johnston laughed boisterously at himself.

At times, Mr. Johnston accent reminded Lily of her Pa's slight accent.

Mr. Johnston and his wife Nora had been the bakers in town way before Lily and Benny came along. Their Ma and Pa told them the Johnston's were already in Caruthersville when they arrived many years ago. Mr. Johnston and Nora settled in Caruthersville a good long while before their own two sons came along.

"Me lovely Nora," Mr. Johnston would say when he spoke of his wife, who had not lived beyond the first year of their youngest son's birth, "tis the baker from the heavens." Much to the dismay of the town widows, Mr. Johnston never remarried. He raised his sons alone, teaching them the art of baking and book-learning. Both sons turned out to be hard workers, and highly educated as well. His eldest son was named Mo, after the state he was born in, and his youngest was named Noraman after his mother.

Mr. Johnston was one of the proudest parents in town. His boys had gone off to war, met two Yankee sisters and decided to stay back east, marry the sisters and raise their families. Having opened several bake shops in and around Boston, both of Mr. Johnston's sons were doing quite well in life. He wasn't too happy about their decisions to stay in the east, but there was nothing he could do about it. So, every year he sent all of them Christmas presents and asked them to come live in Missouri with him. Every year they would decline his offer, but would promise to visit for the holidays — which they did. Every other Christmas, his two sons, daughter-in-laws and grandchildren would fill his house and bakery with laughter and noise. On the off years, Mr. Johnston would travel back to Boston and stay with his sons for the whole month of December and well into January. When he returned from seeing his grandchildren he was the happiest man in Missouri. Every time he returned from a visit, he would contemplate moving back to Boston, but once he got back into the running of his own bake shop, he just couldn't leave Missouri.

"One day," he would say with a jovial laugh and a smile on his face, "I will leave this wilderness and once again live among the civilized citizens of proper society. But for now, I love it here among the rowdy, uncivilized hooligans of Missouri."

Then he would laugh and say, "Tis the Viking blood runnin' in me veins. I fit right in with these wild and wooly folks in my Missouri."

He was a tall, stout man with white-blond hair and sparkling bright-blue eyes. His eyebrows and eyelashes were the same color as his hair, which made his stunning blue eyes seem to jump right out of his face. When a person looked at Mr. Johnston, they always looked him straight in the eyes because they were mesmerizing and at times, seemed to be hypnotic. They had the look of the clear blue waters off the Caribbean islands; at least that was what the sailors all said. If Mr. Johnston had warts and toads living on his face, no one would notice. All a person remembered about him was his blue captivating eyes. He was a very nice jolly man, always ready to laugh.

At the moment, he was covered from head to toe with flour as if he had been throwing flour in the air and catching it. He must have tried to wipe it off his face when he heard Lily and Benny come in, because small parts of his face were the only areas not powdery white. Clumps of flour was still attached to his mustache and eyebrows looking like snow tipped trees in the winter. Every time he moved his head, flour would sift slowly from his hair and eyebrows like a soft winter snow.

"Thanks, Mr. Johnston, but these eggs are from Granny so we really can't buy anything today. But, they sure do look good...and smell even better," Lily said.

"Well here, take these four pitiful, sad-looking tarts who din't mind their manners and bake the way they should have. They are a pitiful looking lot, aren't the. And, they won't sell so I'll end up throwing them out to the hogs. Take one to your little sister and one for Granny. I hear ye children are staying out at Granny's house for a while. What's going on with that? Nothing is wrong at ye own house now is there?"

Lily and Benny looked at each other. "My goodness," Lily thought. "Nothing is a secret in this town."

Replying quickly, Benny said with a smile, "We just decided to visit Granny for a bit."

"Well then, take all these cherry tarts and here's a word of advice..." Mr. Johnston lowered his voice a bit and leaned over the glass case, "Stay away from that Aunt Birdie of yours," he said in a whispery voice, "something ain't right with that woman, I tell ye, something ain't right. I can feel it in me old bones."

"Here, how 'bout ya take some apple tarts ta go 'long with the cherry. The rest of 'em are looking mighty poorly too. They make a wonderful, tasty treat with your milk in the morning. Just don't mention it to that aunt of yours; I'm not giving anything to that woman! Pardon my saying so, but she needs to stop eating all those bitter greens. Maybe she would sweeten up a bit."

Mr. Johnston winked and chuckled at his own joke as he handed Lily and Benny a bag full of tarts.

When he laughed, a clump of flour fell off his hair and tumbled down onto his face like a snowball.

"At times," he laughed as he brushed the powdery flour away from his eyes, "she scares the heebie-jeebies outta me. Here ye go, here's the money for Granny's eggs and let her know I be thanking her. She is a woman sent straight from heaven for letting me buy her eggs at such a low price. Be sure and bring me all the eggs ye can spare, ya hear."

Flour was covering the counter and floating around the room as Mr. Johnston moved his head; Lily was sure the floor behind the glass case was also covered.

"Well, children, I be running off at the mouth again, I am sure Miss Bidy — sorry, Birdie — is a right nice person if one got to know her."

"I highly doubt that," Benny mumbled.

"It's okay. Thanks Mr. Johnston," Lily said, "We'll be sure and give Tessa and Granny some tarts."

The two of them walked out the bakery door and started up the road to Granny's house. As they walked past the door to the *Ruby Slipper Saloon*, Lily caught Benny craning his neck to look in the door.

"Don't be a baboon." she hissed at him. "Stop acting like a donkey's hind-end."

"Itty-bitty brains must come with all baby boys," Lily thought to herself, "No wonder God decided to create a woman. He sure messed up on that man he started with. All they can see is the way a woman looks. They seem to forget God really did give us brains. If all the men in this town put their brains together in a bucket, it wouldn't be enough to fill a thimble.

"Stop acting like a simpleton, Benny Quinn," Lily said as she jerked on Benny's sleeve and pulled him away from the *Slipper's* door. "You don't have the brains God gave a goose."

As they turned the corner behind the *Ruby Slipper*, both of them began running until — *SMACK*! they slammed right into Aunt Birdie's derrièrere.

"WHOA!" Lily and Benny gasped at the same time.

Immediately they spun around like tops and took off running back around the corner as Aunt Birdie flung herself around and started moving as fast as she could in an attempt to nab them.

"You two stop this instant!" she yelled, "Get back here right now! Someone help me! Those two bra—uh—children are mine! Help me s-stop them! Bring them b-back!"

Birdie was huffing and puffing as she tried catching them. Her legs were pumping up and down and she was breathing so deeply she could barely yell. Her face turned bright red and sweat began running down her neck. It ran down her back and soaked into her shirt-waist dress.

Whizzing loudly, Birdie had to stop, "Those wild heathens are like animals! I am going beat them when I finally get my hands on those creatures. Where is that little Tessa? She'll be easier to handle. Those two are just too wild. That is exactly what comes from being the spawn of that no-good, backwoods mother of theirs!"

Birdie kept mumbling to herself as she stopped in front of the bakery and sat down on one of the benches in front of the large glass window. She had a difficult time catching her breath and her heart was pumping so fast she could see her bosoms moving up and down.

"I'm going to get rid of those woods-colts if I have to do away with them myself," she muttered.

She didn't feel one bit of shame about getting rid of Daniel and Molly's children. All she could think about was the fact that she would finally be rid of all Molly 's children and pay her back for taking Daniel away from the plantation and leaving her alone. Daniel had left the plantation for that wild woman with the awful red hair flying around her head. She was like a feral cat in Birdie's eyes. Always laughing and touching Daniel's arms or hands in front of God and anyone else who happened to be around.

"What a floozy she had been." She rambled on as she sat on the bench, "Well, Daniel fell for her wily-ways and look what it had gotten him. Dead! That's what it got him. That wicked woman was the reason Daniel died. The woman he thought was such a beautiful lady killed him."

"Ugh," Birdie thought, "Lady? Not in the least. Molly Donaldson was nothing but trash and a conniving tramp who tricked Daniel into marrying-up with her."

Birdie kept right on muttering to herself as she sat in front of the Bake Shop. She was unaware of the other pedestrians staring at her as they walked quickly past her.

"Molly Donaldson was worse than a saloon girl," she continued ranting, "She pretended to be a high-society lady and all the time acting like a trollop. From the wrong side of the tracks was what she was. She may have lived in a big, fancy house with all the servants she wanted, but that didn't make her a lady," Birdie continued on as if she was by herself in her own house, "Yes, from the wrong side of the tracks, is where she was from! She didn't even have a mother to teach her how to be a proper lady. All she had was that foolish old man for a Pa who was more interested in teaching his daughter to ride astride and shoot a gun than to be a lady. What had Daniel seen in that woman? Molly had thrown herself at Daniel, and being a gentleman, he just couldn't resist her witching ways. That had to be the reason, for surely Daniel could not have truly love a woman such as Molly Donaldson."

"Well, that woman will be clawing in her grave when I finish with those wild savages of hers," Birdie muttered. "She thought she was so smart taking my Daniel away and leaving me alone on that farm. Well, I'll show her, I'll have her house and everything in it and her wild, heathen excuses for children will be gone to join her. Ha! I'll show her! Daniel should have stayed on the farm and helped me." Birdie kept right on muttering to herself.

Being so caught up in ranting about her hatred for Molly Quinn, Birdie never noticed the pedestrians passing the bench looking at her strangely. All she could think about was Molly Donaldson and how much she loathed her for taking Daniel.

Sitting there for a good long while trying to catch her breath and talking to herself, she gradually calmed down. It was becoming harder and harder to breathe after doing anything the less bit taxing.

"I'll get them," she muttered as she took a deep breath and stood up, "I'll get them yet and sell them to the highest bidder. And forget that paper money. I want *gold*!" She leaned her head back and laughed hysterically.

* * *

Lily and Benny ran as fast and as far as they could to get away from Aunt Birdie and ended up on the opposite end of town from Granny's house. Now, they would have to walk all the way back through town to get to Granny's — or walk through the woods.

"Wait-up a minute Benny," Lily gasped, "Let me take a minute and catch my breath. That was a close call. I was so surprised to see her I almost wet myself."

"I could feel her breathing right down the neck of my shirt!" Benny gasped. "She scared the heebie-jee-bees out of me! We were so close I could smell her onion breath. Cri-min-y Lily, that was close. I thought my skin was gonna jump right off my bones and take off running on its own."

"Come on," Lily finally pulled on Benny's sleeve, "let's go on back to Granny house and see what's on the stove to eat."

"Okay, but let's take the path through the woods,"

The narrow path was uneven, overgrown with grass and weeds but it was still visible and the sun was shining as the afternoon drew to a close.

10

Mr. Bushy

On the way back to the farm, Lily and Benny didn't have much to say to each other as they contemplated their next move in finding Caitlin while staying away from Aunt Birdie

Slipping her hand into her pocket, Lily thought about Caitlin's comb.

"I wonder where this came from?" she thought to herself. "It just seems strange with Tessa finding it outside the shanty."

The further they walked from town, the thicker the forest grew. Saplings, flowering bushes and shrubs filled in the open spaces between the larger older trees. Here and there, they came upon a path leading out into the forest going to God knows where. Magnolia and Dogwoods were starting to bloom, and wild flowers opened their eyes to the warm, soothing spring sunshine.

Feeling the shift in the spring breeze as it changes directions and began blowing in from the hot southern states, Lily lifted her face and felt the warm breeze brush across her cheeks.

"Well, slap my arse and call me Spanky," boomed a loud voice from the dense forest.

Coming to a startled stop, Lily and Benny whirled around and peered into the shadowy woods.

"Iff'en it ain't them thar' Quinn critters! How y'all been? Mighty fine to see ya critters again, yes sir'ree, mi-tee fine. Wait up fur' an old feller, would'jah? Yur' a'walkin' way too fast. Hold up thar'."

"Hey," Benny called out with a big grin on his face, "How-do, Mr. Bushman. Where you been hiding ya'self? We haven't seen you in a month of Sundays. You been up there in the Ozarks, living with the bears and the hill folk? Or maybe hibernating with the bears? Come on along with us, we're on our way to Granny Tomason's house."

"Ouch! I don't think I can do that thar'," Mr. Bushy...as he was called by his friends...bellowed loudly, "Granny Tomason don't rightly fancy up to me. I'm not clean enough she says. Iff'en I went with ya she would be puttin' me in a worsh tub quicker'n ah lightin' bug's flash and scrubbin' my hide right off'en my bones." He let out another booming laugh.

"Well! Miss Lily, yor a'lookin as pretty as a picture. You sure do look like yor' Aunt Maggie Mae. That Maggie Mae is a mighty fine lookin' lady, I tell ya. She be the darling of me life, the moonlight on a cloudy night and the sunshine on a rainy day. That she is...that she surely is. She stole me heart clean outta me chest, she did. There be an empty spot where me heart used to be," Mr. Bushy put his hands over his heart and looked toward the sky. Sometimes Mr. Bushy spoke with a horrifying fake Irish accent.

Poising as if he were reciting Shakespeare, he continued.

"Well, never mind that," he grinned from ear to ear as he waved his hands above his head as if to scatter his thoughts.

Rumor had it that it was love at first sight for Mr. Bushman when he met Aunt Maggie Mae. He was so in love, it was said, that he pretty much made a fool of himself. He kidnapped her away from Boston and was on his way back to the Missouri Ozarks with her in tow when Aunt Maggie Mae insisted she had to honor

106

her marriage vows and return to her husband. Supposedly, Maggie Mae promised Mr. Bushy that if anything ever happened to her husband, Mr. Bushy would be the first to know and she would then consider marrying him. Reluctantly, Mr. Bushy took her back to Boston to the man he called a coward.

The coward never found out about the abduction and was no more the wiser as a broken-hearted Mr. Bushy returned to his mountains.

"So how ya two critters doin'?" Mr. Bushy asked.

Lily could not keep from smiling and staring at Mr. Bushy. He was exactly what everyone called him: a bushy man! Lily didn't know if Bushman was his actual name or if folks called him that because of the way he looked. He stood almost six and a half feet tall and broad as the side of a barn. His hair and beard reached almost to his waist, and both were copper-red and curly. He had a big, toothy smile and bushy eyebrows. They were so bushy a person could barely see his eyes.

When the days were sunny, he wore his eyeball covers – that's what he called them. He had made them from thin pieces of wood cut to fit each eye. He then cut openings across the middle of each eye patch and covered the slits with sheer pieces of black cloth. They were held to his head with a long strip of very thin leather woven into the side of each eyepiece and across the middle of his nose. He said they kept the sun out of his eyes and made it possible for him to see things in the glare of the sun other men could not see. He refused to leave his cabin without them.

Some days, like today, he wore them pushed back onto the top of his head, making the hair around his face stand on end like a big feathery poof resembling a weird sort of woman's bonnet.

Pa once told them Mr. Bushman was as strong as a team of oxen and Pa was forever asking him if he would pull the plow as Pa plowed up the soil each spring since Mama always fed him when he was at their house, Pa said he figured it was an even trade. Mama would shush Pa and Mr. Bushy would laugh and tell Pa that, on the day Pa talked Maggie Mae into leaving her coward, he would "plow the whole dang field fur' free". With the exception of Granny Tomason, all the Quinn family dearly loved Mr. Bushy, and Lily was quite sure Granny just liked to pester him.

He had arrived in Missouri long before Molly and Daniel Quinn met him. Supposedly, he met the Quinn's while he was on one of his travels which ended up in Boston and immediately took a liking to Daniel and his pretty wife Molly. It was during that first meeting when he talked Daniel and Molly into moving to the Missouri wilderness where they could own their own land and live in peace with clean air, beautiful mountains and crystal clear streams.

That was when he also met and fell in love with Maggie Mae Donaldson-- Beaufone. There were many secrets about Mr. Bushman and Aunt Maggie Mae which Lily could not get out of anyone. But, maybe someday Lily would find out from Granny or Caitlin and her curiosity would be satisfied.

Molly and Daniel had indeed fallen in love with the land and people of Missouri. They built their home and raised their children in the "wonderful wilderness", as Pa called it, of Missouri. Missouri was quite unlike the crowded plantation on which he had been raised.

When anyone asked Mr. Bushy where he hailed from, he would simply say "way down yonder, deep in the Oh-zarks". But, no one knew exactly where "way down yonder" happened to be. He called himself an inventor, trapper, and traveling mountain man and he was a sight to behold that was for sure.

Lily walked over to Mr. Bushman and gave him a big hug. He smelled of tobacco, horses, and sweat. It wasn't a bad smell, it was just the smell of a mountain man.

"Howdy, Mr. Bushy," she said with a smile. "We sure are glad to see you. You see, our Caitlin went missing and we've been trying to find her. She disappeared a few days back and the Sheriff and Pete Turnkey, the ticket master, are helping us find her. Do you think you can help?"

"What's that you say? Caitlin's missing?" Mr. Bushy said in a whispery voice, leaning in close to Lily and Benny.

"Yes," Benny replied as he proceeded in telling Mr. Bushy the details of Caitlin's disappearance.

"Well, you don't say. I'll be a sawed-off donkey's ear. This here is a strange thing for sure. Yep, mighty strange." Mr. Bushy looked around the woods as if checking for other people, then once again leaned closer to their faces and whispered.

"Let's go have a sit-down over yonder on that thar' fallen tree for a few minutes and take a load off while I tell you two critters something ya ain't gonna believe."

The three of them walked over and had a sit-down on the fallen tree and Mr. Bushy looked at both of them for a second or two before saying anything.

"Ya see here, critters, what I'm gonna tell ya sounds right loco. But it is the honest to goodness gol-durn truth! It all started about a week ago when I was down in my mountain a'sittin' outside my cabin gettin' ready to bed down fur the night and all. I usually sleep outside my cabin unless it's too cold fur' a human bean' to last through the night, 'cuz the fresh air of a mountain night is a right fine thin' for the body and soul.

Well, after my horse, Digger, was all set for the night, I et' my supper and got my night far' burnin' real low-like. I lit-up my pipe and sat thar' smokin' and listenin' to them thar' cricket calls and bull frogs a'singin them thar' love songs to each other. The breeze was blowin' real soft-like so I just lay thar' watchin' as the sweet smellin' smoke from my pipe drifted up and disappeared amongst the tree tops. Ever' so often I'd join in and whistle ah tune or two right along with them forest critters. Well, hit' was gettin' on to being close to the witchin' hour and all, iff'en I 'member right."

Pausing for a bit, he lowered his voice and whispered, "Now, you critters know how those mountains have a soul of thar' own and all, and thar's times when

109

you can almost hear, and feel, it breathin' right beneath ya? Well, that night, my mountain seemed to be whisperin' in my ears, like a bumble bee buzzin' around a daisy. It was as if it was tryin' to wrap me up in its warmth and start tellin' me ah secret. Well, I start in being real quiet like; thinkin' maybe I could hear what she was a'whisperin', but I couldn't hear nor feel nary a thing. Now, I love my mountain and when she talks to me that'ah way I listen and feel all warm and safe from anything lurkin' around. So, I go on ahead and clean up my grub dish and pulled out a blanket, in case the night chill got heavy.

"Then lo'-and-behold, the strangest thing happened. Way off from a distance came this lonesome, call from ah big ol' barred owl. It seemed ta go on forever! I stopped what I was doin' and gave a good listen. It was kindly-like that old owl was callin' out ah warnin' or somethin'. I got goose bumps on my arms and down deep in my soul 'cuz I knew that owl had seen somethin' that weren't right. But, I din't know what to do about it so I went on ahead and relaxed and listened to the silence of the night.

"I kindly dosed off a bit but really not sound asleep. Kindly fuzzy in the brain, ya know, when all of a sudden-like somethin' starts bumpin' on my shoulder real steady like."

Bump, bump, bump.

"Well, I slapped at what I thought was ol' Digger there," Mr. Bushy pointed to his horse. "and my hand hit nothing but plain ole air. Then I thought to myself, 'Well, the dad-blame old horse moved pretty durn fast gettin' away from my slap.' I didn't even bother opening my eyeballs none since I was plum tuckered out and all and I went on back to dosing off. I tucked my hand up under my blanket ta get all comfy an all. Well, about two minutes later, I reckon it was, the bumping starts in again. Only this time it pert near pushed me over onto my belly."

"Now, this belly here," Mr. Bushy patted his stomach with a big grin, "Ain't no little bitty thin' like you critters have, ya see, so that was some pretty dad-blame hard pushing on my shoulder. This time I whirled around as fast as I could," Bushy whirled around on the fallen tree, demonstrating, "and I yelled out

'Digger, get on outta here ya bag o' fleas, ya hear me? Leave me be!' Well, it weren't Digger a'tall."

Lowering his voice to a softer whisper, Mr. Bushy leaned in about two inches from Lily and Benny and said, "This here *person* was squattin' right close to me and it was ah sure 'nuf soldier-boy peerin' inta my face. He was a'lookin' right at me and he had on the whole kit-and-caboodle soldiering uniform. Hat, pants, boots, jacket and everthin' else. His hair was long and his face was real thin-like, but I knowed right off who he was."

With his hands on his knees, Bushy leaned back a bit, and in a halting whisper said, as he looked around the forest, "It was Michael Thorne! Yes sir'ree, it sure 'nuf was Michael Thorne. As God is my witness, it was him.

"Well, I jumped right up onto my feet and put out my hand, wantin' ta shake his hand, and I start in a'talkin'. I said 'Michael my boy, what a fine sight for sore eyes you are. I am right happy to see ya, where ya been boy? Come on over here son, let's have us a sit-down. But first let me give ya such a hug your belly button pops right on out.' Well, I reached out to give the boy a belly-button-popper hug, but he stepped back and shook his head. Then I knowed right off, this weren't no actual meeting with a long-lost soldier-boy. Something weren't right and I knowed just what was happenin'. I stopped and squeezed my eyes a bit so I could look at him real close-like, and lo'-and-behold, I could almost see right through 'em, not really good but, kindly-like he was some kinda apparition or somethin'. He was all shadowy, kindly like a thick cloud, but it sure 'nuf was Michael. He smiled and spoke to me with his usual slow, raspy, Tennessee drawl and says, 'Lo, Bushy. How are ya? Sorry, no more belly-button poppin' for me. I'm just here to ask a favor and then I'll be on my way. I need ta ask ya to help find my Cait.'

"Well, I just stood there with my mouth hangin' down to my own belly-button. Then he spoke again in that soft, low drawl, and says, 'They need your help in finding her, Bushy. I know I can depend on ya. When ya find her and she's safe, tell her that she's in my heart for all eternity.'

"Then he reached up, pulled his soldierin' hat a little further down on his head, gives me one of them thar soldier-hat salutes, a smile and a nod as he says, 'Had a mighty fine time knowing ya Mr. Bushy, you're a good man', and then he up and walks away. Not really walkin' away, just kindly meltin' in with the trees and bushes and there we stood, just me and ole' Digger a'lookin' like scared jack-rabbits. My heart jumped right up inta my throat and was dancin' a jig on my tonsils to get out through my mouth. It was poundin' on my ears like a war drum, and I was sweatin' like a buff'lo in a stampede! Digger had backed up and was just a'lookin off inta the forest where Michael had melted away."

As Bushy told his story, he acted out each and every action for Lily and Benny.

"It was the strangest durn thing I ever did see in all my born days. Now, those hill folks say they see spirits and spooks and such," Bushy leaned close again and whispered, "They even say the dead can talk to the livin' and tell 'em all kinda things. Now, I always was thinkin' it was just the jibber-jabber of them thar' women-folk a'talkin and a'squawkin' about ever'thin and them thar tales was just a whole lot of passin' the wind. Pardon me Miss Lily, but now I'm thinkin they may be some grit to them thar tales."

Mr. Bushman was looking off into the woods as if he was talking to himself. "Ya jest never do know, ya never do know fur' sure." Then he blinked his eyes and came back.

"Well, after all that thar' happened, I decided not to sleep out under the stars and all, so I marched right back up onto my porch, turned around and sat right thar against the logs with my rifle handy and watched until the daylight lightened up the sky a wee bit then me and ol' Digger took off lickety-split to check up on you Quinn critters. We spent some scary nights in them thar' mountains while we was a'walkin' and a'ridin' down here. I was kind of jumpy-like, so I had to keep a far' going all night, but nothing happened and there weren't even a whisper of a haint. Next thing I know'd is, I see you Quinn critters and you tell me Caitlin really does need help."

112

Mr. Bushy frowned at them with a look of annoyance, "Now, don't ya be a'lookin' at me like I be gone loco. You critters know I ain't no more loco than your ma and pa was. Why I can't hardly believe the whole thin' myself. But hit's the honest to goodness truth. I will stand before the good Lord in Heaven himself on judgment day and testify that it's all the truth. I couldn't have been more surprised if I'd'ah seen the Mother Mary herself standin' thar' in front ah me!"

"Oh no, Mr. Bushy," Lily whispered. Her throat was tight and her skin was clammy, "I most certainly do believe you. Something similar happened to me on my way out to Granny's house. The person didn't carry on a conversation with me but he did call out my name and motioned for me to go to him. But now I think it must have been Michael and maybe he wanted to talk to me about Caitlin. I was scared out of my skin."

Lily told Mr. Bushman what had happened on the way to Granny's house on the night she had dragged Benny and Tessa out from under the dock.

"Well, I'll be a flap-eared hound-dog," Mr. Bushy muttered, looking at Lily with relief. "I thought you critters would think I'd gone loco. Now," he paused, "are ya sure it was a soldier-boy and not just one of them thar' river rats, hangin' around the town in the fog up to no-good?"

"Nope," Lily replied swiftly. "It was a soldier. I could see that plain enough. I couldn't tell who it was, but it definitely was a soldier, and a scary one at that."

"Well, critters," Mr. Bushy said as he scratched his bearded chin, "I guess I'm gonna have to go on inta Granny Tomason's house with ya after all since it's comin' onta being dark. I can't have ya running 'round here by yourself lookin' for Caitlin and maybe runnin' inta more haints. 'Cuz iff'en that was Michael's haint, I'm knowin' he wouldn't hurt anyone of ya, but iff'en Michael's haint is out there, maybe someone else's haint is out there strollin' around too and they may not be a good'un. Let's go get this torture from Granny Tomason over with." He let out a big sigh and got up from the fallen tree.

"Good Lord on high, please give Granny a kind heart today for this poor wanderer." Mr. Bushy bellowed with his head lifted to the sky.

When the three of them reached the back of Granny's house, Benny called out, "hello the house" since it was now dusky and was was a customary thing to do when one approached anyone's house from the back area (or even the front. If a person did not "hello the house", most farmers would think the person was a thief or someone up to no-good, and may take a shot at them. It was an unwritten law that everyone must "hello the house" to announce themselves. If a person was shot by a farmer because he had not called "hello the house", the law was on the farmer's side. So, Benny called out, just from habit, as they approached Granny's house. Pie-Eater came bounding out to meet them, jumping up and trying to lick their faces. "Hello, Pie-Eater!" Benny said as he rubbed the dog's head.

"Let's get in the house," Lily said, "I'm hungry and we can have these tarts after supper." The two of them took off running toward the house, jumped up onto the back porch and knocked on the door.

"Granny," Lily called out, "it's us, Lily and Benny. We have another guest with us; he came to help us find Caitlin."

Tessa threw open the door to great them. "Well, fellers!" she said with a wide grin, "me and Granny sure are glad to see you. We thought maybe you had gotten eaten up by river monsters or something. We made sweet biscuits and fried apple pie to go along with supper."

"Fellers?" Lily thought, "When did she start saying 'fellers'?"

"Mr. Bushy!" Tessa exclaimed with happiness as she spied Mr. Bushy. Jumping off the porch, she raced into his open arms. "I am sooo glad you came to see me. I sure need your help because my Caitlin is gone and I need you to find her for me."

Tessa considered Caitlin, as well as Mr. Bushy, to be her personal property and Lily was quite sure Tessa thought Mr. Bushy had come to Granny's house just to see her. She figured Caitlin was just on loan to Lily and Benny once in a while.

Tessa leaned into Mr. Bushman's shoulder and kissed him on his hairy face.

"Ah, me lovely, darlin' Tessa. If we ain't careful, someone will steal you away as fast as they did your Caitlin. You be a'lookin more like yor pretty mama each time I see ya. Yor pa was a mighty lucky man iff'en ya be askin' me. He was like a leprechaun with a pot-o-gold tucked under his arm when he was with yur' mama." Mr. Bushy always spoke with his very bad Irish brogue when he was having a conversation Tessa.

"How ya been, ya little red-haired whipper-snapper? Ya been actin' like a young lassie should or a wild honey-bee, buzzin' round ever'body's head?" Bushy grinned at Tessa.

Granny once told them that Mr. Bushy had taken a powerful liking to Tessa the very day she was born. He had lost his wife and his own little red-haired, green-eyed daughter in a fire when the baby was but a couple years old. Both of them had been gone a few years when Tessa was born, and Granny guessed it was Tessa's red hair and mossy green eyes that drew Mr. Bushy to her and created a special place in his heart.

"Oh Mr. Bushy," Tessa giggled, "It's no fun being a proper lassie. It's more fun being a honey bee and buzzing around." She giggled and gave Bushy another big hug.

"Well, Tessa, me darlin' let's go in and buzz around Granny for a while and see if she gives me the boot and sends me packin' out to the barn," Bushy said with a deep laugh. Tessa jumped down, grabbed Mr. Bushy's hand and pulled him towards the house.

As they all walked into the house, Granny turned from her big stove and gave them all a big hello.

"Granny, Granny!" Tessa exclaimed as she pulled Mr. Bushy into the kitchen, "Look what I found! It's Mr. Bushy! Isn't he grand? He'll find Caitlin for us, won't you Mr. Bushy?"

"Well, Alexander," Granny grinned. She always called Mr. Bushy by his given name, "Have you taken a bath since last I saw you? I didn't smell you coming in through the door, so you must be fairly clean."

"Aw, Granny, you wound me heart to me very soul. You be a wonderful sight to behold. Tis that ham I smell cooking? And fresh hot biscuits too? And hot gravy to go with hot biscuits maybe? You are a woman dear to me heart. You are full of kindness for me poor stomach. Me belly is a'bowin' down to my knees, giving ya praises. Your wonderful food and memories of Maggie Mae are me only pleasures in this wild and wooly world, other than these here Quinn critters, that is. I already give thanks to the good Lord above for just the smell of yur' vittles."

With that said, he let out one of his booming laughs and sat down at Granny's table.

"Get on with you, Alexander. You are full of malarkey. All of you have a sit-down and the girls and I will spoon up the food.

11

The Tales

After filling their stomachs with Granny's food and completing the evening work, which needed to be done, they sat down in the parlor and talked the rest of the day away.

Entertaining them, Mr. Bushy told of his adventures and travels amongst the mountain-folk, Indians and wild animals of the Ozarks.

He told of the time he was way back to his cabin from the west side of the Ozarks and a mama bear chased him up a tree and kept him there through the entire night. The mama bear stayed at the bottom of the tree with her cubs until the wee hours of the morning with Mr. Bushy falling asleep in the oak tree's branches; thankful that the tree was huge and the fork in the; three branches was "better than sleeping in a bedroll." When the sun came up the next morning, he climbed down to the lowest branch but just as he let go to drop to the ground, a family of skunks waddled in and stopped right below him in their hunt for grubs. As his feet hit the ground, he landed on the tail of the mama skunk and a crazy frenzy of whooping and hopping began, as well as the continuous streams of skunk perfume saturating his entire body. Leaving their agonizing odor behind, the skunk family scurried on down the path and Mr. Bushy lost what little food he had in his stomach. He threw up on his clothes, on his shoes and all over his beard. His hair was covered with spray and his eyes felt as if they were on fire. Thankfully, he had turned his head in the nick of time so his eyes had not caught the full force of the spray. Since Digger had vanished the night before when the mama bear surprised them, Mr. Bushy walked miles back to his cabin, stopping every so often to throw up and by the time he reached the cabin he was thirsty and his stomach was chewing on his backbone with hunger. And, there stood Digger inside his lean-to, peeking out as he watched Mr. Bushy walk in. When Mr. Bushy got close to the cabin Digger began pawing at the ground and shaking his head. He took a few steps outside the lean-to and snorted, all the while looking at Bushy and shaking his head. Then the cantankerous horse took off down the path at a full gallop trying to get away from the smell and he didn't come back for two whole days. Mr. bushy said he would catch a glimpse of digger peering at him from behind the trees in front of his cabin, but he wouldn't come any closer until the skunk perfume had eased a bit. In the meantime, Mr. Bushy had to shave his hair completely off as well as his mustache and beard, then threw his clothes into the fire and burned them. He scrubbed and scrubbed in the creek until he thought his skin would come plum off, but nothing worked. He just had to live with it until the smell left on its own. He walked around without shoes for a full week until he nabbed a reluctant peddler who was passing by his cabin and talked him into making a trade with him as long as Mr. Bushy stayed back from the peddler's wagon. The peddler gave him a good bargain on the boots and clothing and made a quick getaway as soon as the furs Mr. Bushy traded barely touched his wagon bed. Mr. Bushy told of how the mountain folks and the Indians pointed and laughed at him and wanted him to take off his hat so they could rub his bald head.

Granny, Benny and the girls laughed at Mr. Bushy until their sides hurt. Around dark, Mr. Bushy began telling them about the strange happenings deep in the valley of the mountain where his cabin sits. He told about the evil apparitions which appear to ride in on the wings of the hot winds in the middle of a dark night when the sounds of the forest become deathly quiet and the phantom's wails echo off the valley walls. When the sweltering heat of the afternoon lingered far into the night and the stars and moon would cover their faces with dark clouds, keeping the night air as hot as the mid-day heat. He told how sometimes he would wake up and feel something, or someone, watching him, the presence of which was so intense he could barely force himself up to light his lanterns. He would feel — not see — someone next to his bed but when he managed to light his lanterns he could

118

actually see, out of the corners of his eyes, black shadows fleeing out through the cracks in his cabin walls.

Other times, he said, he would wake up to heavy breathing coming from outside his door as if someone, or something, was trying to slip through the narrow cracks of the heavy barrier.

He told of other nights when the heat was thick and heavy — so heavy it was difficult to draw air into his lungs — with the thick darkness. At times, he said, the black of a Missouri mountain night was so dark it felt like a thick blanket pressing against a body's soul.

It was as if all the worlds' darkness had crept into his house for a visit, and decided to stay the night. Then suddenly the crickets and frogs would stop their singing; and that in itself would wake him from a sound sleep. It was at that point he would hear it — the soft rustle of leaves growing louder and louder as it drew closer. Every time this happened, he would jump out of his bed or, if he was sleeping outside, he would rush into his cabin, shut and lock all the windows and doors, lighting all the lanterns and sitting them all over his small cabin, "lighting it up like a house a'far'" he said. Then he would sit in his chair by the door watching and waiting for something to happen. At times the winds would whip so hard it shook the handles on his doors and rattled the glass on his windows as if trying to shatter the pane so as to get inside.

Mr. Bushy's voice lowered to a whisper as he leaned closer to his captive audience. Granny sat in her rocker with her knitting needles quietly clicking faster and faster, as if unknowingly her heart was beating faster.

"I myself have heard of the evil spirits trying to occupy our mountain-folks home," Granny whispered softly.

Mr. Bushy went on to tell of another time when a strong, black, wind rushed down into his valley, carrying black ash and dirt and strained to slip its black-evil fingers through the small cracks and crevices around his door and windows. He told of how he had sat at his table and watched as the shadowy black powder slowly slipped its fingers along the wood floor, encircling the legs of his table and chairs. He would lower a lantern onto the floor and see the dark fingers jerk back as if they had touched a flame; rolling up like balls and rushing out the same way they had entered. He was sure ol' Lucifer himself would, at any moment, start banging on his door with vengeance.

"I'm thinkin' that ol' fella was low on fuel for his far' lake," Mr. Bushy whispered, "and wanted to drag me off and whirl me inta its flames. I hate to admit being scare't, but a few times I have been so scare't I would start in singing *Amazing Grace* at the top of my voice 'cuz I knew when I did that, the black devils vanished with a *whoosh*! And I ain't foolin' none a'tall. It ain't manly fur' ah man to be so scare't...but I was!"

He laughed and continued with his telling.

"Ya see, I've done more than my share of wrong in my days," he whispered, "but I ain't ready to walk into those fary' flames with that ol' boy just yet. Nope, I'm not goin' any time soon. I still have me some livin' to do on this here earth and I plan on doin' it. That old boy can just wait awhile. Maybe the good Lord on high will see fit to take me up with him. Maybe I can do some good thin's down here a'fore I take my dive in the dirt," he said with a chuckle and a smile.

"Iff'en I help ya find our Caitlin maybe that'll give me some good points and I can tell that ol' feller ta get lost." Mr. Bushy laugh loudly at himself

"But now listen here ya critters. Let me tell ya some more about my mountains. My mountains ain't usually like that. Only once't in a while does ah black wind come a'blowin' and sneakin' through my forest. My mountains are like a wall guarding ever'thing and ever'body who lives there.

"Why, I've seen angels a'walkin' amongst my trees along with the spirits of my long-gone good friends and ancestors, and I've felt the breeze a'whisperin' in my ears warning me of dangers. That mountain breeze has saved my life more than once't, I tell ya, and I sure do 'preciate it."

"Yep it surely does," he sighed

120

Then a huge grin spread across Mr. Bushy's face and laughter swelled up from his chest. "Well, critters," he said with a chuckle, "let me tell ya a story that is the dad-blame truth."

Granny's knitting needles stopped as she looked sternly at Mr. Bushy, waiting for him to stop cussing and start the telling.

"Sorry Granny," he said sheepishly, "Okay, one time I was over yonder visitin' them thar' Oh-zark hill folk, and they was havin' a big 'ol shin-dig cuz some of their kin was marryin-up. I just happened to be there doin' some tradin' and they all insisted I stay around; said it was gonna be the best shin-dig they ever put on cuz this here was a marryin-up between two old folks who had never been married-up a'fore.

"Willingly...I obliged" he laughed, "They didn't even have to twist my arm or anythin', and I started in a'havin' me a grand ol' time. I was a'dancin' and a'talkin' and eatin' the best durn food ever cooked when low and behold I suddenly realized I was as drunk as ol' Cooter Brown himself. So, I decided I should stumble on out into the woods ah ways and sleep it off. Well, I no more than had my first dream a'goin' when I felt someone jest a'smoochin' away on my face. 'Now, this ain't so bad' I'm a'thinkin' to myself. I'd been dreamin' of your pretty little Aunt Maggie Mae fur' such a long time and — what do ya know — here she is in my dream just a'smoochin' on me! Then, in my half-asleep stupor, I start in smilin' and puckerin' up my lips and she's still smoochin' away. I leaned over and wrapped my arms around her pretty little neck tryin' to give her the biggest ol' kiss right on her sweet lips."

Once again Mr. Busy was acting out his tale, "I had me a lip-lock on those beautiful lips of hers and I was a'thinkin' hit' was pure heaven. Then, all of a sudden-like, I hear this here piercing scream right in my ear! It was so loud, my eyeballs started bouncin' around inside my head and it took me a second or two to get 'em back into my eyeball holes and when I finally managed ta do that, I popped my eyeballs open and all I could see was a hog — a big ol' mama hog starin' at me with her beady little eyes and squealin' like a banshee with the biggest

121

ol' snoot I ever did see right up against my lips and that there ol' sow's snoot was covered with molasses.

"I jumped right up from that thar' tree, reached up to wipe my mouth off, and there was molasses all over my face. Then I hear'd this here loud laughin' and I looked up to see four of them thar' skinny little mountain fellers, couldn't be more'n twelve years old, taking off into the woods just a'whoopin' and a'laughin' their dang heads off luggin' a big ol' jug ah molasses with 'em. I start in yellin' at 'em and that dang, oops, 'cuse me Granny, mama sow runs right into me and knocked me down to the ground as she's stompin' 'round trying to get away. Well, I'm fightin' 'er trying to get myself up when that hog gets her foot hooked in my 'spenders and down I go again, but this time I fall right down on top of 'er. She takes off a'runnin' like lightning and thar' I am hangin' on for dear life. She's still squealin' and I start in yellin'. She takes off lickety-split for home with me on 'er back. My 'spenders won't come off'en 'er leg, so all's I can do is hang on and ride it out. That hog was pert near as long as I am tall, so it was a wild ride. I got my arms hooked around her neck and my legs around her middle and she's a'runnin' straight out. Well after a minute or two, I start in laughin' and cain't stop cuz she was swayin' back and forth and gruntin' with ever step and I was slidin' from the left to the right, back to the left and back to the right again. It was the most fun I've had in all my born days!"

At this point, Mr. Bushy was actually standing up acting out his hog ride.

"Then lo-and-behold," he continued as he sat back down, "after about five minutes that ol' sow-hog just dropped to the ground. She was dead! Just as dead as old Abe himself. I thank the good Lord on high I was on her left side when she went down on her right side. But dead she was! There she lay, just as dead as if I'd bonked her on the noggin. Well, I managed to get my 'spenders off'en 'er front leg and stood there a'lookin' at 'er. I got down on my knees and put my ear to her heart area, and sure 'nuf — no heart beat a'tall.

"I stood over there jest lookin' down at 'er then, Land-a-Goshen, I suddenly knew right off whoever owned that hog was gonna be purty mad-as-a-hornet when they found out their breedin' sow was a goner and most likely would come after me with a shotgun. So, I jumped right up and scurried on back to that thar' house where the shin-dig was still goin' strong. I grabbed Digger and high-tailed it right on outta thar'. I still had molasses all over my face and my 'spenders weren't doin' a very good job holdin' my britches up, since that she-hog had pulled them apart. But I jumped on Digger anyways, held onta my britches with one hand and the reins with the other and away we went. I haven't been back to visit them thar' particular hill folk since, and I don't plan on goin' back any time soon."

Mr. Bushy sat there laughing so hard his belly was jumping up and down, and the rest of us, including Granny, were laughing so hard our eyes were watering.

"Now," he said, "one more story of my adventures and I believe you critters better hit the hay."

"You're absolutely right, Alexander," Granny spoke up. "One more tall-tale and that's it for tonight."

"Now, Granny, these here ain't no tall-tales! As the Good Lord is my witness, all these tales be the honest, gospel truth." Mr. Bushy sounded quite offended by Granny's accusation.

"Ok Alexander, start in with the telling," Granny replied.

Granny still had her knitting on her lap, but she was just as enthralled with Mr. Bushy's tales as the rest of us. She didn't pick her needles up; she sat quietly waiting for him to begin the telling.

"Weeelll, this here story happened a while back when I was over on the other side of the Oh-zarks doing some trappin' and such an it was only me, Digger and an ol' pack mule we took along to help carry our load of furs — and that mule was a stubborn old cuss! In fact, I names 'em Cuss cuz that was exactly what he was. We'd just came away from that there big Oh-zark Lake and was headin' down the side of the mountain, when that ol' mule stopped and wouldn't go another step. I tried and tried to get ol' Cuss to move but everthing I tried jest din't work. 'Well,' I said to my Digger, 'let's camp here for the night. It's way too early, but iff'en this ol' mule won't go, he just won't go.'

"So, I set up camp, unloaded Cuss, took all my gear off Digger and turned 'em both out to find their own food. The day was pretty on that mountain, jest as it usually is, so I took my time fixin' my grub and cleanin' it up after I was done and since the day was still young, I decided to take me a walk-around for a look-see.

"I start in walkin' toward the west and got about a mile or two away when I came upon an old burial ground. There was still a lot of them thar' poles with some tattered feathers hangin' all over 'em, and the big body-burnin contraption was still standin'. You know, the thing where they burn their dead a'fore they put 'em in the ground. Well, I guess that's what they do. I ain't never been to one of them buryin ceremonies, so I don't rightly know for sure jest what they do. But, one ah these days I'm gonna go see fur' myself jest how they do thar' buryin'.

"Anyway, I stopped before I got onto the grounds – out of respect for their dead and all – and started in thinkin' 'bout how far around I should walk to stay respectful but not take forever and a day to do it. Plus, I was hopin' none of them warriors were still out there keepin' watch. So, I start in a'walkin' around the place, tryin' to be respectful and all and when I got to the other side...in no time a'tall...lo'-and-behold, there sat an ol' Kickapoo fella just watchin' me real close-like! Well, I made the peace sign of the Osage and the Kickapoo, hoping he's one of 'em. Then, sure enough, he signs back, so I know'd right off he was Kickapoo. They're a friendly folk and all, so I sit down beside him and we just sat thar' for an hour or so sayin' nary a word or lookin' at one another. That's the polite thing to do among the Kickapoo, I guess. If you don't mind someone sittin' by ya, ya just stay, but if ya don't like it, ya get right up and walk away in a hurry. Well, I took it he din't mind me a'sittin' there, since he stayed right beside me fur' so long.

"After a bit, he gets up, nods at me with ah friendly nod and walked straight through the burial grounds and disappears, but I just stay right there cuz the view was nice and the tree I was leaning against was feeling mighty fine. I leaned my head back and decided to take myself a little snooze, ya see. Well, I start in dreamin' about that burial ground. I dream all them thar' dead folks came right up outta their graves then strolled over and had a seat all around me and the tree I was leanin' against. There were warriors, squaws, babies, and all other ages of people and they were all Kickapoo except one. Sittin' right in front, right close to

124

me, was this here little white gal. She had on a beautiful Kickapoo dress and moccasins with all sorts of beads and feathers on both her dress and mocs and her hair was as white as the clouds on a sunny day and long 'nuf to almost touch the ground and I remember, as clear as day, seeing her hair blowin kindly soft-like in the breeze and she had a big smile on her little freckled face. Her eyes were as blue as ah robin's egg and sparkled with laughter. She was as cute as the little pup she was a'holdin' onto. She looked to be about nine or ten years along. She sat with her legs crossed, like most Injuns do, and I could see the markings on her ankle were the ankle markings saying she was of the Kickapoo tribe.

"She just sat thar' fur' a while smilin' an starin' at me and sayin' nothin' a'tall! Kindly made goose-bumps jump up on my arms to tell the truth. Then, without seeing her mouth move, I heard her say in a soft little-gal whisper, 'Would you tell my mama I can't go home, 'cause me and Bluebonnet fell into the river. The nice Indians found me and pulled me out and tried to get me to breathe again, but me and Bluebonnet were already sitting in the top of the tree and couldn't go back down. Please tell my mama and papa that they buried me here with my Bluebonnet and that I'm sorry I fell in the water. Bluebonnet fell in first and I just wanted to try and get him out. But it's all okay now. The Kickapoo gave me the name Sooleawa, which means Silver — they didn't know my real name and they said my hair looked like silver so that's what they named me and then they gave me a pretty new dress and shoes and drew a pretty picture of a little girl, like me, and wrote the name Sooleawa on my ankle. Tell Mama, Papa, Granny and the boys that I love them. Would you do that for me, mister?'

Mr. Bushy stopped talking and stared at us as his eyes got a bit misty.

"Can ya believe that? So then, in my dream, I told her that yes, I would certainly do that, but I didn't know who her mama was or where her family lived. She told me her name was Hannah Barnes and her mama and papa's names were Anna and Jonathan Barnes and they lived in Eden Bend along with her granny and her brothers. She told how she had gone on over there and tried to talk to them after she drowned, but no one could hear or see her. She didn't know why, but she was able to talk to me but she truly wanted her Ma and Pa to know what happened to her."

125

"I told that little Hannah gal that I sure would do just that, as soon as I could get over to Eden Bend. Then, she did the strangest thin'. Ya know how young'un wink thur' eyes when thur' learnin' how ta wink? Well, that's what she did. She scrunched up the left side of 'er little face and gave me a grin and one ah them strange little gal winks and said, 'thank you kindly, Mister,' and then... she and all the rest of them Kickapoo up and vanished into thin air!

"Well, in a flash I woke right up with sweat pourin' down my back in a stream. I looked around that thar' burial ground and nothing had changed. I told myself it must have jest been a dream and then I took off back around that thar' burial ground to my camp where Digger and Cuss were still a'choppin on the grass. I started makin' up my sleeping blankets for the night even though I was a little uneasy, cause of the dream and all, but kept right on tellin' myself, 'it's just a dream, ol' boy, it's just a dream.' Well along about midnight I finally fell asleep and I din't dream a single thing! And seeing that I always start in a'dreamin' as soon as I fall asleep, that was mighty strange. I got up the next morning and I had the vigor of a fifteen-year-old boy!"

"To shorten up this here adventure story ah bit, I high-tailed it down that thar' mountain as fast as that mule would go, stashed my furs and started in huntin' for Eden Bend, since I ain't never in my life heard of such a place. I asked everbody I met-up with but nary ah one of them had ever heard of such a place. Finally, I gave up and started on back to collect my furs and go on inta St. Louie to do some tradin'. I surely felt mighty bad about not being able to keep my promise to that little gal, I sure did. But, I was thinkin' it was just a strange dream is all.

"After collectin' my furs I get a day or two closer to St. Louie and along the way I run into a feller comin' down from St. Louie goin' towards Naw-leens area to do some trappin' and tradin' and one of his pack mules had lost a shoe, so I stop to help the feller unload the mule and fix it right up with a new shoe. Well, we strike up talkin' and he seems like ah right-nice fella, so we decide to set up camp together for the night. And what do ya know but lo'-and-behold, he had some homemade 'shine with him. So, we started in sharin' it and we start-in talkin' and laughin', and gettin' purty dang gabby when we decide ta swap our stories about spooks and haints and the like.

126

"After he told me a fist-full of his strange happenin's, I start in. I started right-off tellin' my tale about that there little white gal. Well, he sits there a'starin' at me with his mouth and eyeballs wide open, and when I'm all done with the tellin', he kindly swallers and says in a low whisper, 'We looked for little Hannah for weeks. We never did find hide nor hair of what happened to 'er. We ended up thinking some mountain man snatched 'er right up or maybe a bear or panther got ahold of 'er. Her ma and pa grieve for 'er still and that was nigh on a year ago. I'm 'er Uncle Benjamin.'

"Then, much to my surprise, he stopped talkin', jumped up, whipped out that thar' long skinnin' knife he was carryin' and says, 'Bushman, if you took our little Hannah and are just making this up, I'm gonna skin ya alive!'

"Right away I shook my head, held out the palms of my hands towards him and told 'em, 'No, Benjamin, I didn't take yor little Hannah. I lost my own little gal some years back and I'd never do that to any ma and pa's young'un.'

"Well, he stared at me for a good, long while then sat right back down and started in weepin'. Now, I don't mean jest some tears runnin' down his face, I mean he was sobbin'! I din't rightly know what to say to help him, so I just sat there and let him weep for a while. I din't want to embarrass him, seeing that he was a grown fella and all."

By that time everyone was staring at Mr. Bushy waiting for him to continue his tale so they could find out what happened.

"After a while," Mr. Bushy continued, emotionally, "he stopped his weepin' and shook my hand and tells me he would let Hannah's ma and pa know what happened to 'er but I told him no, I had to do it myself since I made a promise to that little gal. So, along about daybreak we started on out for Eden Bend. Eden Bend is jest a few homesteaders out on one ah the points in the Mississippi, not too far from St. Louie. When we finally get to the Barnes farm, Benjamin walks right in and pulls me along with him. The whole family was sittin' around the table eatin' with food piled high enough for the whole Union army. The two women got right up and gave Benjamin a hug and he introduced me all around. There was the little gal's ma Anna, her pa Jonathan, her little brothers Seth and Jacob, and her granny, Pansy. Well, her pa invites us to have a sit-down, and so we did and we all start in eatin'. Good food and plenty of it. I hadn't had good food like that in a coon's age. My belly was a grinning from my belly-button to my backbone."

"Come on Mr. Bushy," Tessa says, "tell us what happened when you told her ma and pa about little Hannah."

"Okay, Okay. Well after we all 'et, Benjamin asked if the two of us could speak to Hannah's pa in the barn, so the three of us went on out.

"Then, Benjamin gave me a nod and I started in with my tellin'. At first Jonathan looked angry as if maybe he wanted to pick up his gun and shoot me, but Benjamin told him how he run into me on his way down to Naw-leens an I helped 'em with his mule an I had never heard of Eden Bend in my life.

"Finally, Jonathan calmed down a bit and started-in askin' me all kinds of questions about that little gal and answered 'em the best I could remember. He wanted to know how she looked and if she looked happy. I told him about her little pup she had in her arms and he shook his head yes, he had just found her a pup and sure enough she had named it Bluebonnet.

"I don't think Jonathan knew what to do, but he did know he had to tell Hannah's ma about it, so we all went on back inta the house and he tells his boys to go on outside and do the evening chores. We all sat back down at the table and he starts in tellin' Anna and Pansy about the dream I had.

"Weeelll," Mr. Bushy drew the word out slowly, "Anna just stared at me fur a few seconds then all of ah sudden-like tears start pourin' down her face like water coming out of a bucket. Granny Pansy just sat there the whole time noddin' her head as if she already knew what was being said was true, then she spoke up and said she had kindly felt Hannah one morning when she was standing at the cook-stove singing one of Hannah's favorite songs but when she peering around, she couldn't see hide nor hair of little Hannah spirit. But she sure 'nuf had a feelin' little Hannah was standin' right there beside 'er. Then Granny Pansy leaned

128

over and put her arm around Anna's shoulders and says, 'Anna girl, I know'd she was happy. I know'd it all along. She's gone from us, but she's doin' fine now. She's at home with our maker. He always knows what's best, Anna my daughter, He knows what's best.'

Mr. Bushy stopped telling his tale for a minute and sat there quietly.

"Let me tell ya, it was all I could do to keep my tears from pourin' outta my own eyeballs like ah big ol' baby as I watched Anna in her grief over her little lost gal and my heart was a 'breakin' for her. Now, that is a true story, and the good Lord in heaven knows it is. I will never, in my life, forget that thar little gal and her family. Not everbody would believe it, but it's the truth."

Mr. Bushy hesitated before continuing.

"Then, low-and-behold, after all that weepin' and cryin', Anna got up and walked away from the eatin' table and returns from ah bedroom with ah lil' bitty baby. She handed me that little gal and thar' she was, a spittin' image of that little Hannah. That lil' gal looked straight inta my eyes and I do swear, that itty-bitty baby gal gave in the same scrunched up wink little Hannah had given me. It was kindly like she and me had a secret nobody else knew about. Hit' was the strangest thin' I ever did feel. Ta' tell ya the truth, hit' gave me the shivers running up and down my spine."

Everyone sat there staring at Mr. Bushy waiting for him to continue.

"Well," He said as he once again looked around at his captive audience, "that's it. That's the whole tale,"

Everyone let out a groan as if to say they wanted to hear more.

"Alexander," Granny finally spoke up, "That truly was a wonderful thing you did by going to her ma and pa. I surely do have more respect for you now. You are welcome in my home, whether you are clean or dirty, anytime you want."

"Mr. Bushy," Tessa said, as she climbed up onto his lap, "You are an angel come down from heaven, aren't you?"

"Now Tessa me-girl," Mr. Bushy chuckled as he grinned at Tessa, "don't be a'goin that far. I only did what any good man would do. That's what the Good Book be tellin' us to do, so that's jest what I did." But everyone knew Mr. Bushy was delighted at what Tessa said to him.

After a moment's pause, Mr. Bushy said, "Okay critters, off to bed with ya. I'm a'goin out to the barn and havin me a good-night's sleep for once," Mr. Bushy announced.

"No, you are not," Granny said as she stood up, "Alexander, you will sleep in my fourth bedroom down the hall. No one is sleeping in there, and I insist. Let me put another blanket in there for you and you can just take yourself right on down there and crawl into that bed, or you won't be getting any breakfast in the morning."

"Well, Granny," Mr. Bushy said with a beaming smile, "if you put it that ah-way, I guess I'll have to oblige ya. thank ye ma'am."

12

Yoder's Farm

"Oh Lord, what happened to my head?" Caitlin moaned as she tried turning over onto her side.

"Nope, that's worse than on my back," she mumbled to herself.

Laying there for a few minutes with her eyes closed, she couldn't help but wonder where she was and how had she gotten there and she felt sick, as if someone had beaten the side of her head with a board and then taken all the food out of her stomach, since her stomach was growling like a grizzly and she was also hungry as a grizzly.

"What happened to me?" she mumbled.

Trying to remember where she was and what could be causing her misery she closed her eyes and went over the events she did remember. After a few minutes of heavy thinking, it all came back to her.

The last thing she remembered was opening her bedroom window for Benny, or so she thought. She had wondered why he was knocking on her bedroom window instead of coming in through the back door. She remembered thinking maybe Aunt Birdie had locked the door on him again, and since his bedroom was on the second floor, he was trying to come in through her room. She had opened her window and leaned out to give him a hand as he climbed in, and that was all she could remember.

Cautiously she opened her eyes and looked around the room. This was not her room – that was for sure. It smelled of musty old wood and dirt and the only thing in the room was the bed she was on. There was dirt around the edges of the floor, as if someone had made an attempt to sweep and decided just to leave the dirt there. No one else was in the room and the door was closed, so she moved her head to get a better look around. "Where in the world am I?" she mumbled.

Slowly sitting up and trying to keep her stomach from coming up into her throat, she carefully eased herself out of the bed. Being careful as to not let herself fall, she stood there for a few minutes and steadied her spinning head. Once she got her bearings she tiptoed quietly over to one of the rag covered windows. The rags were drawn shut, but the sun was shining through the ripped and deteriorating material. Slowly she moved the edge of the rag and looked out. The sun was straight up, so it must be around noontime, she thought to herself.

"Great jumping Jehoshaphat!" she muttered. The entire horizon was nothing but trees on either side of the building.

"I must be looking out a back window from a room on the second floor of a house," Caitlin thought, "because there were outbuildings and a faded grey barn in full view. Most of the outbuildings had fallen to the ground and were now overgrown with tall weeds and brambles. The barn itself looked as if it was ready to join the outbuildings at any given time. It was leaning to one side with boards bracing it up and so many planks were missing it resembled a skeleton. It looked like an old, grey skeleton leaning on a cane. Looking straight through the barn's skeletal remains, Caitlin spied two horses inside the corral and the thick forest beyond began right at the back fence and it too continued as far as her eyes could see. The trees were thick and dense with weeds and wild brush covering most of the tree trunks.

Turning to the other window, she tiptoed quietly over to have a look. There she could see what looked to be the roof of a wrap-around porch coming from the front side of the house and extending around the backside. A dirt road, partially covered with grass, ran from the barn into a thick pine forest facing, what she assumed was east. The forest in front of the house was full of the tallest pines she had ever seen with heir branches started twenty feet or so above the ground and so thick and close together it was quite dark under the branches.

Wherever she was, it had been abandoned for many years by the looks of it.

"That must be the road back to town," Caitlin thought as she looked at the weed over-grown path. "I'm in the middle of nowhere!"

With nothing on her feet but her night stockings it was easy for her to walk quietly across the room and put her ear to the door. She could hear faint murmurings of voices and the clanking of dishes downstairs.

"Dishes! I'm starving," She whispered softly as her stomach gowled.

The voices grew louder and angrier.

Slowly and gently she opened the door. As she peeked through the tiny crack, all she could see was a hallway. Slowly pulling the door open a bit wider with her heart pounding in her ears like a war-drum, she held her breath then eased her head out the door and looked down the hall. She was in the last room at the end of a long hall covered in faded peeling wall paper with some of it peeling off in coils hanging halfway down the walls. The sun was shining brightly outside, but the hall was dark and musty smelling, five other doors in the hall were closed. The hallway smelled of wet dirt and the feeling of neglect hung heavy in the air, as if the soul of the house had left with the previous owners who had once called it home. Along the hallway, the floors were covered in thick dust along the edges.

"Thankfully, the darkness in the hall will cover my footprints when I decide to leave," she thought to herself as she stared down the dark gloomy hall.

"This must be the Yoder's place," Caitlin frowned as she tried thinking of another abandoned farmhouse around Caruthersville, "I don't know of any other abandoned farms around here unless I've been taken further away than I hope."

Opening the door wider still, in hopes of making it easier for her to hear the angry voices coming from the downstairs rooms, she listened carefully.

"You say I stupid because I ask you how close you get to New-Awlean in two hour? It because I Chinese? You think all Chinese stupid?" A man yelled at the top of his lungs. "You the stupid one, cow-pie!"

Then a second man's voice yelled back, "No, ya id-jet, what I'm a'sayin' is, ya Chinese think ya have all the brains. I'm a'sayin that I cain't figger out how fur I can get to Naw-leens in two hours, and that doesn't mean I be stupid! It means you cain't figger it out either, so ya must be jest as stupid as I am!"

With her heart pounding faster, Caitlin tiptoed down the hall to the top of the stairs but staying back enough so no one could look up and notice her.

At the top of the staircase someone had, at one time, knocked holes in the walls. Some holes were large and some were small. Squatting down and peeking through a small narrow hole, Caitlin was able to see three men sitting at a large, round, kitchen table.

One of the men was sitting with his mouth hanging open looking at the other two as they yelled at each other.

"No! You ask stupid question because you think I stupid. I know what you mean!" yelled the Chinaman. Then the second idiot stood up from the table and leaned across to get closer to the Chinaman's face as he shook his fork at the Chinaman, almost hitting him in the nose, all the while flinging food all over the table.

"No! I'm a'callin' ya a stupid donkey-behind 'cuz ya think only Chinamen have the high-flutin' privilege of havin' more brains then ever-body else in this here country, and yur always a'takin' advantage of everthin' in this here outfit just

134

whenever ya be a'wantin to!" At this point, his voice was getting high and squeaky, and he put his hands on his hips and swished his hips around. Evidently, he was trying to act like a high-society woman.

"I hate Chinamen!" he continued loudly, "You always be a'thinkin yur better'n everbody else and a'hoggin' all the brains, and, as a matter of fact," his voice went back to normal, "yur always hoggin' all the coffee up! Ever mornin', no matter if we're a'campin' or in some ol' house, I'm havin' ta snatch up my coffee just as soon as I'm thinkin' hit's done, or, iff'en I don't, by golly, next thin' I know hit's all gone down yur gullet."

As he was yelling at the Chinaman, food was flying out of his mouth and landing in the bowls of food sitting on the table. He was leaning so far over the table his dirty shirt was hanging in the gravy bowl. His pants were up under his armpits and his suspenders looked as if they had, at one time, belonged to a five-year old. They drew his oversized pants up in peaks at the front and back of his body. From where Caitlin squatted, she could see that his pant legs were rolled up to the middle of the calves of his legs. In previous years, his pants must have belonged to a much heavier, taller man.

"I going to kick you all way to China, you STUPID cowboy donkey! You too STUPID to get coffee when ready, then no coffee for you!" the Chinaman yelled back, waving his arms around as he yelled.

The Chinaman was a short, wiry, fella with a long, black thin braid hanging down his back. His hat was so big it was resting on the top of his ears, making them stick straight out from his head. He took his hat off and threw it on the floor as if getting ready for a fight.

"Well jest come on over here, ya sawed off little woodpecker, and give 'er a try iff'en yur a'thinkin' ya can whoop me! I'll whoop ya so hard you'll be eatin' with yur belly-button!"

Then the third man, who had been in a trance watching the two idiots argue, shot to his feet, picked up their full plates of food and slammed them onto the tops of their heads without missing a beat. He dropped the plates back onto the table, whipped out two pistols, pointing them at the arguing men and started in yelling.

"SIT DOWN! SHUT UP AND SIT DOWN! You two are dumb as dirt, and I'm getting tired of hearing your yammering. I've met smarter buckets of mud. Where in the world did you find these two characters, woman? I'm thinking they left their brains a'flappin' in the breeze on some woman's clothesline. Between the two of you, you don't have enough brains to fill a thimble! So, do as I say or, I swear, I'm gonna shoot ya both!"

"What woman?" Caitlin mumbled with a frown.

Both men stood there looking at the plate-slammer with their mouths open and food sliding down their heads. The Chinaman had a fried egg slipping down his forehead; almost covering his right eye, and his other two eggs were sitting on top of the bacon, which was sitting on top of his head like a little brown greasy hat. Gravy already covered both sides of his face, hair and shoulders and his biscuits were on the floor. The cowboy had one egg on his head and one egg on his right shoulder. His bacon was stuck on his ear and gravy was slipping down the front of his shirt. They both looked like two mud-ugly women with greasy gravy hair.

The two idiots looked at each other, looked back at the plate-slammer and apparently decided he was serious. Then the Chinaman took the egg from his eye and put it back on his plate, then leaned over to let the other two eggs and bacon slip onto his plate.

The Cowboy snatched the eggs and bacon off his head and chest and slammed them back onto his own plate. They both wiped some of the gravy off their faces with their shirt sleeves, not bothering to clean their hair or hands, then sat back down at the table, picked their forks off the floor and started eating again without saying a single word.

Bending over to pick his biscuits up off the floor, the cowboy let out the loudest fart Caitlin had ever heard in her life. The eruption went on forever, or so it seemed. The sound was like the rumble of thunder before a storm. He stayed

136

bent over until the blast ended then acted as if nothing unusual had occurred. Sitting back down in his chair he released a long, reverberating burp, sighed and said "Ah that felt good," then shoved a biscuit in his mouth, turned his head toward the floor and spat out a chunk of something which had, evidently, stuck to his biscuit when it dropped onto the floor.

Caitlin sat there in amazement as she watched the plate-slammer sit back down and quietly look at the two idiots for a few seconds, then muttered "filthy pigs", before picking up his fork and once again began shoveling food into his mouth.

The Chinaman sat staring at the cowboy. "Stupid stinking cowboy," he said and went back to eating.

A fourth person moved into Caitlin's line of sight but all she could see was the person's shoes. It was a woman all right.

"Come on, come out and let me see you," Caitlin thought to herself.

With a loud *"Ugh"*, the woman stomped out of the kitchen and into another room.

The plate-slammer sat down his fork, looked up at the two other men and calmly said, "If you two make her mad and she stops cooking for us, you are both going to become pig slop. And by the time I get done with you, no one will ever know what happened to you or where your bones are buried."

Again he calmly picked up his fork and returned to eating as the other two men looked up from their plates with eyes wide and mouths open.

"Sorry, boss, hit won't happen again," stammered the cowboy.

"No, boss," the Chinaman quickly agreed, "not ever again."

Slowly and quietly, Caitlin stood up and tiptoed quickly back down the hall to the room she had woken up in. It was cold in the room and her feet were

137

freezing, but at least she still had a winter nightgown and wrap on, so her body was okay. She started looking around the room for something to keep her feet warmer — maybe some regular socks or shoes. Under the bed, she found an old pair of boots. they were worn, holey and looked way too big, but they were better than nothing at all. Caitlin picked them up and sat them on the bed.

"If I manage to get out of this place, these will do fine," she whispered.

"Okay, what am I going to do next? And how long have I been here? My stomach says months, but probably not that long since I can still walk and my brain is still working. And why am I here?"

Squeezing her eyes shut, she tried remembering what had happened after the hit on her head. Nothing. Nothing at all came to mind. She felt around on her head and – "ouch!" There it was— a bump on the side of her head above her right ear.

"Well, they must have known just where to hit me," she thought. "It's as big as a goose egg. No wonder I was out so long."

"Those dirty stinking polecats!" she whispered softly. "they knew just what they were doing. I'm probably not the first person to experience their handiwork. I wonder who else they've done this to."

Caitlin walked back to the door and listened. No sounds were coming from outside the door. Slowly and carefully she turned the knob and opened the door again.

No one came running up the stairs, so they must not have heard her during the fracas.

"Well, cri-min-y," Caitlin whispered to herself. "Somehow I'll just have to find a way out of this mess and get back home. I sure hope they haven't taken Benny, Lily or Tessa."

Stepping gingerly out of the room again, as softly as possible, she was tip-toeing back down the hall when one of the floor boards squeaked.

Instantly Caitlin froze. Holding her breath with her heart thumping so fast she could feel it in her ears, she waited a few seconds. Other than the stairs leading down to the kitchen, there was not another way out, that she could see. Maybe one of the other doors led to another staircase, but she couldn't risk making any more sounds and the doors were all too old to open quietly. She would have to wait until it was dark to try again.

Suddenly she heard an outside door open and slam shut and all the men started talking again. A different male voice floated up the stairs.

"I'm as hungry as a horse and dog-tired. Give me some grub, woman, or I'm gonna start chewing on old Fernando here," the man's booming voice rang out.

"Yeah, well you just give it a try, Mac and I'll shoot your knees caps off. I've put up with these two, stupid jackals all morning and I'm in no mood to put up with your mouth." The plate-slammer said quietly.

"Whoa doggies, what got into you, Ferd? Had a bit of a ruckus maybe? Give me some food, woman!"

"Get your own food," the unseen woman mumbled. "I'm not one of your servants. I'll cook the food but I'm not waiting on you." All the men laughed loudly. Once again Caitlin heard the woman stomp out of the room and slam a door.

Afraid to take another step forward, she turned around and went back toward the bedroom.

"I can't do this right now. There's no way for me to get out without going through the kitchen!" she told herself as she returned to the bedroom. She put the boots back under the bed and laid down. She tried to remember which way she had been when she woke up. Not being able to remember, Caitlin decided to lie on her side facing the wall.

"I'll wait until dark and then try again," Caitlin told herself. "Maybe after they all go to bed and are sound asleep, I can sneak out of here."

Slowly the hours ticked by.

"Oh chicken-poo, if I don't use the privy soon," she thought, "I'm going to have a big problem. There's going to be water dripping downstairs any minute". Quickly she got back up and looked under the bed for a chamber pot.

Nothing.

"Well, chicken-poo" she whispered. "What am I going to do now?"

"I guess there's just one thing to do. I'll have to use one of those old boots as a chamber pot," she thought. "Wait, wait, wait; maybe there is something else around here." Caitlin looked around the room and spied an opening that looked as if it had once been a clothes closet.

"Ah-ha! Here's something!" In the corner of the closet was a glass canning jar with something brown growing in the bottom. Picking it up, she unscrewed the top and looked inside. Only mold. "This will work just fine," she thought with a sigh of relief.

"I'll leave it in the kitchen when I get out of here and maybe one of those polecats will be drunk and think it's a jar of whiskey." After using the jar, Caitlin screwed the top back on and placed it under the bed with the boots. She couldn't help but quietly laugh about her idea.

"I sure wish I could see their faces when they pick up that jar and take a big swig," she thought as she sat down on the bed and tried to arrange the blanket the same way it had been before she woke up.

Next thing she heard was the sound of someone coming up the stairs. Her heart started thundering in her chest.

"Oh Lord," she thought, "They're coming up here to get me." Quickly she forced herself to lie down on the bed, but her body wanted to open the window and jump out.

One of the doors down the hall opened and slammed shut. Next, she heard the same door open and the fourth man's voice yell out.

"One of you better check on that gal. I'm not gonna do it. I've been up all last night and this morning watchin' for the dang Sheriff. Who, by the way, never did show up, and I'm dog-tired."

Slowly Caitlin got out of the bed and walked to the door. Hoping she could hear a reply from downstairs she put her ear against the wood.

"Okay," one of the men yelled up from the kitchen. "We'll do it. Just shut up and go to sleep or you're gonna wake her up and then there'll be hell to pay as we fight her into that carriage."

"You stupid donkey's hind-end," came a woman's voice, "That girl will be out for another day or two. Did you see the size of that bump on her head? She may never wake up – and then she'll be worthless. Did you two idiots think you were handling a grown man?"

"Just shut-up Bird," the man named Fernando yelled, "Next time maybe you can do the dirty work and handle it better. Let's see you lug a limp body from Caruthersville all the way out here and not make anyone suspicious as you're doing it. That was the hard part. Thank the devil himself for the dark clouds and all the city folks being either at home or at the saloons. We better get a lot for this one, or I'm about done with this work."

The man from the second floor yelled down, "We've been here too long and that Sheriff is gonna start sniffing around. Mark my word. We never should have taken that gal. Those two younger kids are slicker than snot and seem to be

141

everywhere, asking questions, looking into every shack along the river. Yesterday I saw those two under the train depot platform. What in tarnation were they doing under there? What's the matter with you, Bird? Can't you keep a handle on those two? And where's that little sister of theirs, huh? She run off too?"

Caitlin eyes opened wide as she put a hand over her mouth trying to stifle a gasp as she whispered, "Bird? Did he really say 'Bird'? And did that woman say 'Donkey's hind-end'? That's what Aunt Birdie calls Elmer whenever she gets upset with him. That's Aunt Birdie down there! What is going on here?"

"I guess Aunt Birdie will do anything for money. Why isn't she down on the farm? ," Caitlin thought to herself.

Caitlin thought back to when Mama and Pa were alive. She and the other children had never seen Aunt Birdie, as far as she could remember. Pa had said it was because Aunt Birdie felt she had to stay on the farm to prove she could run it properly. Every Christmas, Aunt Birdie sent all of them beautiful gifts, as well as on their birthdays. But not one time could Caitlin remember meeting her. Mama and Pa saw her when they went downriver to New Orleans for business every month or so and would come back with tales of their trips to the plantation and their visits with Aunt Birdie. There were no pictures of her and no one had ever commented on what she looked like. All Pa mainly spoke about was how well she was handling the farm. Mama always talked of how she missed Aunt Birdie and would love to have Birdie closer so they could visit like old times. But it seemed like Aunt Birdie was always way too busy with her farm, and Mama and Pa were too busy with their own farm to make any arrangements.

Late at night, when Mama and Pa thought all the kids were asleep, they would sit in the kitchen and talk in quiet whispers. Caitlin remembered once, as she got up to use the privy, hearing Mama say, "I hope Birdie is doing better, I worry about her so," then Pa replied, "Don't worry about her, me Molly, she's a grown woman. There's nothing we can do to change her at this time in her life." Pa always called Mama 'me Molly' when he had his arms around her or was trying to make her feel better about something.

"Maude is there with her, and she'll let us know if Birdie gets worse. Maude is a good keeper," he had whispered to Mama.

Now Caitlin wondered what had happened to Maude. Had she run off and left Aunt Birdie? Maybe Aunt Birdie was not the nice sister Pa remembered. Maybe she had some emotional issues going on.

Tears flooded Caitlin's eyes as she thought about Mama and Pa, and how terribly she missed them. Why did they have to die? Why couldn't it have been someone else?

Life was not fair. Lily, Benny and Tessa were way too young to be left without parents. All these questions and concerns ran through Caitlin's mind as she stood by the bedroom door listening. She wondered if anything had happened to Benny, Lily and Tessa. Had Aunt Birdie sent them off on a ship? Had she and Elmer hurt them?

"No, I don't think Elmer would hurt the little ones," Caitlin whispered to herself, "He may get drunk most nights, but I don't believe he would hurt children. Hopefully he won't. I sure hope they're all safe. Maybe they went to Granny Tomason's house when they discovered I was gone."

"Okay," she whispered, "What am I going to do now? I have to leave as soon as it gets dark. That's the only chance I have."

Walking back to the bed, Caitlin sat on its edge and pondered her choices, "If anyone comes up here I'll act as if I'm still asleep and then I'll try and get away from this place as soon as it's dark enough. This place has to be west of Caruthersville. It must be Yoder's farm. Either that or some other abandoned farm. If I had a horse, I can make it back to town."

Caitlin crawled back under the blanket and faced the wall. "Maybe they won't come up and check on me until tomorrow," she thought to herself.

No such luck!

Within a few minutes, she heard stomping feet coming up the stairs, then down the hallway coming towards her room. Whoever it was stopped outside the door as if listening. Caitlin shut her eyes and tried to breathe normally.

"How does one breathe when they're asleep?" she thought wildly.

Quietly the door opened and someone slipped softly into the room. The person seemed to stand there at the door for a few seconds, then slowly walked over to the bed. Caitlin felt as if she was going to throw up. She willed herself to calm down and stop shaking.

"Well girlie," Caitlin heard Aunt Birdie whisper, "when are you going to wake up so we can get rid of you?"

"Caitlin! Wake up girl!" Birdie said in a harsh whisper, "Wake up!" She gave Caitlin's shoulder a sharp shake which made Caitlin's arm fall off the edge of the bed but she forced herself to leave it be.

"Thank God you're still breathing," Birdie muttered, "Don't become a worthless poke of trouble by dying on us, girlie. At least stay alive until we can get you on that train tomorrow."

Aunt Birdie gave her shoulder a sharp shake.

"You're a complete waste of a girl," Birdie said, "I should leave you here to die. Well, if you don't wake up by tomorrow, that's just what I'm going to do. I'm sick to death of dealing with these four butt-ugly men. Let them take care of getting rid of you and all the rest of this mess for all I care. I'm going home in the morning."

With that said, Birdie stomped out of the room muttering to herself about bags of gold and riches as she went. Then Caitlin heard the door slam and Birdie stomp back down the hall, she let out her breath with a deep *whoosh*.

"Well chicken pooh! What a mean, old witch she turned out to be! Well I'll show you, Aunt Birdie, I'm getting out of here tonight before you try getting me on that train tomorrow, or I'll die trying!"

She stayed in the bed a little longer, then got up and walked around the room trying to stretch her legs. The hours seemed to drag by, she heard the three men leave the house and not return until late afternoon. Aunt Birdie came back up once in the late afternoon and just stood at the end of the bed muttering.

Once again, she tried to wake Caitlin before she went back down to the kitchen where the sound of pots and pans rattling carried up the stairs. Aunt Birdie must be cooking again because she could smell the wonderful fragrance of Aunt Birdie frying ham.

Staying away from the window so as to not be seen by any of the cowboys passing by, she quietly walked around the room until it began getting dark and she heard Mac leave his room and stomp down to the kitchen. It sounded as if all the men were back in the kitchen eating. Aunt Birdie was yelling at one of them to stop eating out of the pan and sit down at the table like a civilized human.

Opening the door a crack, she tried her best to hear their voices a little better. Aunt Birdie and the men were not talking loud enough for her to make out what they were saying. She would have to walk down the hall again and maybe find out what plans they had for her.

When she got to the top of the stair, she again peeked through one of the narrow holes in the wall.

She heard Aunt Birdie say: "Mac, you go on into town and ask around in the saloons and see if you can figure out what that Sheriff is doing about finding Caitlin."

"That's a right-fine idea," Mac replied. "I can wet my whistle while I'm at it."

Quickly Mac got up from the table and walked out the door. The rest of the men sat a while grumbling because they weren't the ones going into town.

"We're taking her into the train tomorrow," Aunt Birdie spoke up, "and if she still isn't awake, we're leaving her here to die. I'm tired of dealing with her and those smaller children are much easier to handle. You men get ready to leave first thing in the morning."

"Good idee," all three men said at the same time.

Caitlin crept back to the bedroom and eased the door shut. She walked to the window and peeked out through the crack in the rags to watch Mac as he rode away. So, the road leading to town was exactly the way she thought.

Standing at the window until the sky turned shades of pink and purple, and the clinking of dishes, along with the sound of voices, stopped drifting up to her Caitlin wondered what had happened to make such a drastic change in Aunt Birdie.

Waiting as long as she could with her stomach still growling like a mad dog, she decided it was time to leave. The night was chilly but sweat was running down her body in streams. She was nervous, hungry and thirsty. She went back to the window to make sure it was completely dark and listened for a door to shut downstairs. Surely Aunt Birdie slept downstairs.

Opening the bedroom door just enough to see the light in the kitchen, she finally saw the light move away from the stairs and heard a door shut. Aunt Birdie must have carried the lamp into her bedroom. Quietly she closed the door and heard the men, one by one, climb the stairs and enter a bedroom.

At long last all the shuffling and bed squeaking stopped and the snoring began.

Quickly the night became quiet and the snoring grew louder. After a few minutes, she was able to determine three different snores and she knew all three men were sound asleep.

Still, she stayed in the bedroom until she was quite sure they were all in a deep sleep, including Aunt Birdie, and wouldn't be easily awakened.

It seemed like an eternity before she was confident enough to take the chance.

"Okay, here we go," she told herself with determination.

Silently she tiptoed to the window once more. The moon was flooding the forest with shimmering splotches of light scattered throughout the trees. Everything on the farm was clearly outlined in shadows.

"Okay," She thought to herself, "let's do this. Get yourself out of this fine kettle-of- fish and away from this horrible nightmare."

Collecting the boots and canning jar from under the bed, she crossed to the bedroom door where she opened it just a tiny bit and peeked out. No sounds, except for the snoring, came from the rooms. Again, Caitlin grinned as she thought of those scallywags opening the canning jar. She felt a nervous giggle coming up in her throat and had to swallow it back down.

"Serves them right!" she thought.

Reaching the door, she slowly turned the knob and eased it open, it slid open without a squeak but when she took her first step, the floor creaked; she stopped instantly. Holding her breath, she listened for movement from the other bedrooms.

Nothing.

For some reason, the darkness of night amplified sound so she would have to be extremely cautious getting out of the house. She opened the door a little more and finally had enough room to squeeze her body through. Grimacing, she pulled the door shut. If they didn't discover her absence until morning it would give her more time to make it into town. Standing outside the door until she worked up enough courage to start walking down the hall, she drew in a deep breath. Looking down the hallway, she decided to walk along the edge of the hall floor again just to make sure there would be no squeaks or creaks.

"Okay, me-girl. Let's go," she whispered.

She was so hungry and scared her legs were shaking as she tip-toed down the hall past two doors, then past another two doors. Stopping at the top of the stairs, she cocked her head and listened. Nothing moved and the snoring continued, somewhat louder than before. And, thankfully, the loudest snoring was coming from Aunt Birdie's room.

The kitchen was lit up like it was high-noon with the bright moonlight flooding the entire room.

Taking a deep breath, she took one step down and waited. No squeaks and nothing moved within the house. Stepping extremely slow, she warily continued down the stairs. When she got to the bottom of the steps, she was finally in the kitchen and the first thing she did was walk to the water pail and drink from the nasty ladle.

"Ah, that's the best water I have ever tasted," she thought. "No telling what was in it, but it sure felt good going down."

Sitting the dirty ladle down, she looked around for some food. Not only did she find biscuits on the stove but thick slices of ham were covered with a dish cloth.

"Oh yes, I'll just take most of these with me," she thought as she stuffed five biscuits and most of the ham into her night-wraps pocket, along with the clean dish cloth. There were dirty dishes stacked in piles all everywhere. Dried food was stuck on the table and the floor. Some of the breakfast food from the day before was still on the floor — bacon and smeared gravy. It looked as if someone had slipped on the gravy and landed on their backside. It certainly wasn't the sparkling clean kitchen Aunt Birdie kept at their house — that was for sure.

Sitting the canning jar down next to the pitcher of water, she smiled. Then she turned and tiptoed to the back door with her sock feet sticking to the grimy floor with each step and there was no lock-bar on the door so the door should open easily, Caitlin thought as she gently eased the door open a little at a time. It squeaked softly a bit, so each time she moved it and it squeaked, she stopped and waited a few seconds but she eventually got it open enough to slip out and stand on the back porch. Instead of closing the door, she let it stay where it stopped on its own then stood on the steps and looked around the farm buildings. About fifty feet in front of her was the barn and it looked as if the horses were still in the back corral.

"Now for the get-away," she mumbled.

13

The Getaway

Running quickly and quietly to the barn, Caitlin slipped through one of the open slats. The barn smelled of rotting hay and horse manure. Moonlight streaming from the holes in the roof brightened the barn and created a cathedral effect. Heavy shadows lingered in the dark corners and rafters. Some of the support beams holding up the loft had decayed and crumbled and were now lying on the barn floor. As Caitlin looked up at the highest peak in the dilapidated barn, she spied two huge owls sitting in an opening with their glowing eyes —almost unnaturally— staring back at her.

A slight meowing came from the deteriorated loft.

"It must be a mama cat and her kittens," Caitlin thought as she bent down and pulled on the old boots, and immediately, or so it seemed, there sat the five kittens and their mama all of them standing within two inches of her face staring intently at her as if expecting something. She reached over to pet the babies but they quickly scattered.

"If Aunt Birdie thinks she's going to get away with this she's in for a big surprise," she murmured to the mother cat who was sitting quietly looking at her with big eyes as if she was waiting patiently to be petted

150

Fear clinched her heart with an intense grip as she heard one of the windows in the house shatter.

"Chicken-pooh," she thought as she jumped to her feet and hurried to the barn wall.

Peering around the edge of a missing board she looked out; fully realizing if she didn't stay hidden, whomever was looking out that window would be able to see her in the bright moonlit night.

One of the men was peeing out a bedroom window! "Oh, yuck!" Caitlin gasped as she jerked her head back inside the barn. Shuffling to an upturned barrel, she sat down with a disgusted sigh. She would have to wait until the man was once again sound asleep before she could make her move.

Holding the mother cat on her lap, Caitlin began thinking of how she was going to escape and get back home. Maybe she should just start walking? She could stay in the woods and maybe they wouldn't be able to find her. Nope, that wouldn't do because she had no idea where she was, and the men had horses and Aunt Birdie had a carriage. They would quickly find her.

"Maybe I should take one of the horses. That's what I'll do," she thought to herself. But the men would probably catch up with her since she didn't know where she was going, "Well, I'll just take all the horses."

Growing tired of waiting and getting antsy, she walked to the back of the barn where she picked up a bridle and some lead ropes. She had ridden bareback many time before and hopefully these horses were gentle enough they wouldn't start a ruckus when she tried putting the lead ropes on. Out through a section of the missing boards she slipped and stepped into the horse corral.

All five horses turned and looked at her, "Well," she spoke in a whisper, "I wonder which one of you will let me ride you?" As she looked at the horses, one of them trotted up to her.

"Tabby!"

Aunt Birdie must have hitched Caitlin's very own horse, Tabby, to the carriage when she rode out here.

"Well, Tabby girl," she whispered, rubbing the horse's nose. "Aunt Birdie did me an unknown favor when she brought you out here, didn't she," Tabby nickered back at Caitlin and bumped her shoulder.

"Shhh, Tabby-girl, we don't want to wake Aunt Birdie and her trolls," Caitlin said quietly as she slipped the bridle on Tabby and led her to the fence where she stepped up on one of the rails and slid onto Tabby's back. She trotted her over to the other four horses and put lead ropes on the two mares. The other two didn't want anything to do with the leads as they began snorting and prancing away.

"Okay boys," she spoke softly to the two big black horses. "Calm down. I won't try again. With any luck, you'll follow us through the gate.

"Come on Tabby, let's go." She held the two lead ropes and the two mares began walking calmly beside them. Trotting Tabby to the corral gate, she leaned down and pulled the gate open. The gate screeched loudly and at the same time she heard the back door of the house bang open. Looking towards the back door of the house her heart skipped a beat.

There stood the blurry-eyed, dirty, cowboy. His hair looked like something had built a nest in it and the dried gravy was plastered on one side of his head causing part of his hair to stand on end in thick clumps and the rest was slicked back. His eyes were squinted and his face was furrowed with a frown.

"HEY! Get back here, girl!" he yelled in a high piercing screech, "Get down off'en that horse and come back in here!" He jumped down from the porch and began running toward the corral.

"HEE-YAA!" Caitlin screamed at the horses as she flung open the gate.

She gave Tabby a sharp kick with her heels and the horse took off like a shot. She didn't look back as she bent low over Tabby's back, holding onto her mane with one hand and the lead ropes with the other. She knew if she looked back she might lose her grip or balance, and that would be the end of her. Then the slimy cowboy yelled again.

"I'm gonna beat ya when I citch ya, gal!"

One of the other men must have heard the yelling and ran down the stairs and out the door, because now a different voice was yelling.

"You be sorry you was ever born'd!" yelled the Chinamen.

"Get back here ya stupid gal, Bird is gonna tan yor hide less'en ya get back here, now!" yelled the cowboy.

Caitlin kept right on pushing Tabby as best she could, but then, she heard the echoing hoof beats of another horse coming up behind her. Her heart began hammering faster and faster.

"Oh no!" she thought. "That ugly buzzard has caught one of the other horses and is catching up to me." She kneed Tabby trying to make her move faster. Then she turned her head to the left, and out of the corner of her eye, she could see one of the black horses coming up fast. All of a sudden, the big black horse shot past her with the smaller black tight behind him. Thankfully, both horses were riderless. They passed Caitlin as if she and Tabby was standing still.

"What a gorgeous horse," she thought to herself.

The bigger black stood almost seventeen hands high, or so she figured. And, his coat was black as midnight and shiny as satin. His mane and tail were flowing almost horizontal to the ground as he ran in a full gallop. His mane and tail hair was not the normal straight hair of a horse, it was wavy almost to the point of being curly. His gait was smooth and even as if he barely touched the ground and the long, feather hair growing around the tops of his hooves made him look as if he were floating.

"What a beauty! That horse must have been stolen. Such a magnificent horse could not possibly belong to any of the riff-raff back at that farm. I'll make sure he gets back to his owner as soon as I can get myself to safety," she thought as she pushed Tabby further.

Again, she nudged Tabby to get her going a little faster. Caitlin and the three mares ran for a long time. There were no forks in the road and no paths leading off into the woods. The road kept on going straight as an arrow.

"I sure hope this is the right way to town," she whispered.

Hearing the sound of heavy breathing coming from the two mares on the lead ropes, Caitlin pulled back on Tabby to slow them down a bit. The last thing she wanted was to have one of these horses collapse and die on her.

"Okay Tabby-girl," Caitlin said loudly, pulling back on the reins a little more, "let's give these ladies a rest." She let the three mares walk for a good long while as she watched the night change from darkness to the gray shadows of the early morning pre-dawn. In no time at all the sun would be slipping its gold fingers over the horizon and across the Mississippi river into the Missouri Delta and ease its way throughout the farmland.

As Caitlin and the mares walked further along the road, the abundance of tall pine trees began thinning and gave way to giant oak trees, and approximately a half mile further it looked as if the oak trees were leaning across the road, blocking out the glow of the early morning light and creating an emerald tunnel.

By this time, all three mares were voluntarily trotting at a faster pace and the big black horse and his buddy were long gone. Not even an echo of their distant hoof beats could be heard. For some reason, Caitlin felt more alone without the two big horses. She would have felt safer had they stayed with her and the mares.

"Where is that feeling coming from?" she said out loud. "I think I'm losing my mind. They're just horses, the same as these three."

But whatever the case, she kept her eyes on the road ahead looking for the two of them. The deeper they went into the forest of oaks, the colder she felt. Goosebumps popped out on her arms and the back of her neck tingled. She gave a shiver and felt as if someone was watching her. A feeling of unease started to build in her stomach like a hand squeezing her body tightly as it worked its way up to her throat.

Guardedly she led the mares into the emerald green tunnel. Further ahead, she could make out a turn in the road which blocked the open end of the tunnel from sight.

The two mares trotted up beside Tabby and began pulling on the lead ropes as if wanting to run creating anxiety in her chest. Maybe she should wait.

"Wait for what?" she asked herself in a sharp whisper, "Wait for Aunt Birdie and the river rats to catch up with me? Not a good idea," she said loudly. "Let's go girls. We're going to make it through these woods and into town."

Giving Tabby a gentle nudge, she realized the early morning sounds of the forest were gone. Something was amiss...it was too quiet.

Calls of the early morning birds could no longer be heard and the scurrying of small creatures hunting for breakfast had vanished.

The dark tunnel was as quiet as a tomb. Only the soft echo of horse hooves trotting along the narrowing road bounced off the trees. Slowly, Caitlin urged the mares further and faster along the lonely road into the forest tunnel, with fear building slowly within her soul.

She knew the trees were not as close as they seemed, but in her mind, it felt as if the forest was closing in on them. The end of the tunnel was not yet visible, and the oaks were growing larger and thicker as the tunnel of trees began feeling like a dark cavern. When she turned her head to look back, the entrance was also hidden from view, the green canopy made an arc over the narrow road which in turn formed the tunnel of emerald leaves. She could not see the beginning or the end of the passageway. She and the mares were totally enclosed.

155

All three mares began pulling on their lead ropes as Caitlin struggled to hold them back.

Then, with a fear unknown to mankind, she heard the very sound the horses and other forest creatures had already sensed. From the hills and valleys surrounding them came the scream of a black panther echoing off the wall of trees. Black panthers were abundant along the Mississippi river bottom and they were black as midnight and their screams were like that of a woman.

Everyone knew the stories of men going out during the dusky late hours of the day trying to find the woman they heard screaming, only to never return.

It was unusual to hear them this early in the morning, so this one must be hurt or still hunting. Whatever the case, Caitlin wasn't about to stick around and find out which one it was. Seldom did the panthers come close to civilization; but then again, this area was not civilization.

The scream came again, louder this time, as if the panther was on the run, coming closer and closer to her and the mares.

All three horses had become skittish and anxious to run faster and when the second screams echoed off the hills, Tabby and the other two mares needed no urging to run. Tabby took off like a bullet, with the two mares right behind her. All Caitlin could do was hang on tightly to Tabby's mane. She knew if she fell off she was a dead woman — either from the fall itself or from being panther breakfast. She held onto Tabby's mane with one hand and hugged the horse's neck with the hand holding the lead ropes.

All of a sudden, the leads were jerked back; instantly she either had to let the ropes drop or be pulled off Tabby. Without hesitation, she dropped the leads and grabbed Tabby's neck with both hands. As she hugged the horse's body she turned to glance back. One of the mares had stumbled.

"Come on girl, get up! Get up!" she screamed loudly, "You can do it, get up!"

The second mare was keeping up with Tabby; in fact, she was less than a necks length behind them. Seconds passed and Caitlin glanced back again, she could see the fallen mare getting to her feet and, amazingly she began to run.

"That's it girl, come on now, catch up."

When the panther scream rang out again, the fallen mare needed no encouragement. Her head came up and immediately she was in a full gallop.

"Good girl, come on up!"

Caitlin turned her head back around to see where Tabby was taking them and she spied the big black horse. He and the smaller black had returned for some reason.

He was prancing around in a circle and looking back as if to make sure they were coming. The smaller black horse was standing further down the road waiting for him. When Caitlin got closer, both of them once again took off running at a full gallop. Caitlin felt both surprise and relief when she saw them.

"Okay, come on girls, let's get up there with our boys," she mumbled to herself. The horse seemed to realize what was being said because she increased her speed.

As they came around the bend in the road, Caitlin spotted the end of the tunnel. Relief flooded over her body as she caught sight of the early morning sun with its golden fingers tickling the tops of the trees and softly tumbling into the field ahead. The dense forest had thinned into a meadow with only a scattering of clustered oak tree among the tall field grasses.

They were able to run another mile or so before horses began slowing down. All three were lathered with foam and breathing heavily and the two big blacks were once again out of sight.

Gently she pulled back on Tabby, slowing all of them down to a walk.

Unless she had missed a horse, Aunt Birdie and the river rats had no way to get away from the farm unless they were walking, and if they were walking, they would be quite far behind her and the mares.

The horses needed to stop and rest for a bit and it would also give Caitlin time to wipe the foam off their bodies and find a stream of clear water for them to drink.

Spotting a large cluster of oak and aspen trees up ahead, she decided to stop and rest of mares. The trees started at the edge of the road and went back more than two hundred feet.

Slowly she walked the horses through the line of oaks and discovered a small clearing within the circle, well hidden from anyone passing by. Giant oaks encircled the clearing like a fortress wall and there were probably more than one hundred trees surrounding the clearing which was covered with spring grasses and fallen trees trunks. It was a perfect place to rest and hide from prying eyes.

Stopping Tabby in the center of the clearing she slipped off her back and picked up the lead ropes for the other two mares and tied them to a branch on the fallen tree, just in case they decided to stray. She truly didn't want that panther to have them for breakfast and the good Lord was the only one who knew where that black devil was lurking. She probably shouldn't linger in these trees too long.

Bending down, she pulled a hand-full of tall grass and began wiping the foam from Tabby's coat. When she was finished with Tabby, she pulled more of the tall grass and slowly approached one of the other mares.

Whispering softly, she calmed the nervous twitching muscles of the horse.

Quietly the two mares stood watching her with big, brown, solemn eyes. The first mare waited patiently as Caitlin wiped the foam from her body.

"Well now," Caitlin spoke gently as she rubbed the mares nose and head. "You haven't received very good care, have you? You probably belong to one of the filthy rats out there with Aunt Birdie. What a shame. Well, if I have anything to do with it, you aren't going back to any of those rascals. They don't deserve to own a pig, much less a beautiful horse like you."

Caitlin pulled more grass for the third mare and began singing a soft Irish lullaby her Pa had sang to his "wee lad and lassies" many years ago. She stood up and looked off into the forest.

"It all seems so long ago," she thought to herself, "Sometimes I forget how Mama and Pa looked when we were all together around the table and Pa was making us laugh. At times, it seems like a fairy tale and I should be able to go home and there they would be doing their daily chores and waiting for me to get back home."

Once in a while, when Caitlin visited her parents grave, it seemed as if she could hear her mama speak to her in a gentle voice telling her, "Go on home now Caitlin. Live your life to the fullest and don't worry about your pa and me. We are together and happy, so go along my sweet girl, and don't cry over us. Your sisters and Benny need you."

Softly she began singing to the mares, hoping it would help calm the third mare so she could wipe the foam off her coat and also calm her own nerves. The events of the last few days seemed to come crashing in on her as she stood beside the waiting horses.

> *My Mother sang a song to me*
>
> *In tones, so sweet and low.*
>
> *Just a simple itty bitty ditty.*
>
> *With soulful heartfelt pity.*
>
> *I'd give the world if she could sing that song to me this very day.*
>
> *But alas, my lass...those days have gone away.*

Taking her time, she rubbed down the third horse, enjoying the pleasant warm breeze coming through the clearing. The balmy sun warmed her still cold hands and feet and seemed to enter her very bones. All three horses were now calmly munching on the lush grass growing in the meadow, so Caitlin took that as a sign the smell of the panther had vanished.

Picking up the leads to the two mares, she tugged on Tabby's halter and led them over to a tree stump where she slid onto Tabby's back again.

"Okay, Tabby girl, let's get going again. We don't want to be panther-food if we can avoid it," as she began walking the horses toward the road,

Then, she heard the sound of a horse approaching from the direction of the farmhouse and immediately she pulled Tabby to a stop, slid off her back and twisted the lead ropes for all three horses around a tree branch then scurried out to the edge of the road where she squatted down behind an oak tree surrounded by thick brush and watched for the approaching horse.

14

The Road Home

Caitlin heard the voices before she spied the riders.

"Slow down would ya, I'm a'fallin' off'en his hind-end. Pull up and slow down ah mite, would ya?" one of the riders yelled loudly.

As the riders drew closer, Caitlin was dumbstruck. The horse was not a horse at all, it was an old, sway-back mule whose coat was graying with age. The old mule had a long, drawn-out body, short legs and huge ears and he was carrying two men. One man was guiding the mule and the other was lying stretched out his stomach with his long skinny arms wrapped around the waist of the fella in the front. His feet were flapping out behind the mule's hind quarters as he hung on for dear life and much to Caitlin's surprise, it was the cowboy and the plate-slammer!

The poor old mule was running as fast as his short legs could manage and with each stride of his legs, the cowboy would flop up and slam back down onto the backbone of the poor old animal. The cowboy's hat, evidently, had fallen off since all of his hair was slicked down on his head. His pant legs, which were rolled up to begin with, were almost above his knees due to flopping up and down on the mule's back. His filthy socks were so big they were hanging down completely covering his shoes. His legs looked like sticks flapping in the wind. It was one of the funniest sights Caitlin had ever witnessed. His skinny body kept flipping and

161

flopping like a dead chicken tied to the back of a running dog, and the plate-slammer wasn't paying one bit of attention to the cowboy's complaints; he just kept right on kicking the sides of the poor old mule. All three went right on past the spot where Caitlin was hiding without the slightest glance into the forest around them.

"Good Lord on high, what a sight to behold," Caitlin laughed to herself, "Where did that mule come from? I sure didn't see a that mule around the barn."

"I guess that ends our journey for a bit, we'll have to stay here until they go back to the farm. I sure don't want to meet up with them on our way into town, that's for sure." She whispered to Tabby as she picked up the three lead ropes.

Turning the horses around, she led them back to the clearing hoping with all her heart that the panther from this morning was well away from the river. With a sigh, she sat down on a big fall tree trunk.

After a while, the forest once again came alive with the sounds of early morning life along the Mississippi river. The sky was crystal clear and as blue as Michael's eyes had been. Bees were again buzzing around the early spring flowers while a woodpecker, high in one of the trees, began its rhythmic knocking and the rustling and scurrying of small critters disturbed the silence of the peaceful little clearing. Singing birds once again flooded the forest with their cheery calls of the morning as a warm, soft breeze moved gently through the aspen bringing in the sweet summer fragrance of wild honeysuckle and producing the familiar murmuring of aspen leaves which would grow as loud as a waterfall and then soften to the whisper of a bubbling stream as the breeze lessened.

Caitlin lay down on the flat smooth surface of the large, fallen oak and watched two eagles soaring and gliding through the tree tops. They would catch the wind as it brushed the tops of the tallest trees and let it carry them to higher heights...so far up she could barely see them as they swirled and glided in circles. After they were carried a good distance they would flap their wings and swoop down to catch another updraft and once again be carried far into the blue sky.

The oak trees stood tall and majestic as they stretched their branches out, creating a canopy of shadows almost covering the entire clearing. It was as if they were guarding the smaller aspen and flowering bushes scattered throughout the glade. Flowering bushes filled in the gaps between the giant oaks, making the clearing a perfect place to hide from prying eyes.

Dove coos and the chattering of squirrels lulled her into a state of tranquility. She closed her eyes and felt the sunshine caress her skin and sooth her anxieties.

"This is so nice," she thought as she curled into a ball on the fallen tree, "there is absolutely nothing in this world better than a nap in the warm morning sun."

As she closed her eyes, her mind wandered back to the days she had spent with Michael. She smiled as she remembered his smell when he came to visit and the warmth of his arms around her when he hugged her before going off to war. She could visualize that day so vividly; he had stood so proud and anxious to defend his country.

"Oh to have Michael back one more time," she smiled softly, "along with Mama and Papa. That would be wonderful." She lay there for a while daydreaming about the people she loved who were now only memories and the people she loved who were still with her.

The sun was now completely up and warming the tree trunk; its warmth intensifying the heady fragrance of spring flowers. Her night-wrap was almost too warm and she could no longer keep her eyes open—slowly she slipped into a slumber.

Caitlin awoke with Tabby pushing at her shoulder with her muzzle. The two mares were standing on the other side of her with their faces less than a foot away from Caitlin's face as one of the mares kept lipping her hair. The sun had passed the high-noon point and was on its way down. It was probably three o'clock, or there about. The birds were still singing but the eagles had moved on. The clearing seemed so peaceful; Caitlin did not want to move. But she knew they had to start out for town again because she sure didn't want to be out here during the dark of night with no protection.

As she stretched and sat up, Tabby and the mares moved back as if they knew they needed to be moving on. But, in the distance, she heard the sound of rapidly approaching hoof-beats. The three horses must have sensed the approaching danger and that was why Tabby had awakened her. This time the sounds were coming from the opposite direction.

"It must be the plate-slammer and the cowboy again," she thought as she scrambled off the fallen tree. She picked up the lead ropes for all three horses and wrapped them around a branch so they wouldn't follow her out to the road and expose their hiding place. Quietly she hurried to the same large tree she had previously hidden behind and crouched down to wait.

And, there they came. Sure enough, it was the old mule, the plate-slammer and the cowboy. The cowboy was still holding onto the plate-slammer and the plate-slammer was still kicking the old mule trying to make him run faster.

"Where is that stupid gal?" the plate-slammer yelled to the cowboy.

"I cain't hardly hold on, Mac, much less think 'bout whur' that thar' gal is." Yelled the cowboy.

The cowboy had managed to get his legs up and around the belly of the old mule and again his long arms were stretched out around the plate-slammer's waist with his behind sticking out over the mule's behind. His skinny legs were clamped around the mule's belly so tightly Caitlin could see the depression in the poor, old mule's side. Thankfully, the cowboy had his face turned to the opposite side of the trail or he would have been looking right at where Caitlin was hiding.

Quickly she walked back the horses and led Tabby to the fallen tree and slipped onto her back without struggle. Slowly she guided the three mares back to the road.

164

"Well," she muttered to the mares, "this road has to lead into a town of some sort, let's just hope its Caruthersville. Come on, girls, let's get going and see how far we can get before it turns dark. Hopefully this is the way home."

Off they went with the two mares following close behind Tabby as if they knew there could be danger awaiting along the road. Caitlin started the horses off in a slow trot so as to not alert the mule riders of her whereabouts. She sure didn't want them to turn around and begin chasing her.

After a while, the road turned and ran along beside a stream where Caitlin stopped the hoses and let them drink their full, as did she. She ate some of the biscuits and ham she had stashed in her pockets then got back on Tabby and began her trip home. This time she urged the mares into a faster gallop seeing that the afternoon was getting away from them and soon it would be too dark to chance traveling. The last thing she wanted to do was stay in the forest and encounter one of the black panthers roaming the countryside or any other wild animals wandering about during the night hours.

Within minutes the giant oak tree clusters totally disappeared and the land became full of tall prairie grass with a few trees scattered along the sides of the road. They came to a fork in the road and Caitlin stopped the horses.

"Tabby, which way should we go?" she said, as if expecting a reply.

Not getting an answer, she laughed and bent down to have a good look at the prints in the dusty road. Walking Tabby a short distance in each direction, she soon discovered that the road leading to the south seemed to have more hoof prints than the one leading north.

"Okay girls, this is the way we are going to go," she said to the mares as she urged Tabby forward. They looked at her with wide solemn eyes, not realizing she had made a huge decision for all of them.

Not wanting anyone ahead or behind them to see the dust they might create, Caitlin kept the hoses going in a trot. They must have gone maybe five miles when Caitlin spotted a wagon coming towards them. Quickly she pulled back on Tabby and strained her eyes to see if she could make out who was driving the wagon. It looked to be a man and a woman sitting on the wagon bench with a small child squeezed in between them.

She led her horses into the tall grass at the side of the road and waited for the wagon to approach and pass. The man driving pulled his wagon to a stop beside her and the mares.

"How-do," ma'am," he spoke with a thick southern accent, "Are ya okay way out here by ya'self? We sure will help ya if need be. Ya know yur ah long ways from town. Hit's 'bout ten more mile inta Caruthersville and hit's gonna be dark here just in a jiffy. I'm David John and this here is my lovely wife Katie Nicole. We be the Levi's and we hail from way over Georgia-way. These here young'uns be Mary Queen of Scotts, Henry the Fifth— we'd a'named 'em Henry the Eighth, but my Katie Nicole tells me ol' Henry the Eighth weren't a very nice fella. And sittin' right next to Henry there is Jethro John the Baptist, and Arthur Coydon is the one sleepin' on the floor of the wagon. We'd ah named 'em King Arthur but Katie Nicole liked Arthur Coydon better. This'un right here be little Josephine Pansy. She be named after ol' Napoleon's sweetheart. Now I know'd Napoleon weren't no fine fella and all, but we figured Josephine might'ah been jest a right-nice lady. Katie Nicole here love the name Josephine so we jest went right on ahead and named our little gal Josephine. We be expectin' another'n in jest a few months."

David John grinned at Caitlin as if he had accomplished a grand deed then kept right on talking.

"And, iff'en hit's a boy child he'll be named after his great-grandpappy and be called King David, being that his great-grandpappy came over from the old country and all. But iff'en hit's a girl child she'll be called Catherine the Great, since Catherine the Great was such a grand woman and all. I know'd they all have grand fancy names but hit's because Katie Nicole here is a fine educated lady from Baltimore, Maryland and knows all 'bout them folks. But we don't never call 'em by their given name; unless Mama here is upset with 'em. We jest call 'em Queenie, Henny, JJ, Bugpappy and Josie. Now if yur wonderin' why we call Arthur "Bugpappy", hit's cuz he truly loves ever' kind ah bug there is. Ever' kind you can

166

think of, he likes 'em. Why once't on a Sunday morning he took his jug-o'-bugs inta the house of the Lord, without us knowin', mind you. Well, that thar' preacher-man started in shoutin' bout how we'll all be free from the earthly cage of sin when we get to heaven and we'll be able to fly 'round with wings in the promised-land. Well, our Bugpappy starts in weepin' and opened-up his jug-o'-bugs and yells out at the top of his voice, 'You're free, bugs! Go on now and fly into the promised-land whur there be lots of skitter for ya to eat.'

"Well," David John laughed loudly, "there was more yellin' and shoutin' and jumpin' up and down on that thar' particular Sunday morning gatherin' that thar' ever was in all them ten revivals put together. Folks were slappin' and swattin' bugs like they was monsters from the deep. Well, the church-folk said our Bugpappy couldn't return ever again and even though he was jest a little'un they was steadfast in thar' saying. So, right then and thar' I decided to move my family and find a good place to farm where everbody loves the gifts God gave us in our young'uns. Ain't no man on this green earth gonna be mean to my young'uns. So here we are headed on up to Eden's Bend where we plan on farming and living for many a year, iff'en the good Lord sees fit and we don't get flooded out."

Caitlin could see why Katie Nicole had fallen for David John. He was a very handsome man and he sure loved his children.

Four little blond heads with grins spread across their faces were still peeking over the wagon rails at her. Then, another little tow-head popped up from the floor of the wagon who was cuter than the others...if that were possible. He had huge, steel-gray eyes outlined with long, beautiful black eyelashes. His hair was white as cotton and it was sticking straight up all over his head and he had a splash of freckles spreading across his nose and cheeks. He looked to be around six years old and was grinning from ear to ear as he stared at her.

"How-do, ma'am," the little tow-head yelled in a squeaky little boy's voice.

"This must be Bugpappy." Caitlin thought to herself.

"It's a right fine day today, isn't it?" he called out, "I'm Bugpappy and I'm almost a grown-up man. I have some nice brothers and sisters here if you want to

167

meet them. And, I even have some fine bugs in my jug-o'-bugs with me. What ya doing out here by yourself? You getting ready for bed this early? It's not even dark yet. I like your horse. She's a beaut' and I'm going to get me one just like her when I'm a full-grown man. Yes, I'm going to get me a dandy fine horse! What's your name ma'am? Do you have a grand name like we do? You probably do 'cuz you're so pretty and all. You want to hold my jug-o'-bugs? I have some beauties in here and they're might fine," he said as he held up his jug-o'-bugs for Caitlin to see, "Right here is the biggest ol' bug you ever did see in the whole, wide, world, I'm sure of it," he was pointing to a big bug crawling around in his jar and continued talking without waiting for Caitlin's reply.

"And, I know you would really like them, I'm sure 'bout that. We're moving to a big farm and we are going to help Pa build it up! I'm going to catch every bug on our farm. In fact, I'm going to have me a bug-farm. I just now thought of that. That's a right fine idea, isn't it ma'am? What'cha doing with three horses? You can't ride all three at one time, can ya? Well, if you see any good bugs send them our way." Bugpappy scratched his head and grinned widely as he looked thoughtful, "Yes ma'am, there will be lots and lots of bugs on our farm."

"My name is Caitlin Violet Quinn and it is very nice to meet you, Bugpappy, as well as meeting your bugs."

"It's mighty nice meeting you too, ma'am," Bugpappy announced loudly as he stretched out to shake Caitlin's hand, "My real name is Arthur, but I like Bugpappy better." He said with a big smile. Caitlin took the small outstretched hand and was surprised at the strength in the little guy's handshake and his mother, or whoever taught the children, was doing a great job. His speech was great for such a small child.

"Bugpappy," his mother turned and spoke softly to him, "Mind your manners now. Pa was talking. Don't interrupt. Maybe you can talk to this nice lady when we finish our visit. Don't release your bugs and please hold onto your sister so she doesn't fall over the side."

168

When little Bugpappy did as his mother instructed, she spoke to him again softly and with a smile, "Think you, son, that's very kind of you."

Katie Nicole turned back and smiled at Caitlin, "I do apologize, Miss Caitlin, he means no disrespect. He loves to talk and gets a little carried away talking about his bugs at times."

"No offense taken at all, I have a younger brother and sisters myself. Your children are beautiful and I'm sure you will all have a wonderful farm. The land up north, closer to St Louis, is quite fertile and the farms always have a good harvest in the fall." Caitlin smiled at the grinning little faces peering at her. Not one of them said a word except for Bugpappy.

"Well, ya be careful now, young lady," David John stated, "Iff'en ya get caught out here in the dark afore you get into town, there be an old, abandoned shack 'bout five miles back on-down the road a bit. We spent the night there last night. We didn't get an early start-out this morning cuz ol' Blue here lost one of his shoes and it took me forever to fix it. These young'uns ain't big enough to help much yet, but they'll get thar' in a few more years. We plan on spendin' this here night just makin' camp out in the forest. Ya don't know of any empty farmhouses out this way, do ya?"

"Well, no, not really" Caitlin replied with caution, "But I do know of a large grove of giant oaks a short way up the road that may give you some shelter. There's plenty of grass for the horse and a good, clear stream for drinking just before you reach it. As a matter of fact," Caitlin made a quick decision, "I would like to give you these two mares of mine. I really don't need them and I was just going to give them to anyone who could use them once I get into town. They often get away from me and I'm tired of chasing them all over the county. If you would take them off my hands I sure would appreciate it. It would save me the trouble of leading them along the next ten miles and maybe having to chase them down again. That way Tabby and I can go a little faster. How about it? Could you use two extra mares on your farm? You're more than welcome to them if you like. I have no use for them anymore."

169

"Well," David John said slowly as he scratched his head and eyed the mares, "Hit don't feel right us just takin' 'em from ya. Let us pay ya in some way. We can make a trade, what would you like? We have plenty of food stuff and all kinds of kitchen things ya might like. Take yur pick. It's up to you."

"Well, I could use some food for the night. Whatever you have, just a little bit will do for me. My horse can live off the grass and stream water."

"Katie Nicole love, get this here gal some food and maybe a jug o' milk and whatever else you think she might need."

With the help of her husband, Katie Nicole climbed over the bench and into the back of the wagon. David John jumped down from the bench, took the lead ropes from Caitlin and tied the two mares to the back of the wagon next to their cow.

Katie Nicole had a burlap flour bag and it was stuffed full of food and other items. Caitlin didn't say anything because she didn't want them to feel as if they had cheated her.

David John handed the bag to Caitlin and smiled broadly as he said, "Miss, you have helped us out mighty fine and we sure do thank ya for it. You be a blessin' to us." Katie Nicole gave Caitlin a beautiful smile and nodded in agreement.

"You are quite welcome," Caitlin replied, "I should also let you know about a couple of things to watch for. Today, in the early hours of the morning, I heard a black panther scream a few times as if maybe it was hurt. And, the second thing is, when you come to the first fork in the road, don't go west. Stay on the road to the north. Down the west road is an old abandoned farm but it's full of every bad folk. They won't hesitant to take everything you have and may even steal your children to sell down the river. They will also take your wife if they get a chance. I know for a fact they are a group of slave traders and they may be trying to walk, or ride an old mule back into town. Keep a sharp eye out for anyone walking or riding a mule. They have one mule, a carriage and maybe more horses by now. So, if they stop you and try to talk you into helping them out or giving them the horses I gave you, don't do it. Don't even stop to talk to them, get away from them as fast as you can. Get your gun out and have it ready as soon as you spot them coming up the road and have your children hide. If I were you, I would also give your wife a gun, even if she doesn't know how to use it, it will be a backup for you. I know for a fact there are at least four men and one woman and there could be more by now and they are all in cahoots with the slavers along the river.

"If the sky stays clear tonight I'm going to try and make it into town and if I were y'all I wouldn't chance running into those evil folks."

Katie Nicole sat looking at Caitlin with wide-eyed fear.

"When you get to Eden Bend, please send me a letter letting me know you made it safely and everything is okay. Just send it to Caitlin Quinn in care of Pete Turnkey at the train depot, Caruthersville and he will see that I get it."

Katie Nicole's face turned a little white and David John seemed, all of a sudden, to be in a big hurry.

"Miss Caitlin, we sure do thank you for these mares and the warning. We wish you luck in getting back to town but we better be movin' along now. We sure won't take the west road and maybe we'll jest keep on movin' along until we get well past that fork in the road. We sure will send you a letter when we get to Eden Bend, won't we Katie Nicole. And you be very careful ya'self, young lady. Thank ya again, Miss Caitlin, Thank ya very much."

With that said, the wagon moved out at a faster pace than a wagon should move.

"Thank you, Miss Caitlin." They all called back

Little Bugpappy was standing up in the wagon bed holding up his jug-o'-bugs as he yelled out to her, "I know for sure you will love these here bugs once you get to meet them! They are right friendly most times. Come on into Eden Bend and give us a visit."

Caitlin laughed and gave them another wave. The five little ones and Katie Nicole all turned and waved at her until they reached a bend in the road and were out of sight.

"Well, Tabby, it's just you and me, love." Caitlin said to her horse, "I know I told a lie, but they seemed to be good folks and they will take good care of the mares. I did the right thing and I sure hope they don't run into those river-rats of Aunt Birdie's. Let's get moving girl and see how far we can go before it gets too dark."

Off they went again and even though it was only the two of them and they were moving quickly, the lengthening shadows of the night were rapidly descending upon the forest. The clouds were rolling across the sky, chasing away any hopes of being able to continue riding in the dark of night. Once the moon was completely covered, the road along the Mississippi would turn black as coal making it impossible to ride a horse and stay on the road.

Pushing Tabby into a full gallop, they went a few more miles when she began looking for the old shack the Levi's had told her about. The clouds were getting thicker and darkness was now closing in on them. Wispy, feathery fingers of fog slipped up from the river and tumbled along the road, and she realized soon it would be too dark and foggy to see the old shack.

Cold air was quickly moving in as the forest sounds changed from singing birds to hoot owl calls, crickets chirping and bull frogs croaking. Along with the damp foggy dusk coming up from the river, off in the distance came the sounds of large animals pushing through branches and underbrush in their nightly hunt.

Tabby must have sensed the urgency in Caitlin's movements, because she started moving faster than Caitlin wanted to go in the dark. In the growing darkness, Caitlin needed to watch for the holes in the road – or anything else Tabby night stumble over.

Finally, approximately one hundred feet off to the right sat the old abandoned cabin. There was no path leading up to the door; only the slight bending of the tall prairie grass gave proof of someone being there recently. The old cabin looked as if it might, at any time, fall to the ground, but at least it had four walls and a roof. The door was still attached and the windows were boarded-up to keep the animals out.

"Come on, girl, we'll both stay inside so that panther won't have us for dinner." She whispered to Tabby as if speaking any louder would alert the forest creature of their whereabouts.

Carefully she walked Tabby across the field and up to the cabin and slid off Tabby's back and landed on the rickety porch being sure her feet did not slip through the weak, weathered boards. Slowly she eased the door open and looked inside. It was better than she had expected. Evidently the Levi's had somewhat cleaned it up. She could barely see, but she could make out an old rusty lantern with a small amount of oil still in the bottom and what looked like a box of matches sitting alongside it. Stepping inside the room, she quickly lit the lantern and sat it on a tiny table leaning against the wall. The light from the lantern lit up the small room and she saw the only furniture was an old table and one chair along with an old feather tick mattress lying on the floor. What had once been a cot was now in pieces next to a pot-bellied stove along with a small stack of fire wood. Caitlin walked to the back of the cabin and opened the back door. It led into a small lean-to which looked to be in decent shape.

"This will be fine for us," she said to herself. She then went back outside and picked up the sack Katie Nicole had filled for her and led Tabby inside the cabin and through the back door to the lean-to. There were walls at both ends of the lean-to; it must have been added on at one time as an additional room for storage.

"Well, tonight it's going to be a room for a horse," she laughed. After closing the door to the lean-to, she walked over and opened the bag from the Levi's. Inside the bag she found, along with food and milk, a blanket, a small knife and an old dress. Caitlin began laughing at herself because she had completely forgotten about being in her night-wrap and the over-sized boots. Katie Nicole must have thought she was a runaway and needed some clothes. and the knife— Katie Nicole knew Caitlin might need some kind of protection. Bless her for that.

A woman traveling alone in the wilderness needed something for her protection even if it was a small sharp knife.

The bag was stuffed with more food than Caitlin would be able to eat along with a jug of milk. The food consisted of sweet potato pancakes, bacon, fried chicken and some kind of sweet bread. It was a feast fit for a king!

Walking to the outside door, she blocked it with the table and pulled the rickety chair up to the table and sat down to feast. The chicken was the best tasting chicken she had ever eaten, she believed, and the sweet potato pancakes melted in her mouth. The milk tasted like honey going down her throat.

With a huge sigh of contentment, she sat back in the chair.

After finishing her feast, she blew out the lantern, wrapped herself in the blanket and lay down on the shoddy old feather tic. She wasn't just concerned with staying warm, she was also concerned about the bugs living in the old mattress. Curling up in a ball, immediately she fell sound asleep.

15

A Night in the Wilderness

Along about midnight, or so she guessed, Caitlin was awakened by the sound of clapping, laughter and music. She lay there for a few minutes trying to get her bearings, then slowly eased herself into a sitting position. But still she couldn't figure out what was going on.

"What is that racket and where is it coming from?" she whispered to herself as she got up from the floor and peeked through a crack in the boards covering the window.

Approximately fifty-feet further down the meadow, in a large stand of tall pines, she saw a large campfire and since the pine branches began twenty feet above the earth, she could easily see the area clearly. The clouds had vanished and the moon was lighting up the entire meadow. Peering out the window, she watched as a group of men moved around the campfire as if dancing with each other!

Knowing sound carried further in the night, she quietly pulled the table away from the door, wrapped the dark-colored blanket around herself to hide her light clothing and slipped out onto the front porch. Realizing the creaking of wood would carry across the clearing to the men she did not pull the door of the cabin closed. Instead, she stood on the porch watching for a minute; just to make sure no one had heard her open the door to the cabin. Swiftly she ran to the edge of the

175

tree line and moved into the thick brush which grew around the tree trunks. Carefully and slowly she edged closer to the campfire. When she was roughly thirty feet from the men, she stopped and crouched down behind a clump of pine trees and brush. Much to her surprise, there stood eighteen to twenty men encircling around the fire. The fire was large and the men were rowdily singing *Camp Town Races* at the top of the lungs.

Wearing a pretty ladies bonnet, one of the men was dancing with one of the other men. The two of them were twirling around the fire between the circle of men and the huge bonfire. The bonnet looked new and was decked out with ribbons, bows and streamers. It was pink with blue ruffles trimming the brim and neck strap. Actually, it was quite pretty — if a woman had been wearing it.

One of the men, a little, short man dressed in a dandy suit and top hat, was standing on a large rock calling out the dance steps for the dancing men. He would call out, "step to the right, now swing to the left, now do-si-so," and the dancing men would whirl around each other Then, after a turn around the fire the little guy would call out, "Switch partners" at which time the bonnet-man would snatch up another man and away they went dancing around the fire. They seemed to be having the time of their life.

After each man had a go-around with that particular bonnet-man, the short little man yelled out, "switch the bonnet" and the bonnet-man would whip off the bonnet and plunk it onto the head of the man with whom he was currently dancing, who slapped the bonnet further down on his own head and snatched-up a different man to be his dancing partner. Then the two of them took off around the fire with the rest of the men clapping and singing as they waited for their turn to be the pretend woman or the fella dancing with the pretend woman.

One very tall, skinny man with a huge nose, long lanky arms and legs and no teeth would — every time he switched partners — repeat an attention-grabbing routine. He would bow, break wind, snatch up his partner's hand, wrap his arm around their waist and take off around the fire so quick his bonnet ribbons would be streaming out behind him. Before he changes to the next partner he would stop, bow, break wind again and yell out enthusiastically, "Thank'ye ma'am fur' the lovely dance!"

This went on for a while until the little man doing the calling yelled out, "Okay, boys, that's the whole lesson for tonight. I can't yell anymore and I have a powerful thirst coming on. Let's all have a drink. Break out the whisky, John T. Let's celebrate our dancing skills."

The dandy little fella continued on with his speech as John T broke out the whiskey jugs, "The next town-dance we come upon, you men will be the envy of every man in attendance. Ever' last one of you are ready to impress every boney-fide lady you happen to meet up with, I do have to say one thing, though – I have done an excellent job of teaching you how to dance, and all of you have done an excellent job of learning." The little fella raised a fancy tea cup in the air and yelled, "Welcome to the civilized world, boys!" At which time the men let out a loud whoop and took a swig of whiskey.

"Yes indeed, welcome to the world of dancing with boney-fide ladies and sipping tea in a parlor. Tomorree we will practice sipping tea one more time before we move on, and I am right proud of you and I do suspect many of you will soon be marrying-up with the best ladies in Missouri. By this time next year, we should be seeing some fathers among us, myself included, I do hope and pray.

"Now, this here calls for some celebrating, if you ask me! Wrap up that bonnet for the next time and we can start our celebration. I salute you all!" he held up another fancy tea-cup with his little finger sticking straight out and took a big gulp of whiskey.

Then the whooping and hollering began again as they sat down around the fire and John T began passing more jugs of whiskey. As the jugs were passed around they began teasing each other. Calls like, "Yur one fine, lookin' boney-fide lady," one fella yelled to another.

"I know'd I am, ya handsome country-bumpkin," the man called back in a mocking high squeaky voice like a female, "but, I jest cain't marry-up with ya, Slim. Ever'time ya change partners ya break an awful smellin' wind and I jest cain't put up with that thar' habit." They all laughed bawdily and kept on passing the jugs and harassing each other.

"Well Jasper, you are a sweet, charmin' lady," Slim replied, "But I don't think I can marry-up with ya either. You be one fine dancin' boney-fide lady but yur boo-soms seem to have dropped right down and turned into a belly."

That comment brought another round of raucous laughter from the other men and more crude remarks were yelled as they pushed and shoved at each other in jest.

"I'm a'lookin' fur me a wife. I'm 'tard ah riding and sleeping on the ground. Hit's a'wearin' on my bones." A bald-headed cowboy yelled out, "I sure hope I find ah better-lookin' wife than yur' ugly mugs. Whew! I cain't 'mangine wakin' up to a face like your'n, Bulldog. It's ah frightin' thing ta think 'bout."

"Right back at ya, Beanpole, I'd rather wake up ta ah mountain lion, I'm thinkin'," Bulldog and Beanpole both laughed along with the rest of the men.

"Me too," the one called Slim yelled out in agreement, "I'm getting' too old for this life ah herdin' cattle. Iff'en I find me a nice, rich lady who'll have me, I'll marry-up with 'er in ah far' fly flash."

"Same here," called out the little dandy man.

All of a sudden, Caitlin heard loud yelling as someone came crashing through the edge of the woods no more than ten feet from where she was hiding. Hunkering further down into the brush, she pulled her blanket over her head. When she looked up again, two men were running towards the campfire holding their hats on their heads and screaming like banshees as they waved their one free hand.

"We see'd haints! We see'd haints! Get out yur guns! We see'd some haints."

Every man jumped up and whipped out his gun while staring at the men as they continued screaming with fear.

"What ya talkin' bout, Bones?" one of the men asked,

"Stop yur yammering and yellin', Jonsey and y'all tell us what ya see'd." one of the other men yelled.

The men had their guns drawn and were staring bug-eyed out into the forest. Then Bones and Jonsey stopped yammering, put their hands on their knees with their heads hanging down as they tried catching their breath.

"Well," the man named Bones finally managed to get out, "Me and Jonsey here, we be over yonder by that thar' old shack just a'nosin' around and all of a sudden-like, thar' be a man and a little white-haired gal standin' right dab in front of us. He was one of them thar' soldier-boys and that little gal was all decked out in Kickapoo clothes and her hair was a'blowin' straight out behind her head and there weren't no wind a'tall. That thar' soldier-boy was a'glarin' right at us with red fary' eyes. Hit' looked like far' was shootin' right on outta his eyeballs shootin' straight at us, ain't that right, Jonsey Well, me and Jonsey stopped dead in our tracks. I was mighty scare't, I tell ya, and my legs started in a'shakin' and a'shiverin'. Then, they froze right up on me and wouldn't let me move nary one bit. Now, me and Jonsey." the fella stopped talking as he took a deep breath then continued. "We ain't no cowards a'tall, but that thar' sure 'nuf was two haints we see'd. Hit was kindly like we could see right through 'em. They was thar' a'right, but we could see the shack right on through thar' bodies, and thar' eyes was on far'! Then the soldier haint calls out and says fur' us to get on outta thar' and stay out, or we'd be on our way to the early gates ta face ol' Saint Pete in a flash. Ain't that right, Jonsey?"

"Yep, boss," Jonsey sputtered out, "that thar' is jest the way hit happened." Jonsey stammered as spit flew out of his mouth in globs the whole time he was speaking, "cept' hit was worst'en that fur' me. I see'd that thar' soldier-boy stretch out his hand and started in a'comin' right fur' me. He was pointin' ah finger at me and the end of his finger was on far' and thar' was lightnin' comin right-on outta

179

hit'. Bones here had done turned 'round and took-off a'runnin' but I was still froze solid right whur' I was with my eyeballs gaping wide open. Well, as soon as I see'd that thar' far' comin' outta his finger, I whipped my legs on 'round and took off a'runnin' after Bones. We never looked back ta see iff'en they was a'follerin' us, but I didn't get struck by that lightnin', so I'm thinkin' we out-runned 'em."

"Hit' were the first time I ever did see a haint up close, and I'm a'hopin' hits the last time." Bones said with a stammer and a sigh.

"Me too, boss, me too. No more haints for me! I'm stayin' right by this here campfar' ever' night from here on out. I ain't even gonna go let water durin' the night." Jonsey stated forcefully. Then he walked over to the fire, sat down with his gun drawn staring out into the woods as he watched for the haints.

Caitlin sat there with her blanket wrapped around her for what seemed like an eternity and she wasn't so calm herself —if there was something strange going on at the shack, maybe she shouldn't sleep over there. Maybe it would be safer staying right here close to the cowboys and their campfire. After all, they didn't seem like such a bad bunch of fellas.

But, she had to go back. Tabby was there and she didn't want anyone to take her and leave. She would have to go back before daybreak.

Gathering the blanket around herself she leaned against the trunk of the tree, knowing the thick brush would hide her body from prying eyes. Her eyes began to slowly close and her head began to nod when she felt a warm hand on her shoulder and heard a soft voice whisper in her ear.

"Caitlin, wake up, love," the voice whispered, "It's me Michael and I'm here to help you get home safely. When the men begin yelling and shooting, run back to the shack as fast as you can and lock yourself in,

Startled, Caitlin's eyes popped open and she was staring up into Michael's face.

"Michael," she whispered with delight, "you're here! Oh, my goodness! I thought I would never see you again. Where have you been?" Tears were streaming down her face as she silently wept.

Crouching down, Michael wrapped his arms around her; holding her close.

"No, love," he whispered tenderly, "I'm not home to stay, I'm here to help *you* get home."

Puzzled at what Michael said, Caitlin whispered, "What do you mean, Michael? Where are you going? You can't stay here with me? Michael, we need you. Mama and Pa are gone and Aunt Birdie may have the little ones. We need you, Michael. I need you to stay home with us."

"I can't, love," he replied with sadness in his blue eyes, "I would love to stay here and take care of you but it's too late for me. I'll be leaving shortly and I won't be back again. You will find someone special to help keep the little ones safe, but I can't be me, love." He sighed deeply, "it can't be me."

Standing to his feet, he pulled her up with him and she felt the warmth of his body and the love in his heart pour into hers.

"I will always love you, my Cait. You will always be with me, but I want you to find another who will love you as much and I do. You will know him when it's time. Please be happy and have a good life, love."

With that said, he kissed her tenderly and backed away once again telling her to run for the shack when the men began yelling and shooting.

"Wait, Michael, don't go. Please — don't go!" she whispered frantically as she held onto him, but Michael had already slipped out of her embrace, turned his back and was walking away. She watched him with a confused frown on her face as he walked towards the campfire.

Then, she realized he was not moving the bushes as he went through the thick brush, and there appeared to be a small child with him. Both Michael and the child seemed to be floating through the undergrowth instead of walking through it. The child was a little girl with the longest, whitest hair Caitlin had ever seen. Her silver shining hair was flowing straight out behind her, fluttering softly in the breeze. She was dressed as an Indian child and had a small pup under her arm as she held onto Michael's hand and looked up at him with a grin.

The little girl's voice floated back to Caitlin as she spoke to Michael.

"Let's give them another really big scare, okay Mr. Michael? That way they won't be bothering your Cait again."

Laughing softly, Michael looked down at the child and replied, "Okay, Hannah, let's do that. You startle them awake and we'll both give them a taste of being scared."

Captivated, Caitlin stood and watched as the two of them approach the campfire and little Hannah glide up to one of the men who, like all the others, had drifted off to sleep; thinking Bones and Jonsey had imagined the haints.

"Yooouuu whooo," Hannah yelled loudly, no more than one inch from the man's ear, "Get up, cowboy. It's the haints and we're here to take all of ya to your maker so you can get your just rewards for all the things you have done in your lives."

Pandemonium was unleashed with a fury of chaotic terror. Men were scrambling up, pointing their guns at Michael and Hannah who were facing Caitlin so the bullets would not hit her by accident. The two of them were waving their hands above their heads and Hannah's hair was now standing straight up from her head with the ends twirling and waving.

The men began running around the campfire shooting into the night air towards the two ghosts. Caitlin notice two of the men had wet the front of their britches but they paid no mind and kept right on shooting into nothingness.

After using up all their bullets, some, instead of reloading, were in such a panic they kept right on shooting empty guns. Looking over at Caitlin with a twinkle in his eyes, Michael blew her a kiss, gave her a big smile and a wink; telling her to run.

Mesmerized with the sight of seeing Michael, Caitlin stood watching for a few more seconds...knowing this would be the last time she would ever see him. Then, she took off for the shack as fast as her feet could carry her and didn't look back until she was standing on the front stoop of the little cabin. With her hand on the door, she glanced back and saw Michael and Hannah had moved around the campfire so the shooting would not come near the cabin.

Floating three feet above the ground, the two of them were swooping back and forth in front of the cowboys to keep them where they wanted them to be. Then, they began clapping their hands above their heads and dancing to unheard music. Unexpectedly a banjo appeared in Michael's hands and he began playing a lively Irish tune as little Hannah began dancing an Irish jig with her little feet moving so fast they could barely be seen and the little pup, who had been wrapped around her neck like a winter muff, began yipping at the top of his voice. Hannah's hair was now whirling around her head like a top spinning out of control, stretching four feet around on each side of her head. Michael began stomping out a tune with his feet and Hannah's laughter, along with the sound of the banjo, echoed throughout the pine forest. Then, the little pup jumped up on the top of Hannah's spinning hair and howled like a coyote.

Quickly Caitlin slipped into the shack, blocked the door and moved to the window. In the few seconds it took for her to cross from the door to the window, most of the men had managed to mount up and race their terrified horses through the forest. Those remaining were struggled into their saddles and leaving. Then, Michael turned his face to the little cabin, gave Caitlin another wink before he and little Hannah began floating up through the trees as their visible bodies thinned into nothingness.

Smoldering embers of the campfire was the only evidence remaining of the large group of men and two haints who, seconds earlier, had possessed the clearing.

Caitlin stood peering out the window for a long time but nothing moved and Michael did not return. Once again, the forest came alive with the sounds of the night. Owls called out to their mates, bull frogs croaked and crickets chirped. The symphony of the wilderness once again enchanting the forest.

Moving across the room to check on Tabby, she peeked into the lean-to and there the horse stood looking at her as if to say, "Go away and leave me alone."

Walking back to the window to take one last look, and once again she saw nothing. She watched as the lingering embers vanished into ash and the last coils of smoke slipped its way through the branches of the tall pines andt into the clear night sky where it too melted away.

Sleep came quickly as she once again snuggled into her blanket and closed her eyes.

16

Elmer's Confession

"Well, Pete," André said, "Ah think maybe Ah should deputize ya and then you and Ah should take a look-see on some of these here'ah boats. What do ya think about that? That way you can point out any of the men ya saw on the train platform."

Replying with a big grin on his face, Pete said, "If need be. I will do that very thing. I would be honored to serve my state and Caruthersville as your Deputy Sheriff."

"Then, let's get it done," Sheriff Beaumont smiled, "Ah can always use ah Deputy Sheriff to help out 'round here'ah. Come on inta the office and we'll get it all set up." André and Pete went into the office and André got out a deputy badge and his book for deputizing. When he finished, André smiled, shook Pete's hand and told him congratulations on becoming a Deputy Sheriff and that he was certain Pete would be the best deputy in the history of deputies.

Smiling broadly again, Pete thanked André and promised to do his level best to uphold the law and help keep the peace in Caruthersville. So, Sheriff André Beaumont and Deputy Pete Turnkey walked across the levee onto the boat-dock and began their search of the boats.

Congratulating and shaking Pete's hand when André introduced him as the new deputy, all the riverboat Captains welcomed both men aboard to search for Caitlin. Those who were probably carrying contraband goods gave them a harder time until André assured them the only thing they were searching for was a missing young gal, then they willingly let them onboard to conduct their search. André didn't think it was necessary to tell them the young girl was in her twenties and he also closed his eyes to suspicious looking goods but kept the name of the boat in the back of his mind for use in the future, if needed.

After each search, the two of them thanked the captains and moved on to the next boat until all the docked boats were investigated. Then they walked back up the levee to the Sheriff's office on Waterfront Street which was busy with wagons lined all the way from the dock-landing, up across the levee and three blocks down Waterfront. Every wagon was waiting their turn to unload their goods and reload any incoming goods. Most of the riverboats were shabby, goods-haulers and spent each day going up and down the Mississippi picking up produce, cotton, and cedar wood planks from Caruthersville. Livestock from the port of New Orleans and machinery from Natchez and Vicksburg along with many other products which could be sold down river in Natchez and New Orleans.

Many of the triple-deck paddle steam-wheelers were passengers only and carried very few goods, the only stops they made along the river was to let passengers off and take passengers on. When they did happen to take on goods, it was because the price was extremely profitable and passenger business was slow.

"Well, Deputy Pete," André drawled slowly as they ambled along the top of the levee, "nothing a'tall here'ah. What do ya think? Any new ideas come to yor'ah mind about where we should look next?"

"Let me do some pondering, Sheriff. I might come up with an idea or two."

Andre and Pete walked the short distance in silence and when they got to the door of the Sheriff's office André pushed it open with his boot then shoved a

186

block of wood against the door so as to hold it open which would encourage fresh air to blow inside.

"What the..." Pete uttered as André's head snapped up. There sat Elmer in the Sheriff's chair with his hat in his hands and his feet on the desk snoring like a hibernating bear.

Surprised, André and Pete stood there for a minute looking at him. Elmer's head was all the way back against the chair with his mouth hanging wide open. As he sucked in a breath his lips and cheeks went inside his mouth; when he exhaled, his cheek filled with air making him look like a chipmunk.

Wide grins spread across André and Pete's faces as they looked at each other.

"Hey! Elma." André said loudly.

Not even a twitch of a muscle crossed Elmer's face.

"Elma!" André shouted louder.

Jerking his head up, Elmer stared glassy-eyed at the sheriff and Pete for a second, "Oh, sorry, Sheriff," he said as he wiped drool off his mouth with his shirt sleeve and shifted uncomfortably in the chair, "I must have dozed off there while I was waiting for ya. Sorry," he stammered as he lurched up from the chair still looking in a state of disorientation.

"No problem, Elma, what can Ah do for ya today?" André drawled with a grin stuck on his face.

"Well," Elmer said slowly as he stood there nervously turning his hat in his hands and acting too uneasy to stand still. His face was beet-red from being caught sleeping at the Sheriff's desk.

187

Elmer's eyes darted back and forth between André and Pete before he spoke, "Uh, I need to talk to ya 'bout something very important and it should probably be between the two of us for now, Sheriff."

"It's a'right, Elma. Pete here'ah is my new deputy. Anything ya say to me or Pete is strictly confidential. We cannot spread gossip or jeopardize the safety of anyone who comes to us in confidence. We have both taken the oath and cannot, by the laws of the state of Missouri, break your confidence."

Nervously shuffling his feet, Elmer blinked his eyes looking back and forth between the two men. André wasn't sure if Elmer was completely convinced about Pete being his new deputy or not because he kept right on turning his hat in his hands and looking as if, at any time, he might bolt for the door and run.

Pulling his desk chair around so Elmer could set back down, André continued speaking to Elmer calmly, "Elma, sit back down here'ah at my desk, and make ya'self comfortable. Let me get ya a cup of coffee and then we can all talk about whatev'ah ya have on yor'ah mind." André walked over to the tin coffee pot hopin to make Elmer feel more at ease.

"As my deputy, Pete will uphold the law and be as trustworthy as Ah am. As yor'ah Sheriff Ah can guarantee that."

Holding his hat firmly in his hand, Elmer stepped over and had a seat in the sheriff's chair once again.

"Alright, Sheriff, I reckon I can trust Pete."

"You surely can, Elmer, you surely can." Pete said as he puffed out his chest with pride.

Leaning forward, Elmer picked up his cup of coffee, took a long drink of the hot liquid and spoke to them in a whisper as if he was afraid someone outside might be listening.

"I think maybe we should shut the door, Sheriff, I know it's getting a mite hot out, but what I have to tell you is for you and Pete's ears only. No one else should hear this."

"Okay," Pete got up from his chair and kicked the chunk of wood away from the door, causing it to shut with a loud slam, then slid the bolt on the thick wood door, grabbed two chairs; one for himself and one for the Sheriff and turned them to face Elmer.

Pete and André sat down straddling their chairs and looked at Elmer. "Okay," André said, "start-in with the telling."

"Well, first off, let me tell you a tale you will both find unbelievable," Elmer began. He took a deep breath and began the story. "This here story started a long time ago. I was about fifteen years old and Maude, a neighbor gal, was around sixteen or so. We both lived with our families in shacks down by the river not too far from the very prosperous Quinn Plantation, down Natchez, Mississippi way. Growing up, our families had very little food to eat and our clothes were always pretty much rags. My eight brothers and sisters – and her eleven—never did have shoes to wear. It didn't matter if it was cold as blue-blazes or not, we had no shoes. We wore hand-me-down clothes from the church poor-box and once in a great while maybe there would be a pair of old shoes we could force on our feet. In the cold months, we wrapped ourselves in blankets to stay warm and shivered 'round the pot-bellied stoves. Both our lives were hard. After my youngest brother was born, Pa ran off and left Ma so she had to spend many a year washing clothes for other folks and selling summer vegetables to put meat on our table.

"After 'bout three years my older brothers got jobs and insisted Ma stop working herself to death and get some rest. The boys made her quit washing those clothes and plowing that garden, hoping she would enjoy the last years of her life but by that time she was a woman much older than her years and she soon passed on due to overwork and a consumption she just couldn't fight off.

"I was too young at the time to to work for much money, so I began stealing everything I could get my hands on. It didn't matter who owned it or what

189

it was, if something was loose and no one was looking I figured I could sell it for money to buy food, so I took it.

"One day, when I got a few years on, ol Mr. Quinn, or Mr. H, as he was called, caught me stealing chickens from his chicken coop and twisted my ears then offered me a job working with his horses. He was a grand old gentleman who was as honest as old Abe himself. He paid me some cash money and supplied me with warm clothes, socks and shoes. The Mrs. sent warm socks, coats and shoes home with me for the young'uns and every day she cooked up a fine dinner for all the workers. If we had to work early she would give us breakfast and if we worked late, she sent food home with us to share.

"Three years after I started working for Mr. H, or there about, I heard tell about Maude's ma and eight of her brothers and sisters passing on from the influenza and her pa taking off with a gambling woman leaving Maude and the last of her two sisters to fend for themselves. Her sisters were a few years older than Maude and both of them jumped right up and marred two old geezers from town who were old enough to be their granddaddies but had enough food to feed their belly's and a decent place to live. I guess they were only thinking about themselves because they went off and left Maude living alone in that run-down ol shack.

"So there Maude was, living by herself in that river shack with nothing to eat but the few vegetables she could scrap up from the garden or steal from other people and since I know'd her since we were young'uns, I went to Mrs. H and asked if there was work for Maude around that big old plantation so she could provide for herself.

"Right off Mrs. H. said of course she could work for them, and in fact, she should come right on into the house and be a live-in companion for their young daughter Birdie since they were of the same age and all."

Elmer leaned back and took another deep breath before he continued.

"I was as excited as a new born pup going out to that shack to tell Maude about me finding her a position with the Quinn's. But when I got there and knocked on the door, it was answered by this here big, old, burly fella. He looked like a grizzly bear and smelled of sweat and whiskey, He took one look at me and slapped me with his big bear-claw of a hand so hard it knocked me clean off that porch."

'Get out and stay out, boy!' he yelled at me, 'Maude is my woman and ain't no one else gonna have her.'

"So I picked myself up and took off running as fast as I could back to the Quinn's place, goes right in and starts in telling the Mister what happed. He grabbed up his gun and took off running towards the river; not even bothering to get himself a horse and I was running right along behind 'em.

"When we got to the shack we could hear Maude screaming at the man to get out of her house and leave her alone. We could hear the man laughing as he chased her around inside the shack. Things were crashing as if Maude was throwing stuff at him when, all of a sudden, out through the front door comes Maude running as fast as a jack-rabbit with that grizzly bear of a man right behind her. But jest as that giant stepped out the door running with all his might, Mr. H stuck out his leg and trips the fella. He went down like a silo falling over and laid there for a few seconds trying to get some air back inta his lungs. Then he rolled over and looked up at Mr. H with murder in his eyes and in a flash Mr. H put his foot on the fella's neck, drew his rifle up and says, "You twitch one muscle, mister and I'll blow you clear to New Orleans and feed your bones to the 'gators and snakes in the Mississippi where no one will ever find you. Stay down until I say you can get up. Elmer,' he said to me, 'get Maude and her things and run on back to the house, son.

"Well, I took off and did as he told me to do. Me and Maude ran all the way back to the plantation without stopping. About half way there we heard a rifle shot but we didn't slow down and we didn't look back."

As if remembering, Elmer closed his eyes, "I can still remember that day as if it all happened this morning." He paused for a few seconds as if off in another time.

"We made it back to the farm," he continued, "and I told Mrs. H the whole story and she took Maude into the house and told me that everthing would be fine and that I should go on back to work. Well, later that afternoon I saw Mr. H walking back through the field but I didn't say one single thing to him because I figured it was none of my business. A few days later Mr. H took me aside and told me not to worry about walking home after dark or coming to work before the sun was up; I didn't have to be on the lookout for the grizzly-bear of a man. Well, I never asked him why and he never volunteered to tell me. And that was fine with me. The less I knew the less I could tell.

"And, that was the start of my knowing Maude Burbank so well. She was the companion for Miss Birdie and I was one of the farm hands. Eventually Mr. H asked me if I would like to live on the plantation, seeing that I was there from daybreak 'til sundown, and sometimes later. I right away accepted and that was the beginning of the time I fell in love with that beautiful farm.

"As time went by, Maude and I struck up a friendly relationship. There was nothing more to it, only friends, mind you. After some years went by, old Mr. and Mrs. H both passed on and young Mr. Daniel took over running the farm along with his sister Miss Birdie. By and by, young Mr. H was spending more and more time in Boston working with investors and the like. Then, he met his pretty wife Molly. She was one fine woman and just as pleasant as a warm summer breeze. Miss Birdie and Miss Molly loved each other like sisters, I do believe. They seemed to have the time of their lives around that big old plantation.

"But, Miss Molly's family lived in Boston so after she and Mr. H were married and had little Caitlin, they kept right on going back and forth to Boston on business. After a year, or so, of doing all that traveling, they decided it would be best if Mr. H and Miss Molly moved to Boston and someone else ran the plantation.

"So, Mr. H turned the running of the plantation over to Miss Birdie, which surprised all the folks around, but Miss Birdie always wanted to try her hand at running the farm and was delighted when Mr. H decided to let her give it a try. She became the sole owner and boss of the whole thing and she was good at it. She loved that farm and through the years her efforts made more profit than at any other time during its existence.

"But then, later on, when Mr. and Mrs. H moved here to Caruthersville, she began to act a little strange. Finally, one day Maude came and told me she had written Mr. H and told him about Miss Birdie's problem and that he should immediately come down to see her. She warned him about bringing all the children because she said Miss Birdie could get violent at times. Now, I never did see that but I wasn't with Miss Birdie all that much. Mr. H right away made the trip to Natchez and after that came down often to check up on Miss Birdie. At times Miss Molly would come down with him but most times it was Mr. H by himself.

"During that time, I didn't actually see much of Miss Birdie but Maude would keep me up to date on how she was doing and it wasn't good. Maude said she wouldn't eat for many a day then she would start-in eating and wouldn't stop for weeks at a time. Strange things were going on and I just couldn't put my finger on it."

Elmer looked off into space as if he was in deep thought, "Just couldn't figure it out," he muttered again.

Andre and Pete sat there waiting with open-mouths. Silence filled the room as Elmer stared past them.

"Well," Elmer finally came back to them and said, as he looked at André, "I surely was stumped by the whole thing. All those things together just kept right on a'pickin' at my brain. And then, the day came when the news of young Mr. and Mrs. H's passing. Maude had just returned from a trip down to New Orleans for Miss Birdie and said she had heard the news while waiting in Natchez for one of the farm hands to pick her up.

"Naturally Miss Birdie was overcome with grief. She took to her bed that very night and that was the last I ever did see her. Early the next morning Maude called me into the house and told me Miss Birdie had passed on in her sleep due to the devastating grief of losing her dear brother. Then she went on and said I was

193

not to mention a word to any of the other farm hands and that Miss Birdie had spoken to her of what she wanted done when she passed on, so Maude knew exactly what was to be done. Miss Birdie wanted to be buried in privacy the very next day and no one should be notified of her passing.

"Now, that sounded mighty strange to me seeing that Miss Birdie had all sorts of friends in Natchez and the children were here in Caruthersville. But I went along with it because it was Miss Birdie's final request."

Andre and Pete's eyes were bulged out and André's face was as white as a ghost and Pete looked as if he had seen an apparition.

"What the heck, Elma? What are you talking about?" André demanded, "You mean to tell me that the woman at the Quinn's farm is *not* Birdie Quinn?"

"Now, hold on a minute, Sheriff," Elmer said nervously as he stood to his feet holding out his hand as if to defend himself, "Let me finish before you say anything else."

"Okay, hurry it up with the tellin'," André said with a growl.

"Well, about that time," Elmer sat back down and spoke a bit faster, "Mr. Spivey, the Quinn's lawyer, arrived to read the Will. He called me in inside and told me I needed to hear the reading of the Will along with Maude. So, I went on in with him and had me a seat in the parlor. Right off from the start Mr. Spivey read the part to me about Miss Birdie's wishes to be buried the day after she passed-on. When I heard that, my mind started in thinking it was a mighty strange thing to do and the big giveaway was the look on Mr. Spivey's face. His face got real red and he was kindly-like stammering around and sweat was running down his bald head...like maybe he was making up the words as he pretended to read. After that was done, Maude told me that was all I was to hear so I was to leave the house and go back to work. Well, I did leave the house for a while. I walked on back to the back door, went out to the porch and slammed the door shut. I stomped around on the porch and down the steps like I was leaving then sat down and took off my boots and slipped back into the house real quiet-like and stood right next to the parlor door so I could hear what Mr. Spivey was saying to Maude.

194

"And, these are the exact words he said. I remember them as well as I remember my name. He read, 'If Miss Birdie passed on before young Mr. H the plantation and everthing with it would go back to Mr. H, Molly and their children. But if Mr. H passed on first it was to go to Miss Birdie, Miss Molly and the children. If both, Mr. H and Miss Birdie passed on it would go to Miss Molly.

"But, this is the interesting part. He read, 'If all three adults passed on it was to go to the children and if by some reason the children also perished the plantation and everything would be sold and the proceeds would be split between Mr. Spivey, Maude and me.'

"After the lawyer read all that their voices got so low I couldn't hear anything they were saying so I high-tailed it out of there."

Elmer sat for a while staring at the Sheriff and Pete.

"Now, Sheriff," Elmer stated matter-of-factly, "I never once thought a thing about getting any part of that farm since I knew those children were all still alive. I saw Mr. Spivey's carriage go on down the way and went back and sat on the back steps again.

"No more than ten minutes later, Miss Maude walked on out the back door and asks me to come on back into the parlor." Elmer hesitated and looked down and started twisting his hat around again.

"Then she up and tells me the strangest thing I ever did hear," he sat at the desk looking at André and Pete and they were looking at him.

"well..." they both leaned forward and spoke at the same time, "What did she tell you?"

"She flashed a piece of paper with some writing on it in front of me really quick-like. I couldn't read it because she kindly had it hidden from my sight while she was reading. She knew I knew she couldn't read very well so she told me Miss Birdie had her memorize the whole thing. The paper was hand-written by Miss Birdie, or so Maude said, and Miss Birdie had written it to her the very night she

195

passed on. In it Miss Birdie told Maude she wanted Maude to dress up as if she was Miss Birdie, go on up to Caruthersville and act like she was Miss Birdie so she could take care of the Quinn children and be their mother. She went on and on about how Miss Birdie told her not to tell a living soul about the plan and Miss Birdie wanted Maude to talk me into joining her in this falsehood. We were to tell all the farm hands that Miss Birdie left the plantation during the night for New Orleans and on to England because of the heavy heartbreak she was suffering after the loss of her loved ones.

"Well, to tell you the truth, I didn't rightly know what to say but if Miss Birdie wanted it that way, I sure enough was going to go along with it. Miss Birdie always treated me with kindness so I sure wasn't gonna disrespect her death-bed wish.

"So, I packed up my things and when Maude was ready to leave, so was I. I didn't question her at all and I was ready and willing to do what Miss Birdie asked me to do."

Andre and Pete just sat there waiting for Elmer to continue. When he didn't, André spoke with and an "and?"

"And here we are." Elmer replied looking at André with solemn eyes.

"Is that it?"

"No, there's more."

"So, what's the more part of the story, Elma?"

"Out with it, Elmer. Don't just stop talking, keep on going, man!" Pete said anxiously.

"I will, I will. Just hold on, Deputy."

"I'm holding on so tight my fingers are numb. I suggest you start in with the rest of the telling!"

196

"After me and Maude arrive here in Caruthersville, I took a boat back down to Natchez to pick up a few things for Maude and while I was there, I heard about the death of Mr. Spivey. He was found dead in his parlor. He had been hit on the head with a heavy object and the authorities thought it was a surprise attack since he was found slumped over his desk. Then I heard no suspects had been found but they ended up settling it as a robbery when his wife soon discovered some gold bars missing from his desk drawer."

Elmer leaned forward and once again dropped his voice, "That there thing kind of picked at my brain too.

"Then, I started putting it all together like a young'un's puzzle 'til last night when I found the master piece of the puzzle." He stopped again and looked at the two of them.

"Get on with it man, or Ah'm gonna arrest ya." André said firmly.

"I was sittin' at the kitchen table drinkin' coffee and just wonderin' where Maude had taken herself off to for the last few days when I leaned my head back to take the very last gulp and what do you know but up on the sidebar with the lid half open was a box with a book kindly stickin' out. Well, I get myself up and went over to have a look-see at what kind of book it was, mostly because I was being nosy and all, and lo-and-behold it was Maude's diary. Now, I know it ain't proper to be reading someone else's diary and all but I sure was bored and it was too tempting."

"And what did the diary say?" Pete asked

Elmer sat there a few more seconds twisting his hat faster and faster and tapping his foot against the wood floor.

"Elma!"

"Well, ya ain't gonna believe this here, but, it was for sure her diary. It was a diary of all the evils she has done during her many years of living with the Quinn's at the farm and even things she has done here in Caruthersville. It has names, dates and each and every little thing she schemed. She wrote down which acts were completed and which acts were not and the reasons why it was not completed.

"Wher'ah is this diary, Elma, we need to see it. It will be your word against hers if we don't have the diary and we can't prove anything without it."

"It's hidden in a place no one will ever find."

"And where might that be, Elma?"

"Right her in this room, Sheriff."

With a frown André looked at Elmer, "Here?"

"Right here, Sheriff, right here under the floorboards beneath your desk."

"How did ya get it in ther'ah?"

"When I came in and found you gone, I couldn't risk sitting here holding it. Someone else might have walked in and seen it, so I pulled up a board and stuck it inside then stomped on the nails to push the board back down. It's safe and sound. Ain't nobody going to come in here and pull up the floorboards of a sheriff's office, now are they?'

"Well, Ah reckon not, but get on up and let's get it out and have a read. Come on, what are ya waiting for?" André demanded.

Elmer stood up, pushed the chair out of the way and began stomping one of the boards with the heel of his boot.

"Come on, Pete. Help me get this here board up."

"Okay," Pete got up and pushed the desk back a bit more, "Move on over and let me get a hammer."

He walked to the back of the jail and returned with a hammer and began pounding on the opposite end of the board Elmer had stomped. When the board popped up a bit, Elmer reached down and pulled it the rest of the way up. All three men squatted down and stared at the book as if it were a strange foreign object of some kind.

"Well," Elmer whispered softly, "Go on ahead and pick it up, Sheriff. It ain't no snake but it's kindly deadly, at least for me it is."

Gingerly André picked up the book and walked back to his chair and sat down. The book was quite thick and some of the pages were tattered and torn with age. He could tell some of the last pages had not been used, but the majority of the book was filled with writing.

"She sure did a lot of writing for a person not knowing how to write, Elma."

"Yes, she did, Sheriff, but when you read it you will understand. You may not be able to read the words really well. Maude was taught to read and writer by Miss Birdie, and I remember her whining about not needing to know that kind of thing since she would never use it. She said it was a great waste of Miss Birdie's time. Miss Birdie also taught me how to read and write and I kindly caught on really quick-like so I tried helping Maude but she had no interest a'tall. But I can read her writing pretty good seeing I was the one who tried and tried to correct her spelling. She can write most words but she's a mighty poor speller. It wasn't that she wasn't smart a'tall, she just didn't want to learn. But, go on ahead and if ya can't read a word or two, I'll help ya out and I'll kindly explain some of the things she says."

Andre open the book stopped, looked up at Pete and said in a quiet voice, "Deputy, Ah think ya bett'ah lock the door."

"Yeah, I better," Pete said as he got up and stepped to the door where he slid the bolt across the thick wooden door.

May— I will kil hre. I hate hre. I put som posin in hre
watr. It wil kil hre lic it kilt Josie. She is a bad grl. Jest lic
Josie and Salie. Al she wants to do is lok at mi Daniel
and he is mi man. I wil hav hem and no bode else wil.

"Josie and Sally were two other house servants," Elmer explained, "They worked right along with Maude and Miss Birdie. Both women were married with families of their own and their husbands worked in the fields and horse barns, but Maude thought they were in love with Mr. H," Elmer shook his head as if he couldn't believe what was being read, "I remember when Sally died, everyone thought she died of consumption. She just kept getting sicker and sicker until she was gone. The next year came along and the same thing happened with Josie. Then everyone was in a panic thinking it was some sort of influenza and we would all die.

"Miss Birdie finally had the old doctor come out and gathered us all up and he told us both women had died of a blood disease and it wasn't contagious. He wasn't quite sure of the reason they had contracted the disease, but he assured us we would be fine.

"Now, the woman she is talking about in this first writing is named Anna Wallace," Elmer pointed out the paragraph André had finished reading. "Anna was a friend of Miss Birdie's and quite often she would come to the farm and visit Miss Birdie and young Mr. H because her family had a large plantation not too far from the Quinn's. Every time Anna came to visit, Maude would storm out to the barn and tell me how much she hated her and wanted her to die. I would kindly laugh and think she was just being a jealous young woman, but I guess it was a lot more serious than I thought. Luckily, Anna was not in love with Mr. H at all seeing that she up and married a fella from back east and moved to Boston before Maude had a chance to do her evil deed.

"I never, ever thought she really meant it. I figured it was all a bunch of women talk. I knew all along she was in love with Mr. H but not one time did I think it would eat away at her brain.

Andre looked back down at the book and read the next entry.

May — that ugle Anna is gon. I am hapy. I do not want 2 kil hre but I wil if I have to. She wants mr H and that kan not b.

Looking up at Elmer, André asked curiously. "Does this tell anythin' about the disappearance of Caitlin Quinn?"

"Yes, sir it does."

"And wher'ah does it start the tellin' of that?"

"Turn to the last pages with writing, Sheriff. Here, let me show you."

Andre handed Elmer the book.

"Right here, start in reading right here on this-here page and it will tell you everything you want to know. But, if you start out on-back a couple pages you will find out how Miss Birdie passed on and how young Mr. and Mrs. H died in that carriage accident.

Andre looked up at Elmer again and frowned then flipped to the back of the book and Elmer showed him where to begin reading.

Febary – I did it. That terbel Molly is gone. But I lost mi tru love. He wood not com to me becas of that woman so he had to be gon to. Ha! It wer so ese no body wil evr gess I did it. Cutin a carage strap was eze. Ha ha Now al I hav to do is get rid of Miss Birdie. I don't want to but I hav to. Nothin can stop me now. I wil use the same posin I usd with Josie and Salie.

Febary – I did it again! I got rid Miss Birdie. It was not so bad. She died real quik like. Now I will go and get rid of the wood colts of mi man and that woman. It wil be eze. I can do anythin I want now. I wil tak this big plantaton and it wil be al min. I wil get rid of Mr. spiveu and Elmer. Ha! And I wil get rid of them brats.

March - Mr. Spivey was eze. All I did was walk aroun behid him and hit him in the head.

May - Ha! that Caitlin is goin to be gon in a few days. She is almost ready to put on a tran.

May—thos brats ran a way. Oh wil it is ok. I hav already a lot of monie sellin those small children down the river. I wil get them bac and whin I do I wil sell them to.

I AM MOST DONE!!!!

May - I hav to do now is git rid of Elmer. That wil be eze.

Andre and Pete looked at Elmer with disbelief, "You better be careful, Elmer," Pete said in a whispered, "until we find her."

"Oh, I am, Deputy, I am. I'm not going back out to the farm until y'all catch 'er. And then I'll stay and help those young'uns until they tell me to leave. I've known that lil' Caitlin since the day she was born and she's a mighty fine young woman is all I have to say about her. But for now, I'm staying right here in town. I can bed down over at the livery with the horses. They suit me just fine. I'm not rightly ready to meet my maker yet, I've got a lot of living to do before I check in up there."

"When was the last time you saw Miss Bir - Maude?" Pete asked.

"A few days ago when she high-tailed it out from the farm in the carriage. She had me hitch up Caitlin's horse and off she went lickity-split. She hasn't been back since. I'm thinking she's out at one of the farms tending to a new mother she's been telling me about for a while. It's kindly unusual for her to be gone overnight. Most times she lets me know what time she'll be back so I can be there to help her down from the carriage and unhitch the horse but this time she just took off flying down the lane and didn't say a word. Something ain't right and I bet it's got something to do with that lil' Caitlin gone missing. The only time Maude stays overnight is when she's helping out some sick folk, and she always tells me not to go looking for her because she can take care of herself goin' and comin' home.

"Sheriff, I really don't know what she has to do with Caitlin's missing but I ain't feeling good about it. It's kindly strange."

Andre and Pete looked at Elmer then back at each other. Then André turned to Elmer and said, "Elma, let's go find that gal a'fore Miss Bir— Maude does somethin' evil again."

Standing to their feet, Pete reached out and slid the bolt-lock off the door and...

SLAM

The door flew open with a crash, hitting Pete on the shoulder and knocking him back about a foot and in flew Lily, Benny and Mr. Bushy.

Sheriff," Lily yelled, "Michael Thorne's ghost came to me last night as I was sleeping and told me, straight out, that Caitlin is trying to get home! We have to go *RIGHT NOW* and help her. Him and that little haint-gal Hannah came to me and told me she is out at that abandoned farm called Yoder's and she is trying to get home. Come on, come on let's go!"

17

Home

In the vast wildernesses of the world, where large animals roam freely throughout the night hunting for food, whether it be another animal or human, there is a thin window of time; a moment right before dawn, when darkness is at its blackest and the night is so thick even nocturnal creatures cannot see. This narrow portal is often referred to as the *Void of Silence.*

African Tales of long ago claim that during the *Void of Silence,* animals cannot be heard, night-birds are silent and every river, waterfalls and rapids lay unmoving in respect for those few seconds of rest. After that fleeting moment has swiftly passed, darkness begins its rapid flight from the dawn, leaving behind a few hidden tendrils of blackness scattered among the forest trees, hiding in its nooks and crannies. Quickly the night flees to the west dragging its long, dark tail behind. Then the new day will slip its radiant fingers over the land, stretching further than the eye can see as it flicks hidden shadows off to the west. Within minutes the newborn day opens its sleepy eyes wider and brings a smile to the souls of all mankind. Interestingly, before dawn makes her appearance, the night feels her coming and begins thinning and pulling its body from the light as if feeling the burn of dawn's glittering fingers touch its soul. Eventually, the only sign of night is the fading hues of gray in the western sky.

At first, the thinning of the darkness is not visible to the human eye, but the animals of the night feel the air warming and quietly begin their own rapid departure before the creatures of the day begin their morning hunt.

And so, it was in that very moment Caitlin woke from her deep sleep in the little shack in the dark Missouri wilderness.

Listening to the silence, she lay still as thoughts of the previous night danced in her mind like a faded memory. The appearance of Michael and the little girl captured her early morning thoughts. Now her heart felt crushed – she realized the possibility of Michael returning, after all these years, was gone forever.

Looking around the tiny little shack, she knew she had to get up, get back to town and wipe the past from her mind as she turned to the future.

Thump, thump.

Caitlin heard Tabby bumping against the wall of the lean-to. "Okay, Tabby girl," Caitlin called out to the horse, "I'm coming, hold on a minute."

Pushing herself up from the floor she walked to the lean-to door. As she pushed the door open, Tabby pushed her way through and headed for the outside door before Caitlin could get the lean-to door closed.

"Whoa, you must be hungry!" Caitlin laughed as she opened the door and let Tabby out into the shadowy early-morning dawn. "Here you go, find your breakfast."

Going back inside she dug through the burlap bag the Levi's had given her. Inside she found the dress Katie Nicole had slipped into the bag. Pulling off her night-wrap, she pulled the dress, which was a bit too big, over her head. She found more food and a little milk was left from the night before, along with the biscuits and ham from the farmhouse.

Realizing how hungry she was, she gobbled up as much food as her stomach could hold and repacked the rest. Then she gathered up her meager belongings, sat them on the porch and sat down on the front steps, she relaxed and watched the slender fingers of warm sunshine slowly slip through the trees and cover the dewy wet grass.

Finally, she stood up and closed the front door of the shack, picked up her bag of belongings and slid the bridle over Tabby's head.

"Let's go girl," she spoke softly to her horse. "Let's go home," she said as she led Tabby over to the porch and pulled herself onto her back.

Slowly they walked through the tall grass toward the road leading into town with the still-damp grass brushing against her legs and weighing her skirt down a bit, but she knew it would dry in no time at all once the warm morning sun came up.

Starting out in a slow walk, they both enjoyed the early morning. Gentle dove coos came from the forest as soft fingers of the early morning sun reached further and further through the forest, caressing each tree with its warm embrace as it wound itself west in its leisurely fashion. Heady smells of wild flowers and sage began drifting up as the forest warmed. Caitlin figured she had about four or five miles to go before she would reach town. Being eager to get home, she nudged Tabby into a gallop. Maybe she would make it into town without running into anyone else.

But, as she rode along the road, she looked down and noticed there were a lot of hoof prints on the dusty trail, so she pulled back on Tabby to get a closer look. It looked as if quite a few horses had traveled this road in the early morning hours because the prints were fresh and the grass still pressed into the dirt. They were all going in the direction of the abandoned farmhouse. All she could think about was; Aunt Birdie and those men now have horses. She and Tabby would have to make these last few miles in a hurry. Maybe they were already on their way back into town the same as she was. There was no way she was going to let them catch her and take her back to that farmhouse or the train.

Once again, she gave Tabby a sharp nudge to get her going, and off they went in a full run. Every so often she would turn around and check the road behind her, but no one was in sight.

Quickly she and Tabby covered the ground as Tabby stayed in a full gallop. As they approached the outskirts of town, farms begin to appear more frequently. Some of the farm families were up doing early morning chores and they stopped to wave at her. Others just looked at her as if wondering what she was doing out this far from town so early in the morning. She and Tabby were approximately a mile or so from town when she saw them. They looked to be about a mile behind her, but they were quickly closing the gap. It looked like Aunt Birdie was riding astride with every one of her men right beside her and Aunt Birdie was having no trouble staying on her horse.

"When did she learn to ride astride?" Caitlin wondered as she turned around and gave Tabby another nudge with her heels.

"Come on, Tabby-girl!" she yelled out. "Let's get going!"

Caitlin knew if the men, or Aunt Birdie, had found the big black horse she and Tabby were goners. There was no way Tabby could out-run that horse. Tabby took off like a shot with Caitlin lying flat against her back hanging on for dear life as she said all the prayers she had ever learned.

Suddenly she felt Tabby slowing down to a limping walk, "Land-o-Goshen," Caitlin said loudly, "What's wrong, girl?" Looking down, she noticed Tabby had lost a shoe and must have picked up a stone along the road because she was limping heavily.

Nervously, Caitlin looked back; her pursuers were still closing the gap. Panic took over as she tried urging Tabby forward but the poor horse couldn't do it.

From the right side of the road came the sound of a large animal crashing through the brush and instantly she thought of the big panther but out onto the road, right in front of her, burst the big black horse with the smaller black right behind him. Slowly the horse walked over to Tabby and nudged Caitlin on the shoulder. It was as if the two black horses were intentionally there to help them.

"Alright boy," Caitlin whispered nervously. "Come on over here and let me slide onto your back."

As if understanding exactly what she had said, he walked over and stood alongside Tabby. Caitlin reached over, grabbed his beautiful, long mane and slid herself onto his massive back. "This is one giant horse," Caitlin said to herself, "Come on boy, let's get going!"

Just before the big black took off, Caitlin turned to look back. Aunt Birdie and her men were less than a half-mile behind her yelling loudly for her to stop and a couple of them had their guns drawn. Caitlin gave the horse a nudge, and off he went in a flash. Leaning down, she buried her face in his mane and hung on. When she dared to look back, Tabby and the smaller black horse was nowhere in sight and the big black was pulling away from Aunt Birdie. But they continued to chase her.

"Let them come," she thought, "Maybe the Sheriff will catch them red-handed."

After a few seconds, she sat up a bit to see if she could tell how far they had to go. They were going to make it. There was only one more decision to make: should she go to the train depot and get Pete Turnkey, or should she just go to the Sheriff's offce and hope he's there?

Both places were on the other end of town so she guessed it wouldn't make a difference which one she ended up at, as long as she found help. By now, Caitlin and the big horse was in town and the Sheriff's offce was in sight.

Sheriff Beaumont, at that very moment, was walking out the door of his offce with Lily, Benny, Pete, Elmer and Mr. Bushy. They all stopped and stood in front of the offce as if discussing something.

Caitlin started crying as she realized she was going to make it home. Tears were streaming down her face as she yelled for Benny and Lily.

Turning to see who was calling them, Lily and Benny took one look then sprinted towards here. The Sheriff, Pete, Elmer and Mr. Bushy stood there a few more seconds, then they too began running.

Suddenly, a loud whistle ripped through the air and the horse came to an skidding stop and Caitlin felt herself flying from its back. In her mind's eye, she was moving in slow-motion. Calmly, her arms went out from her sides and her legs were pulled straight out behind her. Leisurely, her entire body seemed to flip slowly over and she could see the beautiful, blue morning sky. "What a pretty blue," she thought to herself. White clouds were floating against the robin's-egg blue sky, and small black birds were flying above the tree tops. In the distance came the familiar cooing of a Mourning Dove and Chickadee's were chattering. Once again, her body slowly turned over and she could see the ground coming into view and she gently floated down...at least it felt as if she was gently floating.

Then, with a force she had never felt before her body slammed into the ground and everything went black.

"Caitlin... Caitlin." Someone was shaking her.

"Oh, don't shake me," she moaned. It felt as if every bone under her skin was shattered. It hurt to breathe, it hurt to move; it even hurt to think.

"Can ya open yor'ah eyes, Caitlin?"

Forcing her eyes open, she found herself staring into the beautiful black eyes of Sheriff Beaumont.

"Yes," she said, smiling up at him. "I can open my eyes.

"Good," he said with a smile, "I was thinking I would nev'ah be able to have ya sit on my desk."

Glossary

Fracas	a noisy scramble of people or proceedings
Consumption	a word used to describe any disease a doctor could not identify
Vittles	food
hit'	it
Frippery	something showy, frivolous or unnecessary
Levee	a man-made embankment built to prevent flooding
Haint	ghost or apparition
Privy	outside bathroom
thar'	there or their
fur'/fer'	for
Shanty	a very small abandoned shack or shed
jest	just
tinny piano	a well-used, out-of-tune, piano which sounds like a tin can.
Haint	ghost, apparition

Continue reading Lily's Ghost Adventures

2014 - Lily and the Ghost of Michael Thorne

2015 - Lily and the Ghost of Tillie Brown

2016 - Lily and the Ghost of Peg-Leg Paddy McGee

2017 - The Audacious Ghost Adventures of Phineas A Pennypacker

Coming in 2018 - Lily and the Ghost of Anabelle Bloome, a *Shapeshifter* book

Coming in 2019 - My Name is Lucy, a *Shapeshifter* book

All books are available on Amazon, Kindle, Goodreads and your local book stores

Contact the Author

Email: nphaley@outlook.com

FB: NP Haley

Twitter: NP Haley@NPHaleyBooks